Tome 1

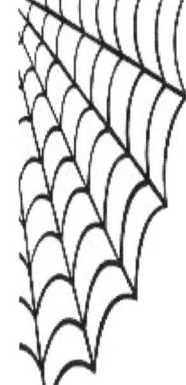

Dr. Weaver

The World of
Empty Glasses

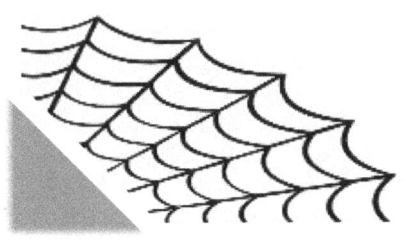

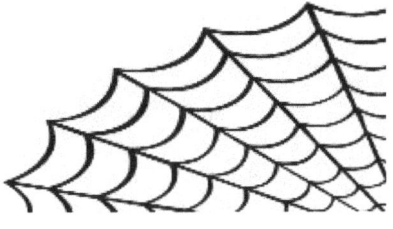

Dr. Weaver (The World of Empty Glasses, Tome 1)
(www.ebhood.com)

Copyright © 2018 by Eric B Hood.

Alley Cat Publishing
alleycatpublishing@gmail.com

Paperback
ISBN 978-0-9884100-7-7

Cover Art By: **Mirella Santana** www.mirellasantana.com.br
©FlexDreams | ©kopitin | ©gorbovoi81 |©digitalArtB

Editors: Joyce Cummings, Bill Staton, Robin Hood and Terri Hood

Special thanks to my wife and my daughter. My wife's support, and my
daughter's input.

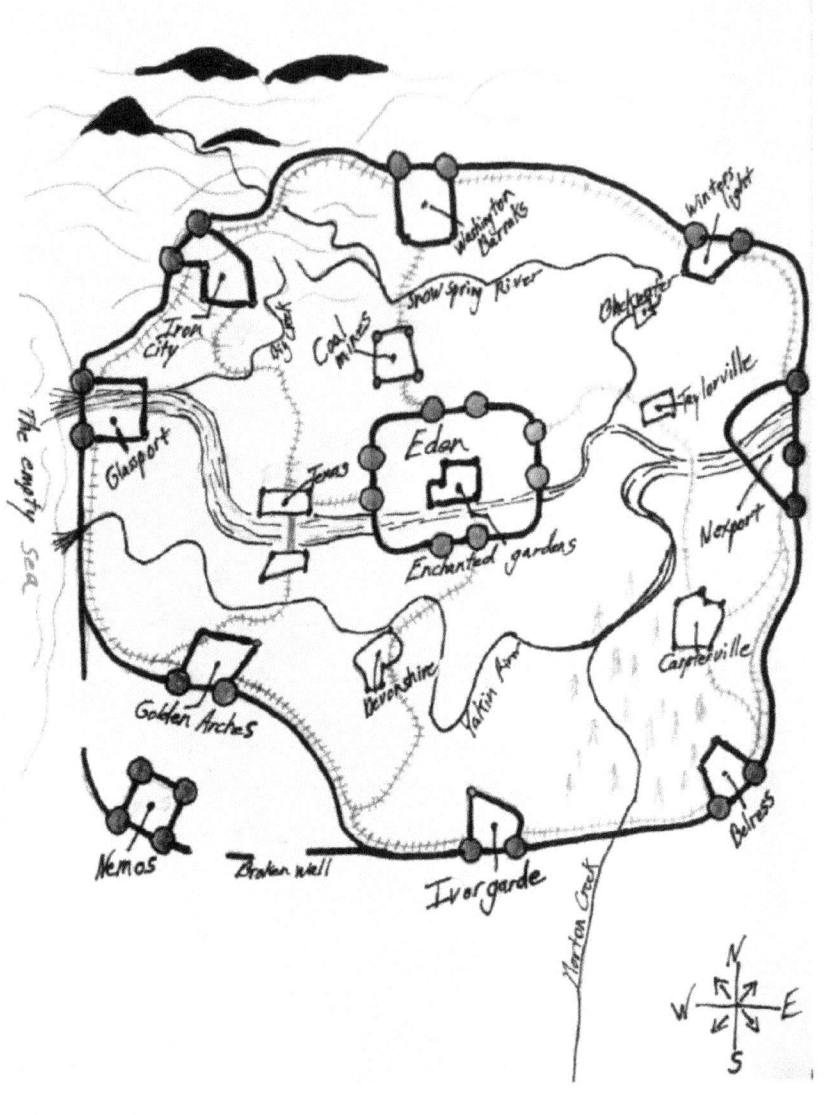

Prologue

Death, it comes to us all. I had lived two lifetimes. Back then, I was not ready to give it up on life entirely. Daughter of death, half angel, half human and sometimes part monster. My death meant something, yet no one remembers my name. Melabeth is my name, lost in history. My death, brought on by men and their hatred for things they don't understand. My death was the end of the world.

I looked down upon the people; hiding behind walls. The earth was now the playground for the dead. They rose up, and killed the living, what a horror show. They killed me for being a murderer. Perhaps I was, but I was the daughter of death and death was my business. In their blind hatred they came for me. I could have killed them all, that is until they killed Adam. My husband, my lover, my life. They were welcomed to take my life after that.

After my mortal body was destroyed I came to the land of the dead to my father's house. Here in the place all the lost spirits came before they moved on to the great beyond. To heaven or hell, don't ask me, I've never been to either. My Adam is in heaven, if you ask me. His spirit had not been lost, he died happy with a complete life. He left without me, for it is not my time and I cannot follow him. I am tasked with the job of reaping the dead, as my father has done for tens of thousands of years.

Feels like forever, yet it has only been six hundred years since the fall of man. Six hundred years I've waited to move on from this purgatory. A city named Eden surrounded by walls fights on. How much longer can they live before joining the dead? Then I will finally be able to move on. If their walls fell, then would I be free of this place? I would be with my Adam. Yet, the humans still have the power to resurrect me, then I could return all the dead from where they came. Why would I help them do that? The earth would return to them and once again I would be a reaper of the dead.

My trusted spirit cat purred on my lap, I looked down in the pool of seeing. There in the water I could see the world. I watched as a young girl with agent blood, engaged in an act of bravery. She will die, but she is brave. The power that runs through this family, especially the girl. What a waste?

I said to my cat Sonja, "Why would I help? The Ghouls will eat her soon enough. I have no need to save this world."

The cat spoke, "Do you have no need to save the girl as well?"

I frowned, "I'm not in the business of saving people." I watched in horror, she was about to be killed. "Oh for God's sake. I will be sorry, I just know it. Go Sonja, save her. I will make a deal with her. Perhaps I will find a use for the girl."

Sonja purred, "Careful, help them too much and we'll be stuck here for another six hundred years." She jumped off my lap, and down into the pool of water. There was no splash as her spirit headed toward the land of the living.

Yet help them, I would. Not personally, not this time, but rather spread my power around. I had made one, now I'll make another. I do believe there will be seven. They will have their seven Gods.

Book 1
Chapter 1 The Day After

Tom Jones

I looked at today's paper, February 5th 2604. The headline reads; The Largest Attack in Twenty Years. Someone knocked at the door, but I didn't want to talk with them. I heard the knock again, but this time much louder. I could hear the impatience as each knock came louder, and faster. It didn't hurry my steps, feet felt as if they were made of lead.

I felt numb and empty, if this was my father, he wouldn't have knocked. I opened the door, and I was not surprised to see two soldiers standing there. Both of them young men, both looked like they had just left the fight.

The two men still wore their armor, dented, covered with dirt and blood. They wore no helmets and their dark skin had deep lines where the sweat removed some of the filth from their faces. None of that bothered me. It was the look in their eyes, for their eyes were empty. I knew they were like me, in shock, tired, and still too confused to really take it all in.

The soldier who had been knocking stood back as he spoke, "This here is Lieutenant Brown, and I'm private Sandford. We are here to deliver a message to a Mary Jones. Is she available?"

"No," The man was about to say something else when I blurted out, "She's dead."

This time the lieutenant spoke, "No! How?"

"Ghouls, they got in, almost killed my sister." My voice held no reflection, it felt unreal, like repeating a random fact.

The man's eyes widened, "Was Mary, your mother?" I nodded, "Oh, dear. Are you the oldest in the house?" I nodded again, "Well, son… How do I put this?"

I answered for him, "My father is dead."

His eyes said it all as he tried to explain, "He died a hero, you should be proud."

"I am," I could feel the tears sliding down my face.

"Look, this isn't a good time, come and see me when your head is clear. I would like to tell you more, but not now." He handed me a parchment, it was a thick paper rolled tightly with a string keeping it together. He also gave me a small paper bag with something wrapped up in it.

I shook my head, "Thanks," I said it so quietly I could not be sure he heard me. I shut the door without awaiting a reply.

Darrell was like a robot, he looked at me with those cold eyes, "Father is dead too. What we will do without Mom and Dad?"

Darrell was such a cold person. It made me so angry his calm caused me distress. Still, he was my little brother and as much as I wanted to scream at him, all I could say is, "We'll figure it out." I pulled the string off, and read the letter.

Dear Mrs. Jones,

We regret to inform you that on February 4th, 2604, Benjamin Jones was killed in the line of duty. On behalf of the men of the 10th, we would like you to know that without his bravery the city of Golden arches might have fallen to the Dead. It was through his bravery that more of the Ghouls did not enter the city. Let it be recorded that his personal sacrifice at the gate saved countless lives.

We have included a bonus in Benjamin's death benefits. I know this does little for the anguish you might feel. If there is anything else you require, please let me know. If it is within my power I would be happy to assist you.

Sincerely, Timothy Bright, Commander of the Golden Arches

I open the brown bag and in it was my father watch. It was dented, I opened it to see that the watch had stopped at 10:10. It had been enchanted no reason to wind the watch, but now it didn't work. I knew what time my father died at.

The letter and watch had been for my mother, but she was dead. That made me wonder; who would be getting father's death benefits? Who would be taking care of us? I crammed the paper in my pocket and headed upstairs, because I needed to check up on my sister Morgan.

I was supposed to sleep. Morgan looked so close to death, so still, so pale, hardly breathing. How could I sleep not knowing if she might wake? If she does wake, she should see me, waiting for her. The clock reads 11:23. It doesn't matter, I can't sleep anyway.

When I entered my parents' room, I noticed the doctor was not there. The big man sitting in a chair in the corner of the room was fast asleep. I was glad I came to check on her. She looked so small in my parent's big bed. They brought her in here because it was the biggest room and gave the doctor the most space to work. Blood still stained the floor. How could she have bled so much, and still be alive?

I took a seat next to her and took her hand. Some fear washed away when I realized her hand was warm and I could see her breathing. I wondered, what did she dream about? Her eyes twitched under her eyelids, for a half second my pulse raced as I thought she might open them. She didn't, I truly hope she is not dreaming of what happened, trapped within a nightmare. She will blame herself for mother… but I don't. When she wakes, I will make sure she understands that, I will take care of her.

Just days ago we all went to have a family portrait made. How could picture day be followed by such madness?

Chapter 2 Picture Day

Morgan Jones, two days earlier.

My head pounded, it hurt to open my eyes and when I did the light was blinding. I closed my eyes, too weak to move, but the pain kept me from falling back to sleep. I could hear voices, not familiar ones. A man was talking, making no sense, "It's truly a miracle. She should be dead, I can't figure it out. She should have at least become infected enough to turn, but perhaps the monster ripped her limbs off before the infection could enter her bloodstream."

Another male voice replied, it was deeper, he sounded like a big man. "I don't know doc. I say it's magic, how else could she be breathing?"

The doc's voice quieted, "For now, I doubt she'll make it through the night."

I heard steps and a door creak open, the voice that now spoke was very familiar. "Dr. V, how is she holding up?" It was my brother Tom, he sounded as if he had been crying.

The doctor's voice changed, more cheerful, "She does well. You and your brother should try to sleep. Jim and I will stay with her."

"I was thinking perhaps I could stay." Tom's voice was brave.

Jim's deep voice filled the room, "Tom, we'll take good care of her. You take care of your brother."

Defeated Tom agreed. Not long after the door shut and the footsteps died away, the doctor spoke with his quiet voice. "Poor boy, thanks Jim, I couldn't have him in here. The last thing that boy needs is to watch the death of another family member."

They were still talking when my world was once again swallowed by darkness. I didn't understand what they were talking about, but I had a bad feeling it was me. I tried to remember, I needed to remember.

My mind slipped back to yesterday and the last things I remembered.

I admired myself in the full length mirror. The mirror itself was large and oval. I had to acknowledge, I looked pretty and fancy in such a nice dress. I looked at the young girl who stared right back at me. My dress was blue with highlights of dark green. My corset was dark green with embroidered vines, crisscrossing across it with the most delicate leaves sprouting from the tips. The vines were just a shade different green from the corset. I felt pretty.

Yesterday my parents took me to the Tailor, on my twelfth birthday. This beautiful dress had been a gift from my parents. Slipping on my black overcoat and my black top hat, I looked upon the image in the mirror once again. I was small, but I would grow. Too thin, but not to the point of being sickly. I smiled a crooked smile, and my image did the same. Today would be a good day.

A loud rap sounded in the doorway. "Come in," I barked.

My brother opened the door, pushing it and allowing it to open fully until it banged against the wall, rattling the photos. Darrell never showed any sign of emotion. He stared at me with that familiar face. His brown overcoat had two rows of buttons, long sleeves, and wide shoulders. It reminded me of a military uniform. This was not only his dress up outfit, but it had been Tom's before he had outgrown it. His short brown hair looked as if someone had put a bowl on his head before they cut it. I am blessed with my mother's jet black straight hair. In the right light it looked purple.

He announced with his monotone voice, "Mother said she'll be ready in two minutes."

I nodded, "I'm about ready." As I returned to straightening my clothes, I looked good, except for my crooked teeth. Darrell just stood there, quietly staring. "What do you want?" I demanded.

"Mother said, she would be ready in two minutes, but it took me eighteen and a half seconds to relay the message. You have less than two minutes to get ready. Of course, there are variables; mother normally is inaccurate. She could be ten minutes off."

I could see the gears moving in his brain, trying to calculate the time we would all be ready to go. Tom gave Darrell such a hard time. I tried my best, to soothe my wacky brother. I tugged on a chain with my left hand, one side of the chain was attached to my coat, the other side my pocket watch. With one hand I caught the pocket watch out of mid air. Flipping open the front I then gave the dial a few twists to make sure it was wound. "My watch says it's, 7:43:35, now. I will arrive in the living room at 7:45. Please let mother know."

Darrell nodded and stress drain from his face. He now had numbers to calculate my arrival. He hurried off without shutting my door, he was on a mission. I smiled, I was not going to allow his nutty behavior to affect my day. Today was family photo day; I was a baby when my parents last had a photo made with the whole family. I couldn't wait. Mother had decided that since father had moved the family out to the Golden Arches, we should mark the occasion.

Father was now third in command of the garrison. The move from Taylorville hadn't been hard for Darrell and me. We hadn't any friends there, Tom on the other hand was angry; he had left his best friend behind. Tom and Charles had been friends since birth, but I didn't care. All it meant to me was, he didn't have his friend to help pick on me. I was hopeful that my brother would hang out with me. Charles had made such fun of me. I had been unable to say anything to Tom without a fight, thanks to Charles. Glancing back at my watch, I closed the lid and slid it back into my coat pocket.

The watch had been last years coming of the year gift. That year we had a decorated steam tree, with fake branches to look like a living tree. The steam tree base powered it, all you had to do was add some coal. It twirled around and powered lights and played music. I've always loved the holidays. Soon afterwards my father announced our move. It was hard to believe it was already February 4th. My hand rested over the watch, it was my most prized possession. Of course I had to wind my watch every day to keep the time. My father had an enchanted watch. Not only was there no need to wind it, the accuracy was down to the second. Darrell thought it was the greatest thing in the whole world. I wasn't worried about the accuracy, I was happy with what I had.

I was down in the living room with ten seconds to spare. Darrell looked relieved that I made it on time. Father was already downstairs looking out the front window. A sense of pride filled me as I looked upon my father. He was tall, with large shoulders and very good looking. He wore his beard trimmed and neat, his hair was cut short. He was an officer, and just one look upon him you knew he was in charge. He was dressed in his best today, a dark green suit with a long jacket, top hat and white shirt. Captain Benjamin Jones, but everyone just called him Ben.

He put his long pipe to his mouth, and with a snap of his fingers, a flame erupted from a match. He lit the end of the pipe while inhaling deeply, letting the air out of his lungs the living room filled full of the sweet smelling smoke. My father's head turned, and when his eyes met mine his face lit up. "Morgan, my sweet girl, you are too pretty for words, and a little taller each day."

My heart filled with pride, "Thank you father! You look the part today. Mom is certain to be jealous of every woman's eyes in town."

My father chuckled as he blew another cloud, "Now Morgan, don't let your mother hear you talk like that."

"Why, the girl is right." My mother entered the room with a giant smile and walk that made it appear she floated across the room. "Oh, my," She looked at me, "Not only will the ladies be ogling my husband and boys, but now I must chase the young men away. Just looked at you," She beamed at me as she inspected every detail, making sure that I had properly put myself together.

My father added, "Perhaps I should bring my sword. You never know when I might need to fight off these young bucks."

I was embarrassed, "Dad."

My mother laughed, as she smiled down at me. My mother was so beautiful, with her long black hair. She was tall for a woman, almost as tall as my father. She may have joked about the woman chasing after father, but there was no doubt that the men would

15

chase after my mother. She was absolutely breathtaking in her dark red dress. The material was shiny and moved like silk, with long delicate sleeves she moved like she was flying. She wore a black corset over her chest and the dress belled outwards at her hips, making her hourglass figure more defined. The dress was absolutely stunning with lots of embroidered designs in the material. All I could think when I looked upon my mother was that she was secretly a princess.

My father grabbed my mother from behind, she let out a squeal as he pulled her into his arms. She complained, "Ben, my dress."

He looked deep in her eyes, "What dress?"

She pushed him away, still smiling, "Not now. Where's Tom?"

Darrell with panic, "He is one minute and thirty five seconds late." He was having a melt down because Tom was messing with the crazy numbers in his head.

Mom smiled at him, "Don't worry darling, he'll be here."

Darrell still looked concerned. I heard loud clomping footsteps coming down from the upstairs. Tom was on his way. My parents were now prattling on about the plans for the day. Tom burst into the room looking like my shaven, starved mini- father. Even his clothes mirrored father's, with the same top hat. Tom had always looked like my father. Darrell started to tell Tom how many minutes and seconds that he was late, but was cut off by mother, "Tom, you look wonderful. Look at all my handsome men."

My mother fussed a little bit with all our clothes, my father asked, "Have you all taken your Zen?" He said this as if we didn't all have to take this every day of our life's. Without it, we would get sick, everyone knows that.

"Yes, father," all three of us replied in stereo. "Make sure to grab your goggles, we will be leaving shortly."

With a, "Yes, sir," we all hurried to make sure we were ready. I grabbed my goggles and gloves from the entryway chest. I was shoved aside by Tom, "Hey, watch it." I complained. He laughed at me, while he gathered his belongs from the chest.

Darrell had wasted no time, he was staring at the clock and panicking about the time. He said loudly to know one in particular, "If the carriage is running slow, we will miss our appointment. There is a thirty-five percent chance, less perhaps, because it is Saturday. It's hard to calculate shopping at this time of year, and what, if any, the variables it might have on arriving."

Mom gently touched his shoulder, "Don't worry darling, we'll make it. We don't have to be there precisely at ten." This of course was meant to relax Darrell, but now he didn't know how much extra time we had, or didn't. I could see the smoke coming from his ears as he tried to calculate unknown variables.

My father understood this, and did a better job of calming Darrell, "He's right, let's get a move on. We should not be tardy."

After donning our goggles the whole family headed out into the cool air. Walking outside and onto the cobble sidewalk, I took in the surroundings. We hadn't been in our home for a week. My father had taken the train from Taylorville, and established the place before my brothers, mother and I followed. Being so close to the great outer wall had brought a lot of changes to the scenery. The Golden Arches had been named after a strange sign that was made during the time of modern men.

I often wondered about the modern men, before the world fell to the dead. What were these things we found, so much stuff and even more questions.

I had not seen the sign yet, but I might get a chance since it was located towards the gate. All the buildings were built with a mixture of stone and wood. In Taylorville, every building was built with smoothly cut stone blocks, but here, all the stones were oddly shaped. It worried me that the buildings might fall over stacked in such poorly cut blocks.

I noticed a few plants and fewer trees as we moved down the sidewalk. The houses were built wall to wall, I couldn't imagine the sun ever finding its way to the sidewalk. Of course it had been overcast for three weeks. Maybe the sun never came out here? My mother was happy go lucky, and found the beauty in everything, no matter how gray, or colorless it truly was. Today was a big deal to mom, and we all knew it. There was an agreement between Tom and I, no fighting, we get along for mother's sake.

My mother only asked for one thing this New Year, a family photo. She had a photo of her and father when they got married, and baby pictures of all three of us, but no others, not even photos of her parents. They had been killed by a fire when she was younger, and what pictures the family had were also destroyed in the fire. Having a photo taken was a big deal, I had never seen it done before. Once our parents agreed to the photo, they would use their meager savings to pay for it. No, there would be no fighting or name calling today, father made that clear, clear beyond any doubt. Today was family day.

Darrell fell in step with me, "Did you know that the diameter of the outer wall that circles the Garden, is 195 miles right through the middle. This makes the wall circumference 612.3 miles long as it wraps around the outer territory. There are four steam engines that repair and build all the sections of the wall. They're so large it takes sixteen train carts to hold them. There are eight gates, each with a city like the one we live in. The Golden Arches are attacked thirty two percent more than any other gate."

"I had no idea," I said, Darrell always knew the craziest information. How he knew this stuff was beyond me, but I truly enjoyed the knowledge, even though it was from my little brother. Tom couldn't stand it when Darrell spoke of things he didn't know about. On any other day, Tom would tell Darrel to shut it, I would defend Darrell, Tom and I would fight. Not today, but I could still hear Tom's huffing as he listened to Darrell rattle off all kinds of small facts about the Golden Arches.

As Darrell talked about Eden it made me wonder. In class we learned the history of Eden, a place of safety as the monsters destroyed the world. The men and women who lived long before us, Modern Man, they had at one time lived in every corner of the planet. Now we were trapped in these walls, at the same time these walls are what set us free. Without them, we would have surely been devoured by the monsters that now freely roam the earth. Are we slaves, jailed within our own walls? Or safe, in our own paradise?

It also made me wonder about Eden, the Enchanted Gardens, where it all began. I heard, but had never seen the walls that encircled the city of Eden. The walls that stood around Eden were taller and stronger than the outer walls. Of course, those walls only encircled a 40 mile area, so they were not nearly as long. Another set of walls stood in the center, encircling the Enchanted Gardens and Castle White. I could only dream of going there one day. Of course I would never be able to enter the enchanted garden. I had seen paintings of the area, I could only dream of such adventures.

Darrell once told me that the Enchanted Garden had been one of the first gated off areas, after man fought their way free from the white castle. The last of the humans had hidden inside the castle. After enough time, we pushed the dead back, and created the Enchanted Gardens. Then they expanded more, making the city of Eden. The same process as been going on for six hundred years. Here we are, on the edge of the outer territory, fighting to take more.

Enchanted Garden was full of the most elite members of society. Full of beautiful homes, and wonderful enchanted plants that didn't die in the outside air. The trees were green, unlike the blue trees I've seen all my life. Whatever made them blue protected them from the toxic air. Magic was everywhere in the Enchanted Garden, and the story of the lights at night filled my imagination. A girl can dream.

My thoughts were interrupted when we reached the corner. There a large trolley cart awaited more passengers. My father hurried us along, since the next one would not arrive in twenty minutes. We would be forced to find a carriage. The carriage cost money and the trolley were free. Personally, I preferred the trolley. The trolley was nothing more than a flat rail cart, with benches on it, and a cover to keep the rain or sun off your head. They were very rustic, made from scrap parts, no two trolleys looked the same. A large steam engine sat at the back with the conductor and his assistant. They refueled the engine at this stop. Covered in black coal, the men toiled away at shoveling the coal from the roadside hopper into the storage bin that hung off the rear of the trolley. A large tube protruded out of the side of one of the buildings, hanging over the road with a bend at its tip. The pipe dropped down and filled water into a large funnel just in front of the steam engine.

Large clouds of black smoke poured upward from the trolley as the conductor took his place at the front. His assistant stood on the rear, shoveling the coal into the fiery furnace. We climbed aboard with several other passengers. The conductor yelled out, "All aboard, next stop, Gate Landing."

The large trolley jerked and shook as it took off. I watched the small city pass by as the trolley rumbled down the track. The houses passed by, thinning out at some spots, filled instead with small plots of lands where people grew different types of crops. Outside of the gates of the city of Eden, the land was full of peril. The great expiation was wild in comparison. Monsters regularly got over the wall and ate people. Here in the barracks there was an added layer of protection, surrounded by its own walls, but that meant less land, stacked houses and very small plots. It was a choice, farm on small plots of land, and be safe. You might starve to death if you have a bad year of crops. You could grow your crops outside of the barracks, more land, more crops. Of course you better know how to use a sword. Bandits, monsters, all kinds of challenges. My father said it was a hell of a living out there, but there was freedom in it.

The trolley was on a loop, the barracks were the size of a large town. In fact, I wasn't even sure how many Trolleys circled around this track. First we stopped at the largest train station in the Golden Gates called Gate Landing.

Our tracks pulled alongside of the platform at Gate Landing. On the other side of the platform was the main line where the large trains that crisscrossed all over the Eden would come to drop off people and supplies. Just north of us was a small lake. Not only was it the water supply for the town, but also the landing site for the large air ships. The ones that landed here, mostly went to Nemos, carrying supplies brought from the trains. Not only supplies, but passengers too, mostly prisoners. There was no train here at this moment, many people just moved about the platform, or sat, waiting patiently for the large train to arrive. Only one airship rested in the water. It looked like pictures I had seen of old naval ships, but instead of masts and sails, a giant balloon floated above, held by many lines of rope. I dreamed of one day flying in one, seeing the world from the sky.

The steam trolley lurched and jerked as it moved forward towards our location. The trolley stopped several more times on the way to Main Street. The buildings in this District lay to my left. To my right lay another set of railroad tracks, larger and wider than the ones we were using. Beyond that was the wall and a gate. The gate was only for the use of the army. Outside the gate were the wastelands. A chill ran up my spine looking upon the giant steel doors.

The large tracks that lay before the great door and wall were empty, but I knew what they were for. They were for a giant steam machine, the wall builders. I had only seen one once, and from a distance. It was long, with many carts, crazy looking machine with many cranes towering above it. Ramps for men moving on the many levels of the giant machine. Smaller trains would come bringing the giant machine, stone, wood and coal. Weapons adorn the machine, with hundreds of soldiers aboard. If a gap broke open in the wall, it was the job of the steam machine to repair it. I had been hoping one might be docked at the station today, so I might see one up close, but no such luck today. Father had said; that they came to the barracks often to refuel and repair, and we would have a chance of seeing one up close. Maybe even get to go aboard.

We unloaded from the trolley. There in front of me was the uptown area of the Golden Arches. The buildings here looked better, mostly metal and stone. The stone was of higher quality and cut to fit with precision. The buildings stood two to three stories tall, with shops at the bottom and high end apartments above. The cobble streets that ran between the buildings were crowded with people and carts. At the far end I could see the depot for carriages. Pulled by a set of bulls, they could seat six people in them. Like the trolleys they were made from scrap, so no two looked the same. Some looked as if they might fit more or less passengers. All of them were colorful, bronze, silver, gold highlighted with brightly painted accents. Each driver seemed to have their own style that matched their carriages.

Each wearing brightly decorated clothing, yelling to the crowd, trying to get them to board their carriage first.

I noticed in the center of the square there was a large fountain. In the middle a pole stood high in the air, and on it was a giant Golden M; that was shaped like arches. Below the M was a red rectangle with what appeared to be faded letters. I could not make them out. It was a relic of Modern Man that they named this city after. Darrell let me know how tall the sign was, and the diameter of the pole.

We strolled down the Main Street. The noises, movement of people coming and going, and the smell, bombarded my senses. The crowd sounded like one long unbroken voice, trapped in a bottle. Every once in a while a voice would break free, "wait for me," or "Fish for sale, come and get the freshest fish in twenty miles." The people were all dressed fine, with their jackets and top hats, dresses of many colors and designs. They called the style, Victorian. Not sure why they called it that, but it sure took a long time to get dressed.

You could quickly see who the hard working settlers were. Dressed in brown and plain clothes with nothing more than a short brim hat. I would see men dressed like that working hard jobs, covered in sweat. Moving the heavy boxes to a train, or building with stone and wood. The adult females would be found in plain dresses that hung straight with no ruffles or embroidery. Flat colors and cheaper material, the women were more common in this part of the city. They worked for a lot of the food vendors and helped with most of the small vendor tables. They would be cutting, boxing up someone's order, waiting on tables, or cooking.

I felt rich today, as my family traveled down the main road, dressed to the hilt. Yet, we were far from it, rather we were middle class and my father is just a soldier. He was very successful and had moved up the ranks quickly. Now he was a Captain, third in line to run this small city. This move to the Golden Arches was a big break for him, and we all moved in hopes for my father's success. We did have more than most, at least we had these fine clothes to wear, even if it wasn't an everyday event. My thoughts were interrupted when we arrived at our location.

We stood out front of a large, very impressive looking building. My father cut to the right of the door, and instead of going into the nice building, he moved down a very narrow alley that lay to one side of the building. When we emerged at the other end of the alley, there was a door to a small building in the back. Standing only two stories, and dwarfed by the buildings around it, you would never see this building from the street. The air was cool and damp, the sun never reached the door, and it was green with mold. Right above the door was a sign, 'Jeff's Picture Palace.'

As we entered, Tom grumbled, "Doesn't look like a palace to me."

My mother gave him the evil eye and not another word was uttered. The next few hours were hell on earth for me. I hated standing still, doing nothing, waiting for others. The dress became heavy, and I became hot. The cameraman kept barking orders, then would stand behind a large wooden box on legs. Dead center of the box was a giant round lens. The cameraman would yell for us to hold still while his assistant would hold a metal pole in the air. The poll had a long flat part at the top, which the assistant would drop powder in. When the cameraman took the photo the powder would burst into a white puff of smoke, filling the room with a brilliant white light. Each time the cameraman would stare into the back of the camera looking at something. Finally, he liked it, smiled, and announced, "It's ready for print."

We all filed into what the man called the viewing room. The man sat us all down in very comfortable chairs. A woman brought tea and cake as we settled in for the printing. We all faced one wall where a large canvas was attached to a strange machine. What surrounded it took my breath away. Two large arms, attached to larger machines, sat on both sides of the canvas. My eyes took in the hundred of gears and wires with brass hoses leading to many different sized tanks. My mind started to try to take it apart, to understand how it worked. It took me a second longer to realize that it was not two machines, but rather one very large machine. Most of it was behind the canvas and as I tried to take it all in I could see large gears starting to spin. Then smaller gears spun, and steam poured out of small holes. The noise was pleasant as it whistled and clunked to life. The two arms came to life. Instead of hands, there were large cylinders.

The arms moved like lighting. Each time the sharp side of the cylinder hit the canvas it would leave a different colored dot. At first I didn't understand what the arms were trying to accomplish, but then the picture started to come to life. My family, my dress, and we are all smiling, standing in a green field with mountains in the background and beautiful trees on the right side of the photo. The large branches overhung our family as the sky above came to life before my eyes. Filling with white puffy clouds and the blue sky, that looked clean and clear. We were standing inside a studio when this photo had been taken. My brother commented on the fact we were all outside without our goggles on. We chuckled at this remark. The magic that this must have taken, I was amazed.

The photographer told my parents that the picture would be framed and delivered in a week. My father agreed, then payed the man, ten gold coins, two silver coins and eight pennies. I had no idea how expensive this was to have made. It made me appreciate our baby photos, even if they were small compared to this family portrait.

We had just left the photo shoot. We were all still dressed in our finest outfits, and my mother felt it would be appropriate to have lunch in the city. We all headed back to the Main Street, where most of the restaurants could be found.

My parents discussed what sounded good to eat when the bells sounded. The city fell quiet as the next ring of the bell filled the air. As if being awaking from a trance, people with no words at all began to move. They moved quickly, the shop owners pulling in their wares and shutting down their shops. People hurried to the carriages, pushing and shoving to get aboard. Half running and walking, peopled hurried down the sidewalks to their homes. My father looked calm and in control, his voice was powerful, "Ok, let's move. Stay together."

My mother asked on the brink of panic, "Do you need to go? Is it not your duty to go defend the wall when the bells ring?"

Father answered flatly, "I will go when I know my family is at home, and safe."

Chapter 3 Shadows of Man

Morgan Jones

I felt like something was squeezing my hand, I looked up, my brother stood over me. "Come on Morgan, keep up."

We jogged through the crowd and down the road. It didn't take long before there were fewer people around us, as we ran straight through the middle of the District. My brother announced that at our current speed we would arrive in twelve minutes. I thought he might be wrong, until twelve minutes later, my father was kissing my mother safely within our home. My father had quickly changed into his armor with his sword hanging to one side. He grabbed his steam rifle and checked over his supplies. He was the captain, so his uniform was more decorative than regular soldiers. His chest plate was bronze with a green swirl that appeared to be under the surface. Splashes of bright red cloth showed under the bends of his armor. He wore a simple helmet that fit tightly. Telling mom to lock up tight, he said he would be home before she knew it, and kissed her once.

I was helping Tom lower the wooded covers for the windows. They slid down from the frame, then locked at the bottom with two large latches. I was at the front window as I watched my father head outside, mother locked the door behind him, securing the main latches. Across the street I saw a middle aged lady. On closer inspection, I recognized her to be one of our neighbors. Her eyes were glazed over with a wild look on her face, and I knew immediately what she was. How she died, I didn't know, but no one must have been around to destroy her brain. She now walked upright, dead but not dead. She now looked upon my father.

She ran towards him, arms stretched out before her, mouth and eyes wide open. The look of rage and hunger made my skin crawl. I yelled out through the glass, "Father, watch out." He didn't appear to hear me, but he was not unaware of her charging across the street. My heart pounded in my chest, he appeared to do nothing. She was almost upon him, now jumping at him. He stopped, then stepped back, while the crazed zombie stepped right in front of him. His right hand shot out, hitting her in the back of the head. I was staring at her face when it went blank as her body fell towards me. Face first she landed, body limp, she was truly dead now. In my father's hand he held a short dagger, which he had used to punch through the back of her skull.

He looked over at me, with a small smile. His voice sounded like he was in a box as he spoke through the window, "Lock up Morgan. You will be safe, and I'll be back." I said nothing as he turned and stepped over the body, it was my mother's voice calling me that awakened me from my trance. I closed the wooden panel and locked it. Then I headed upstairs, my brothers in tow.

My mother stayed down stairs yelling at us, "Lock your doors, and stay up there until I tell you it's safe to come out."

My brothers and I, ran into the same room and secured the door. Tom checked the window and double checked that the board was tightly secured. Now all we could do was wait, wait for the attack to end.

Hours passed, and we sat on the floor playing cards to pass the time. My mother came up several times to check up on us. She seemed more nervous than I was used to, making me wonder if she knew something that I did not. It hadn't taken my brothers and me long to discover that there was a crack in the wooden panel that secured our window. One at a time we would close one eye and stare out the sliver into the empty street. Evening was approaching, and with it, fog rolled in, the gray swirled around making it appear that things were moving in the shadows.

Tom and Darrell had become bored with peeking out the window. They were now immersed in a game of cards. I had a bad feeling, I stared out the crack one more time. At first, all I saw was the swirling fog, but then I realized that across the street the front door had been busted down. I hadn't watched it happen, or heard it. Had I seen the door broken down when last I looked? I searched my memory, desperately hoping that is how the door was, perhaps that home was empty, or perhaps that was the home of the lady that father had to kill. Yes, that was most likely it, I hadn't noticed it, until now, and that's why I hadn't heard anything.

My heart had just about settled down when my eyes caught movement from the doorway. An arm emerged, and at first it looked to be a shadow, but as the figure slowly moved through the door and into the street, I could see that it was no shadow. A shadow of men, perhaps, a Ghoul from beyond the wall. I had only seen paintings until this moment. Even through the fog, my eyes put together the monster's form.

The creature stood upright, limbs appeared to be elongated, but I knew they were not. The Ghouls used to be human long ago. Not a zombie, but much worse, intelligent, fast and strong. It wandered the wastelands, flesh rotting. They did not drink water and the body would slowly dry out, the skin would rip open, allowing the internal organs to spill upon the ground. Skin turned black like coal, as it dried tightly against the muscles and bone. No hair remained, no nose either. The eyeballs were blood red and looked to be bulging out from its dry eye sockets. No lips were covering it's ragged yellow teeth. Teeth were broken and sharp. Its mouth stained red with blood. No stomach remained, as it skin clung tightly around its spine, making it appear to have legs attached to the chest by a stick. Its eyes searched for food. No ears, but it could still hear sounds. It's chest would heave as it pulled air in through the hole that used to be a human nose. Smelling the air, looking for a meal. Ghouls and Zombies had no reason to eat, but yet all they did was hunt for flesh from the living.

The monster's head snapped towards our house. It changed direction, straight for my home. My body tensed, I found it hard to breath. As panic set in, and the creature fell from sight, I could see more Ghouls moving through the fog. Two more followed behind the first. Both soon disappeared as they moved toward what I believe to be our front door.

Tom picked up on my panic, "What's up Morgan?"

I turned and stared at my brother, the look on my face brought panic to Tom's face. Finding my voice, "Three Ghouls, front... front door."

Tom jumped up, pushing me away from the window. He looked through the crack, "Where, I don't see anything?"

"They're at the front door," I explained. You could not see the front of our building from the angle of the window. You would not be able to see them without opening the window and looking down upon the front door.

Tom huffed angrily, "Your full of shit Morgan. There's nothing out there, there is no way they could get over the outer wall, let alone into the barracks."

I started to yell, "I know that," but as my mind registered the fact that noise attracts the Ghouls, I switched to a whisper yell. "I know what I saw, there are three Ghouls out there."

Darrell sounded very unconcerned, "Three. What are the odds of three of them making it this far inside the district." I could see he was now busy working out the numbers in his head.

Tom narrowed his eyes at me, "Don't worry Darrell, Morgan is just making shit up and trying to scare us." He gave me a hard stare, "Just shadows, from the fog, it's in your head."

"Is not," I snarled back. Tom pushed me, I was about to push him back when a loud knock came from downstairs. Tom and I stiffened, we both stood very quiet, straining our ears to every sound. Not thirty seconds had passed, but it felt like eternity. I was about to say something when a smashing noise came from downstairs, both Tom and I jumped. The noise was quickly followed by more loud banging, they were trying to break in. I could hear footsteps running up the stairs, followed by my mother's voice yelling through our door. "Boys! Stay in your room. Make sure your door is locked."

"Yes, mother," We all responded. I could hear her moving around upstairs. She was most likely getting a weapon from her room. Then I could hear her go back down the stairs where the sound of her footsteps was lost in the sound of wood being bashed over and over again. With a new sound shortly following, wood cracking, giving way to the forces being exerted upon it.

In my mind, I knew the door would not hold for much longer. My mother was down there, what could she do against three of those monsters? Wouldn't she be safer with us, perhaps, our door would hold until help arrived… if it arrived. My mind was muddled with fear, still my body moved forward and my hands did my will. I was opening the door, as I pulled it open and started to leave I felt something strong grab my shoulder and start to pull me back. Tom hissed, "Are you crazy? Get back in here, and lock the door."

A gunshot exploded in our ears making Tom and I jump in surprise. I snapped my shoulder forward, breaking his grip. I ran towards the staircase as I heard the door of my room slam shut behind me. Without another thought I ran down the stairs to rescue my mother. I was halfway down the staircase when I came to a sudden halt.

My eyes were seeing it, but my brain was having a hard time understanding. My mother stood in the middle of the living area, with a crystal glowing with a bright blue light. She held it over her head, in her other hand she held a small hatchet. Before my mother, three monsters danced back and forth. They had broken down the front door and entered the living room. Now they swayed back and forth, held back with what I assumed was the light of the crystal. They were searching, pushing, looking for a way through the light. I noticed a gun lying at the bottom of the staircase. She must have dropped it, or perhaps it only had one shot.

One of the creatures turned his head, his bloodshot eyes focused as his body stiffened. He was no longer interested in the women protected by the light. He saw me. My mother noticed the monster shift its attention. Following the monster's eyes to me, my mother gasped, "Morgan." Before she could say another word the creature started towards me. My mother yelled, "Catch."

I looked up, the blue crystal was sailing through the air. Almost instinctively my hand shot out to catch it. The crystal hit the palm of my hand, but it bounced off and flew over my head landing on a step further up the staircase. I turned to head up the stairs, but the sound of screaming stopped me. My mother was screaming, screaming in pain. I turned to see that two of the monsters had pounced upon her. I could not see her under their horrible black bodies.

The light of the crystal had kept the third monster at bay, it was unable to come up the stairs. As I watched in horror, the other two monsters killed my mother. Something grabbed my ankle. I looked down to see the black hand wrap around my ankle. It pulled and I felt myself fall backwards, landing hard against the stairs. The monster pulled me down the staircase and away from the blue light. I must have been on the edge of that light, its hand had reached far enough to get my ankle. My hand shot out, grabbing one of the rails, I pulled, I had to get back up the stairs.

I felt a terrible pain shoot up my leg, I screamed, but held tightly to the railing. The pain was followed by another pain in my other leg, I screamed again. Looking down I could see two Ghouls upon me, each with one leg. Tearing and ripping, they were eating my legs off right in front of me.

The pain came in waves, and my vision was a world of red. The black creatures were now covered in blood. My blood, my mother's blood. I wished to live, my mind was fading, I pulled with all my might. Success, I looked upward upon my goal, I looked upwards towards the blue light. I pulled with one hand, then another. Reaching it finally with my right hand, I grabbed the crystal holding it tight. Rolling onto my back, I looked down at the Ghouls of men.

They huddled together, eating, they were eating my legs. I looked down vision fading upon my legs, right above the knees down, they were gone. My mind was fading out, and was I starting to pass out. Most likely would die of blood loss, I would be joining my mother soon enough. The crystal went out. I could barely make out their hideous faces in the darkness, but I could smell their rotting breath. It took all I had to lift my left arm and try to push the monster away. Instead of pushing it, the Ghoul simply grabbed my good arm, my left arm. The Ghoul tore off my arm as if I offered it up to him for a snack. Another Ghoul came for me, I reached with my right hand trying to defend myself. Then I felt its teeth sink into that hand. It didn't hurt, the world was gone, I felt like I was falling into darkness.

Chapter 4 Dreams of Angels

Morgan Jones

I awoke looking upwards, stars covering the sky. A giant black cloud was blocking out most of the night sky, my mind sharpened, along with my eyes, and I came to realize the cloud had sharp edges. It was not a cloud, rather a building that appeared to float above me. I knew that it was most likely an optical illusion, because I had been unable at this point to move my head.

My legs, the memory of the attack… My mother's death, it came crashing down upon me. I just knew they had eaten my legs off, but yet, I thought I could feel them. In fact, my whole body was now within my minds grasp. I forced myself upwards, to sit up, and see where I was, and what had happened. I looked down at my hands, and more importantly my legs. Not only were they there, but not a mark on them. I pulled up my dress, nothing, not even a scar. Maybe it was a bad dream, but then where am I now? Perhaps this is nothing more than a dream?

Scrambling to my feet, I took in my surroundings. I was standing upon a large, square, gray, unevenly laid block that made up the floor. Broken walls of the same color gray stone, stood as far as the eye could see, nothing but crumbled buildings. No plants, nothing I could make out in the distance, but darkness. The building I had seen in the sky was still there, hanging over my head, hanging over all I could see. No part appeared to touch the ground, I realized that I was under the floating structure. A tall, broken looking tower standing some ways off in the distance, appeared to go up into the floating building. In no way could it hold the massive structure in the sky.

I could see no place to go. No place to go but up to that tower, to see where it leads. This was a dream, strange, but somehow it felt real. As I approached the tower, I noticed a man sitting on a wall. He was old and dressed in rags, face weathered, thin and dirty looking. He stared up to the floating building, not moving, mouth open. At first I thought he might be dead, but his eyes moved towards me when I came closer. Fear crossed his face until his eyes focused upon me. Once he realized I was not what he feared, he turned his eyes back to the sky, his face going blank again. I felt no need to speak to this man, I kept on walking.

I was not far from the base of the tower when I noticed others moving around the base of it. They looked confused, and some of them were talking among themselves. I reached an elderly woman, I knew her, but from where? She looked up at me and smiled, she had been standing there staring at what appeared to be the entrance to the tower. I asked, "Where am I? And where does the tower go?"

The old lady shook her head, then with a solemn voice, "This is death girl." My body stiffened, she added, "I don't know where that tower leads, but I'm afraid to go there. Everyone is. We just stand around here, and no one knows anything. Where are our loved ones? Or, what to expect? Maybe we wait here for God, maybe we wait for judgment? I don't know."

"You're crazy," I said angrily. The woman didn't get mad, she shrugged her shoulders, then she chuckled a dark laugh, turned and walked away. I watched her walk away, too angry, too afraid, to say another word. That's when it hit me, that was our neighbor, the lady I watched my father kill. I fell to my knees, and there I stayed.

Some time passed before I came to the realization that I must have died. The old lady told the truth and this was no dream. I had not survived the monsters attack. Determined to find out the truth, I rose up to my feet. After talking to more than a few people, I found that it only strengthened my fears that indeed I had died. Most remembered some horrible things right before arriving in this strange place.

As mad and scared as this made me, it also excited me when I realized that my mother must be here. Most of these people, not all of them, but most, had been in the Golden Arches. They had died from the attack from the monsters penetrating the wall.

In fact, I noticed more and more people were arriving, most as confused as I was a few hours ago. They were coming from the great expanse of land all around the tower. They were coming here for the same reason I did, because they could see the tower leading to the building in the sky. It was within reason, that mother might be on her way, and this thought made me happy. I would not be alone in this place.

Hours later, more people, and more talking, with no sign of my mother. I thought to go looking for her, but that seemed foolish. I had no idea in what direction to travel, and I might miss her. Also, there was a rumor. A crazy story, a solider had come to warn us. He told us that he too had just been killed, and when he awoke, he was far away from this tower. There he had met a man, this man told him that he had been in this place for a very long time. That when people died, they came to this wasteland. Most went to the tower, but that was a mistake. There was a monster here, and it would destroy us.

He told everyone the only reason he had come was to find his friend, who died right before his eyes. He followed his friend in death shortly. He figured his friend would come here as well, but he had not. The soldier decided that he would not take the chance and hang around here. He left the way he had come.

Most people, including myself, did not take him seriously. We were dead, must we fear the monsters in death? I think not. In fact, what if my mother had arrived here before me? What if she traveled into that tower? If I went that way looking, and she did come here later, she would most likely head the same way. She didn't know I was dead, she isn't looking for me.

I stood before the large arched doorway that led into the tower. No one had gone in. There was no door, just a dimly lit room, I could just make out the base of the staircase leading the way up. My heart pounded in my chest. Why was I afraid? Why were we all afraid? I took a deep breath, and forced myself forward, into the tower. No one followed me.

The climb up the tower was not a big deal. All my fear felt silly halfway up. The tower was in great disrepair, the stone walls held no decoration. Its old stone was solid, and the staircase was wide as it circled upward to the top. It was dimly lit, and the windows were spaced so far apart that in some spots I had to feel the wall. It took a long time, and a lot of stairs, but finally I reached the top. I noted that not only was I not tired, but I felt no hunger either.

I couldn't think about how weird, not being hungry or tired was; because I was trapped in awe as my mind took in my surroundings. Below me was a floor of stone, above me was a sky of stars. I had never seen so many stars, in fact, I had only a distant memory of ever seeing stars. The sky was always dirty and full of smoke, but one night in Taylerville, when the wind was blowing hard from the north, I remembered seeing the stars. But nothing like this. It appeared to be clouds of stars, full of color. My eyes remained looking upon the sky for some time, until I had to tear them away to take in the rest of my surroundings.

I was in the strangest place. Walls stood everywhere, walls with no ceilings. Walls lined with books, thousand of books. Everywhere I looked, books were stacked, or crammed into bookshelves. Fireplaces of all kinds and different designs were on every wall, burning with low fires. I didn't see any wood, nor smoke, just a low flame burning from nothing. Slowly walking, I continued to take in my environment. I could feel the heat of the fires as I passed by. The air was pleasant, sweet, and smelled like a spring day after the rain.

My eyes had been so busy, I hadn't noticed that I was staring at her. When I realized I was, I wondered, how long had she been staring at me. There in front of me, sitting on top of a desk with her legs folded and a book in her lap. Fear washed through me, as my mind put together this Angel who sat in front of me. She wore a simple dress, it was dark red and looked worn. Her long golden hair hung loosely around her head, draped down her shoulders and onto the table. Her skin was a pale white, almost like marble, with long delicate fingers and sharp black nails. Her eyes were blue, with a light that shone through them, making her face almost seem in shadow. The eyes, how long did I stare at them, before I noticed the black wings spread out behind her. Black with large feathers and black smoke rising in small clouds from between those feathers. The smoke floated off into un-felt breezes. She smiled, exposing long, sharp canines, I froze in terror.

The girl's voice was sweet and rang like a bell, "Why, hello." I could not find my voice. She spoke as she set her book to the side and gracefully rose to her feet. "Seldom do spirits brave their way here."

I finally squeaked, "Who are you?"

"I'm the angel of death, but fear me not."

I didn't understand her, but I found my courage and asked, "Have you seen my mother?"

She was giving me a quizzical look, "Your mother has gone on to her final place of rest. Do not be sad, she is happy, and with her ancestors. This is a place for spirits who refuse to move on, and haunt the earth. You my dear, well, let's just say you will be joining your mother soon enough."

I didn't know what to say, and even though I kind of thought I knew the answer I asked, "Why will I join her? I mean, why haven't I?" I must be dead, my mind had a flash of the ghouls eating me alive.

Her eyes narrowed and her smile became a grin, "Little girl, so many questions. Let me show you, let me show you what is happening in the land of the living. Let me show what is happing to my brave girl."

She moved towards me, then around me, without a sound, and far too quickly for me to react. Her wings moved behind her like black clouds, they appeared to be solid, until they hit a wall or a bookshelf. Breaking apart into a cloud, then becoming whole again. One wing hit me, I was momentarily blinded. Next thing I knew, her arm wrapped around my shoulders. She pulled me along saying, "Come now, let me show you." As we walked down the endless hall of books she continued to talk as if we were old friends. "You know you are special. Your blood reaches back, to a different time. Too bad, too bad indeed. Killed at such a young age, never kissed, never loving another." She suddenly looked like she had an idea, "I will send a cat, and give you a chance to live again. Not often I met someone so brave."

I was too shocked to speak back, not sure what to say anyway, or what the heck she was talking about. We arrived in another room of books. This room was much bigger than the hallways and smaller rooms we had come from. In the center lay a pool of water. The tile work around the pool and most of the floor was composed of intricate patterns that highlighted the pool itself. We came to a stop next to the pool. The water was clear, and as I looked down I witnessed another world below me. "Now, dear, look and see," she did not let go of me as we both looked down at the water.

It took me a moment to digest what I was experiencing. I was looking down upon myself, covered in blood with no legs from the knees down. My left arm was missing and my right looked mangled. The Ghouls lay dead in a pile. A gun lay next to my right hand, but that didn't make sense, I was sure it was at the bottom of the staircase. A cat I had never seen before scurried out of sight. I hadn't time to wonder about how the cat got in the house when I realized in that second, that I killed my mother. My heart dropped.

My mother might of held them off, if it wasn't for me. She had thrown her protective crystal to me, to save me… Because I disobeyed her. My eyes filled with water, the Angel gave me a squeeze, then informed me, "I normally don't do this, but… It would not have mattered if you had stayed in your room. She would have died, then you and your brothers. It was unavoidable."

She couldn't understand what I was feeling. Through free flowing tears I cried out, "She was holding them off until I arrived. If she hadn't given me the crystal, she could of held them off until help arrived."

The Angel slowly shook her head. Taking her free hand she reached over and wiped the tears from my face. Her voice was soft, "The crystal was running off a charge that had been left by the enchanter who made it. So see, forget the guilt. You couldn't have saved anyone, not on your own. Your bravery didn't go unnoticed; I could use someone brave."

I sniffle and wiped my face and did my best to pull myself together. The Angel waited quietly, after a bit she led me to a chair. Sitting in front of a desk I leaned against it. Not physically tired, but emotionally. The Angel sat next to me, "There's more."

Unable to cry, "What more can there be. Then again, I'm dead, so what can it matter."

"Not yet," she corrected.

"Soon enough," I retorted.

"A deal," she said with a grin.

I repeated the words back, "A deal?"

"Yes," I could see excitement in those blazing eyes. "I will make you one. I will make you a deal. I have already made a down payment, I have saved your brothers. Here is the deal for the rest of your life. I will let you live, and I will give you a great gift of power. In turn, you will do things for me. When the time is right."

"What things?"

"Does not matter what things. What matters, is you will live." I was about to argue when she went on, "There's more girl." She added bluntly, "Your father is dead."

My body tensed, "You mean my mother."

"No," she said, trying to sound comforting, but not accomplishing it. "He died a hero. The wall fell, and he led the charge to push the dead out, until the great machine came to fix it. He saved hundreds of his fellow soldiers with his quick thinking. In the end he fell to hoards of monsters, but not before ensuring the repair of the wall."

I burst into tears, "Why would I want to live. I want to see my father… No deal, let me die." My mind raced, and I could not wait for death. I wished to be with them now.

The Angel let me cry for a bit, then said softly, "I am not done." I gave her my best death stare, what now I thought. "Morgan, your father didn't die in peace. He died with many regrets. He didn't leave enough for his family, he didn't see his children grow up, and his wife would be alone to raise the children. Most of all, he wanted to protect you Morgan, you had a very special place in his heart. It now means that his spirit is lost in this place." Her eyes narrowed, "And, he is mine."

I jumped to my feet, "Let's go find him. You can help him, right?"

She stood, took my shoulder and pushed me down in my seat, "Not so quick. Yes, I can help him, and I know where he is, but you will never find him. Even if you did, you would not be able to help him. His spirit will remain here for hundreds of years... tormented. Truly sad."

I was dumbfounded, "Why will you not help me? What is it that you want? I will do anything."

A wicked smile spread across her face. I understood her before she even told me. "Then live, and I will see your father's spirit to rest."

She paused waiting for my answer. I stared at her, not sure what to say. In dismissive fashion, she added, "Do not be in such a hurry to die girl. You will, it's guaranteed, and your parents will be waiting for you. Live, make them proud, do my bidding. Then you can all be in heaven, together... forever. If you don't, your poor father might be lost, wandering... forever."

I took a deep breath, then I did as my father had told me, I dug deep for courage. "What must I do?"

The Angel produced a scroll from thin air. It rolled out across the table, the words were in a strange language that I could not read. At the bottom of the paper was a spot to sign. Not sure if it was there before, I noticed a quill in a jar of ink upon the desk. She spoke in a demanding voice, "Sign."

I hesitated, then took the quill out, shaking off the extra ink. "I can't read this."

She laughed, "Great power, you are working for me now, sign, or your father will be lost for all times." I was frozen in indecision, when she whispered, "Save him."

I signed, the room filled with black smoke, and my mind filled with pain. I could feel only one hand and Tom still squeezing. I could hear the doctor saying, "I gave her something to sleep." My mind was falling into darkness, the pain was fading. The last thought I had was, I should have never signed.

Chapter 5 Awake

Tom Jones

Her eyes finally opened. I spoke softly to her, "Morgan, can you hear me." She smiled, and I was forced to wipe a tear way.

With a weak voice she said, "Cry baby."

I laughed, "Yep the doctors were right… Brain damage."

She tried to laugh, but then her face turn to pain. "Sorry, take it easy, sis."

She blinked, she looked around the room, "Parents bed?" I nodded, "Mother…"

It all came out quickly, "You did what you could Morgan. You were a real hero, but you couldn't save her. No one blames you."

She looked confused, then she said as she began to cry, "I killed her Tom."

I knew it, I knew she would blame herself, "Stop that. No one blames you.. In fact, you're kind of a hero. You killed three Ghouls, three… that's amazing."

"What?" her face tightened in panic.

It was not surprising that she might not remember, the doctor told me if she awoke that she might not recall the entire night. "I don't know what happened, but when they found you, you were surrounded by three dead Ghouls. You were lying there, with no arm, no legs and mother's steam gun in your half eaten arm."

Her eyes filled with panic, "No legs, no arm." She tried to sit up, but I stopped her. "What is left of me."

She was crying, "Calm down Morgan, it's going to be ok."

The big man Jim came over, "She's awake." He sounded as if he didn't believe it. "I'll go get the doctor." He rushed quickly out of the room.

Morgan was crying, "Where's dad?"

I couldn't tell her, not now, "He'll be here soon, calm down." Her breathing was labored, and I was beginning to freak out when she closed her eyes. She went stiff as if someone was hurting her. "Morgan... You ok?"

She opened her eyes, wet with tears, "It hurts." She sounded so small I was forced to wipe more tears away, "Don't cry."

"Sorry," I felt ashamed, I needed to be strong, I needed to be the man for her. "Sorry, the doctor will be back soon, he can help with the pain."

Her eyes went blank, like something died inside. With a flat tone, "I need, I need, sleep... I need to rest. Ok Tom, just wake me up when Father gets here."

I squeezed her hand, "Ok sister." I was at a loss of words, what could I say?

I watched her for what felt like hours. I knew she was not sleeping, in pain and misery. I knew she would blame herself about mother, even though it was not her fault. She was twelve years old, yet I wasn't brave enough to chase her out of the room. I hid with Darrel, telling myself it was my job to protect him. I was a coward. She fought the Ghouls all on her own.

Even when I heard my mother's screams, then I heard Morgan scream. Then the gun shots. How did she do it? How did she kill three of them while they ate her alive? Yet, I never left that room, it was our neighbor Jim who had found her. He had stopped the bleeding and found her a doctor. A city of hurt and dying and somehow that man had brought a doctor to my sister.

The doctor was angry about it, he thought it a waste of time. She was already dead, he claimed, but Jim would hear none of it. Her breathing changed. She had finally fallen back to sleep. I squeezed her hand.

Chapter 6 Train to Backwater

Morgan Jones

I must have fallen asleep again, I realized there were several people in my room, "How is the patient doing today?"

Tom's voice answered, it sounded hollow and broken. "She's still sleeping. What day is it?"

Jim's deep voice soothed him, "The sixth, it's only been a day. Don't fret. She'll wake up again, and when she does you'll be right here waiting for her."

Tom's voice was full of pain, "She knows mother died, but after all this, how can I tell her about Dad?"

Jim sounded thoughtful, "Tell her, he was a hero. Without him, many more would have died. The whole city, owes him a debt of gratitude. In fact, thousands of families throughout the southern region owe a debt to him."

It felt like someone had stabbed me in my chest. A mixture of sadness and fear washed over me as I realized two things. One, my father was really dead, and two, that the angel might not have been a dream. I eventually opened my eyes, wishing in some ways I didn't have to.

The next six weeks I spent in bed. Mostly drugged to numb the pain and lost in nightmare filled sleep. My despair was the only thing I felt, I barely spoke with my brothers when they came to visit. My brothers were in the house alone, Jim came by daily to check up on all of us. He also managed to drag the doctor in every other day. The city rewarded my father's family with a nice sum of money and a plaque for his sacrifice in the line of duty. We were too young to manage our own affairs, so Tom informed me, when I was strong enough for travel, we would be moving from the Golden Gates to Backwater. In the small town of Backwater, my uncle Tony Jones lived. My father's brother, a man I knew little about, and my father had barely mentioned.

Tom came into the room, pushing a wheelchair, I told him, "No way."

Tom barked, "I'm not carrying you, and you can't stay in bed forever."

It was the first time I had ever ridden in a wheelchair. I hated it immensely, yet this would be my home for all times. Never to walk or run again, the depression swallowed me whole as Tom pushed and then bounced me down the staircase. Once in the living room, I closed my eyes, I couldn't stand being in here. The room reminds me of mother's death. Tom informed me that the doctor felt that I wasn't well enough to travel, but we were to board the train in the morning. He explained to me that the landlord won't give us one more day, it was already March 14th, our parents had died on February 4th. We need to get to Tony's house right away. Apparently we ran out of money, the rest of it went to my uncle. He hadn't felt it necessary to pay a second month, even though the doctor was against the long travel in my condition.

Our property would be picked up the next day by an auction house, it was all going up for sale. All we were able to keep was what we could fit in our bags. This should have upset me, but it didn't, I was too numb and didn't care. I don't remember the last night in our house, nor the ride to the platform, or getting on the train. It was all a blur.

Once we boarded the main line out of the Golden Arches, we had a ten to twelve hour trip to look forward to. It wasn't a straight shot, and there would be stops along the way. Darrell was not his normal number maniac self, ever since he laid eyes on me, he had barely spoken. Perhaps that should have bothered me, perhaps it did, I felt empty.

Once Tom carried me to my seat, because the wheelchair had to be stored, Darrell broke the silent treatment. He had never really showed emotion, that I could remember. In fact, his silence was the closest thing that I had ever witnessed.

He started in, "It should be an interesting trip Morgan. We will be taking the route through Texas, I've always wanted to see that city. Did you know that it is the largest city outside of Eden?" I didn't answer, he just continued, "After that we will travel north to the Coal mines. I bet it will be cold that far north. Then we will head east to Iron city, District of Washington and finally to the Winters Light. We have rooms in Winters Light. The next morning we will travel by coach for the next fifteen miles. Finally, we will be in the town Backwaters. So, I've calculated the trip, of course I don't know how long we might be at any stop, but if they hold a traveling speed and do not exceed thirty minutes a stop, we'll be there in twenty hours."

My voice was empty, "Sounds great."

His eyes narrowed, he even looked a little upset. I knew I was the only member of the family besides father that listened to him. He tried again with me, "I keep all the important numbers memorized for mother. Like, all our height and weight, so mom can keep a growth chart. Not sure how much you weigh since you lost your limbs, and I guess we will need to remeasure you for your height."

My face heated with my anger, I yelled, "Shut up, you nut. Mother doesn't need you to keep records for her… She's dead. And never, ever, ask me about my height and weight again."

At this moment Tom had returned from storing our luggage, "What's going on?"

"Nothing," I said nastily.

Darrell said nothing, Tom shook his head and joined us. The cart was loud, we couldn't afford private rooms so we had to sit on benches. Each bench could sit three across, two sets of benches faced each other. Across the aisle there were more benches. We all shared one bench as some workers sat on the one across from us. Tom and Darrell fell into conversation with the middle aged men as the train started the journey.

Aside from my little brother hurting my feelings, and the complete awfulness of boarding the loud, smelly train, I rather enjoyed watching the countryside go by while the train rattled down the track. We hadn't been on the train for an hour when I realized Tom had stopped talking to the men and was speaking to me. "Hello, hello, anyone home? Morgan!"

I narrowed my eyes, "What?"

Tom smiled, he has been strangely nice to me ever since the loss of my body parts. "You're being rude to these men, they were introducing themselves."

I stared the men down, and looked back at Tom, "So? I don't want to know them." With that, I went back to staring out the window.

Tom started to yell at me, when the men stopped him, and told him to have patience with me. Obviously Tom had been telling them my life story. Tom softened his tone, "Morgan, I thought, well, you might get bored. I got you a book." He pulled out a rather large book, on the front it said, Olden Fairy tales. "If you need help."

I cut him off, "Thank you," it had been the first happiness I had felt in a long time. "Truly, thank you brother."

Tom added, "Darrell helped pay for it, it's from the both of us."

I gave Darrell a big smile, then kind of felt bad for being mean to him. "Thank you too, brother."

I pulled the book from Tom's lap to my lap with my good hand. It was heavy, and I had some difficulty opening it with my one hand. Tom tried to help, but I stopped him as sweetly as I could, "I can do it, thanks."

He smiled, "Of course you can."

The boys went back to their conversation with workers and left me to my book. I found nothing in this book about Fairy tales. The entire book contained nothing but information on how to enchant. Secrets of enchanting that I had never heard about before. Of course, how could I hear the secrets from the wizards that lived in the Enchanted Garden. That is where all the magical items came from, like my father's watch, or the crystal my mother had. How could I be holding a real magic book?

The train rumbled down the tracks, stopping, loading and unloading. The men who had sat across from us, departed in Texas. They had been replaced by an old couple. The man was skinny, with a gray beard and balding, his wife was plump and wore layers of makeup to hide her age. Her bright black hair obviously colored, and her dress appeared to be at least one size too small. She had to pull on it, just to sit down. She complained loudly to her husband, he responded with, "Yes, dear." He must have said this a dozen times a minute. She acted as if the train company had made a mistake, and they were not poor like the rest of us, they should have been in first class. Everyone, pretended that they couldn't hear them.

I went back to my book. Tom made the remark, "I had no idea you loved fairy tales so much. What story are you reading?"

I looked to make sure no one could hear. The old lady and man had fallen asleep, slumped up against the window. "Have you looked inside this book?" I whispered.

Tom gave me a funny look, "Yes, what's wrong with it?"

"Nothing, just, well, look," I had the book open to how to create an etching rod, also known as an enchanting wand. It is the magical instrument that enchanters use to mark the symbols needed to enchant an item. This was amazing, because I had read that the knowledge had been lost. There were a handful of these rods in the Enchanted Garden, how many, few would know. Then again, perhaps this book has been just a Fairy Tale.

Tom stared at the page for a second, "Peter Pan, I love this story."

I looked down at the book, and nowhere did it say Peter Pan. There were sketches of symbols and an etching rod.. Paragraphs with instructions and notes in the borders. Every page was full of the same. "Wait, that's not what it says. This book is full of magic spells. Nothing about Peter Pan."

Tom just laughed, "Peter Pan is magic. Speaking of which, do you think that our uncle will use our parents' money to send me to school?"

I didn't understand it. I noticed that Darrell had been reading the book from the other side of me. I asked, "What are you reading?"

He gave me a funny look, "Your Peter Pan story."

Tom yelled over my back, "She's playing a game, it's a magic book."

Darrell shrugged, "Ok."

Not understanding what was going on, Tom distracted me by changing the subject, "Well, what do you think uncle will say?"

I was confused because my brothers could not see what I could see in the pages of this book. Tom had asked a question about uncle sending him to school, I put the thought aside and answered him. "Yes, I mean, why won't he send you?"

Tom sounded worried, "Dad never told you about Tony?"

"No, not really," I admitted.

"Dad never really liked to talk about him. See dad grew up in Backwater, poor, a son of a pig farmer. Every day we get our daily dose of Zen. You may not know this, but Zen cost two cents, per person, per day. Being military, father could afford it, but that wasn't true when he grew up."

I was surprised, "I had no idea. What happens if you don't take it every day?"

Grimly Tom answered, "Well, you can get the cough."

The cough, the sickness that plagued the land. Once you started coughing, you would only stop when you died. I remember once, when I was younger, going to the market. There I saw an old lady coughing so hard she was racked with pain. She coughed again into a red rag, and at first I thought the rag was red because of the color of the material. Then I realized, it was drenched with blood. She pulled her lips away from the rag, and the blood dripped from her mouth. Death, then a zombie, then someone one would destroy her brain.

Tom went on with his story about our uncle. "Our Uncle Tony was not blessed like our father. He wasn't very... physical and couldn't pass the military exams. Shoot, the way dad puts it, the man would trip on a flat surface. Dad also said that Tony felt like the parents liked him best, and treated him better somehow."

I hadn't heard father speak much of his parents, "Grandparents are dead now, right?"

"Oh, yes, died when Dad was a teenager. See, Dad showed such promise that he was able to get into the academy. That's inside Eden. He left his brother with the pigs. Father sent Tony money, when he could. It was enough that Uncle could get out of pig farming and start a small supply store. Even though father helped him, Tony was still bitter. Being the older brother he thought he should have gotten the grant to the academy. Now he has the early signs of the cough, most likely from getting too little medicine and having to work outside in the air. He can't afford to go to Eden to get the medical help he would need to survive. Father wanted to help him, but he didn't have enough money."

This didn't sound good, not one bit. I couldn't help but wonder what might become of us. I wouldn't let Tom know my fears, "Don't worry." I lied. "I'm sure Uncle will help us, and take good care of us."

Tom nodded, "Yeah, you're probably right." His voice didn't match his words, he knew there would be trouble ahead.

I turned back to my book. I wonder, looking upon the page of the book. How to make an etching rod? It was a long train ride after all.

Chapter 6 Moonlight

Tom Jones

Morgan looked happy with her new book. If I would have known, I would have given it to her earlier. Darrell is impossible to have a conversation with. After the miners left, they were replaced by this annoying couple. Her ridiculous husband, pretended to be asleep, I would have played dead if I would have married her. I had no interest and speaking to either of them.

I really wanted to talk to Morgan, but she hasn't been the same since our parent's death. Then again, I haven't been the same. I can't even recall crying, it didn't feel real. I was still half expecting my parents to reappear. When it hit me that I would never see them again, the tears would start to rise, but then I'd remember my sister. I had to be strong, so I pushed the thoughts away. Still, whether she knew it or not, she was my best friend and I needed her as much as she needed me.

She had been staring at a page for much too long to be reading it. It was some kind of story about a Troll under a bridge. I decided she wasn't really reading and asked, "How are you doing? Comfortable?"

She looked up at me like I had interrupted her, "Legs feel asleep." I nodded, then realized what she said and laughed. "Well, what legs I have, feel asleep. And not to mention my butt fell asleep too."

"Well, that heavy book can't be helping."

"True, what's your lap doing?" She said this with a grin.

I shook my head, then picked up the book, placing it in my lap. "Better?"

"Yes," She had a strange look in her eye. Then she asked, "What do see when you look at the pages in the book?"

It was the second time she asked me this. The first time I thought it was a game, but this time I was not sure. I looked down at the book and really studied it. "All I see is a story, not even that good of a story. What do you see?"

Her eyes narrowed, "Funny, that's what I see..." She reached with her only arm over her body and touched the book. "That's weird."

At first I thought perhaps a joke, but she hadn't been joking. She would snicker and giggle when she was up to something. "What is it? What do you see?"

She smiled at me, "I see hope. Maybe I have magic, just maybe."

"Maybe you have brain damage, just maybe." She pinched me, "Ow."

"Sorry brain damage causes my fingers to close involuntarily."

I smiled, not because she pinched me, but because I had hope that my sister might overcome this.

Morgan Jones

The book didn't work with just anyone. Could the book be enchanted? This is why my brothers were able to buy it for me, somehow the magic book got mixed up in normal books. This means that the magic in this book could be real.

I dove into my book, reading everything about making an enchanting wand. If I had one, I would be able to magically make... Anything I wanted. Of course, only if this book is genuine.

The first thing I would need was an enchanting rod. Some materials won't work, silver was the best, or a piece of silver on the tip of white oak. I had neither of these things. Further down the list was steel, and steel I had. Father, long ago taught me how to employ a knife. He would say, "This is a dangerous world, and those who do not practice to guard themselves, practice to be a victim."

He handed me a knife on my birthday, but this was no ordinary knife. It was about six inches overall, long and thin, mostly made for stabbing. The handle was flat, and made of steel, in fact, the blade and handle was the same solid piece of steel. This made the weapon thin, and easily hidden within the folds of my clothes. I could sense it, squeezed up against my side, hidden under my corset. Ready to be pulled out at a moments notice. To turn this into an enchanting rod, I would need to draw symbols upon its blade with my blood. Then chant the words, under the light of the moon. The last part bothered me, I won't be able to do this now, and I couldn't remember the last time I saw the moon under the cloud of smog.

Disappointed, I put the book down, and finished the last few hours just staring out the window. It was already March 14th, hard to believe that it had been over thirty days since my parents were killed. Of course I was asleep during much of this time. Snow was now falling, along with my dreams of magic. We arrived at the walled city of Winterlight. The snow was coming down in large white snowflakes, making it hard to see through the wall of white. The city reminds me of the Golden Arches as far as construction and layout. It took minutes to unload, but some time to get my wheelchair and our trunks out of the baggage car. By the time we were ready to leave, my teeth were chattering. Even though Tom covered me with a large blanket, I was still freezing. It was now dark outside, Tom never complained about having to push me through the snow. He had to stop every twenty feet, go back and pull our trunks, and then repeat the whole process over again.

My voice chattered in the cold, "Just, leave me."

Tom was sweating from the effort. He said none too nicely, "Hush it. I will not leave you to freeze to death. I will leave these damn trunks first."

Darrell couldn't do much more then pull his own trunk. I swear I was about to freeze to death when Tom finally pushed me through the door of the inn. I was useless, all I could do was sit there and chatter my teeth and shake. That night I slept poorly. There had been only one bed, we all piled together. It had been so cold, but now with the heat of my brothers' bodies, I was now too hot to sleep. The morning only brought more bad news, we were snowed in. Uncle had sent a young man by the name of Fin to fetch us. Tom met with him, right before bringing me some breakfast. We would never make it out today, maybe tomorrow.

The day had been boring, and I mostly caught up on much needed rest. My brothers spent most of the day with Fin throwing snowballs. I could hear them laughing and playing, it made me cry. When Tom came in to check on me, which he did often, I would pretend to be asleep or reading. I would give him big fake smiles and lie to him about what a wonderful day I was having. That evening, Tom and Darrel burst into our room carrying dinner for all of us. Behind them Fin stood, he was handsome, and shame washed over me from the state of my hair and clothes. He was much older than me, perhaps twenty. Big brown eyes that matched his hair, and a pleasant smile. Even with him watching, I ate, I was starving. He didn't say much and shortly bid me Goodnight. Then he invited Tom to a game of cards in the tavern. Tom's face lit up big, he asked me, "Sis, you think…"

I didn't let him finish, "Go ahead, take Darrell. I will be busy, reading."

He had been too excited about playing cards at the tavern to notice my lie. Or how much it hurt to be left alone again. They left, and all I could do was watch the red sky from my window. The room was cold, I wrapped the blanket around me, staring out at the city covered in white. Really, there wasn't much to see, the window only allowed me to look at what appears to be the back of another building. Still, I could see the sky, which was now dark. The moon lit up the white snow, casting almost enough light to read by. It took me way too long to realize that the storm had cleared the sky. A few stars poked out, but more importantly the moon was out, and it shined through my window! I quickly pulled out the book and my knife. The excitement made me forget about the cold, I was going to try magic!

My work had been hard, with one hand, I found it even difficult to cut myself for the blood I needed for the knife. Pushing the handle of the knife into the side of the bed frame, I could rub my finger against the blade. After cutting myself, I found it just as hard to wrap my hand to stop the bleeding. Realizing I had cut much deeper than I attended to, I cursed my life.

Hours later I looked down upon my knife with a new hope. Following the instructions had been harder than I thought. Perhaps I was just delusional, but I swear it glowed. I felt the magic it had taken, I felt like it sucked out my life force. I would be too tired to try anything else tonight. Tomorrow I would hope to find the time to enchant something.

Chapter 7 Welcome to Backwater

Morgan Jones

I had barely put the knife away when my brothers returned. Tom looked at me, eyes wide, "What have you done?"

At first I couldn't understand how he knew that I was practicing magic, but then I realized he was talking about the blood. "It was an accident," I declared, with my best innocent face. I hadn't noticed what a mess I made. There was blood on my shirt and the bed.

Darrell added in his robotic voice, "She lost six ounces of blood. It looks like more, but it is only six, she should be fine."

Tom snapped at him, "How could you know that?" Tom came over to nurse my hand. I tried to tell him he didn't have to, but he would not take no for an answer. Tom complained as he worked, "I should have never left you alone. You only have one arm… I'm sorry."

This of course made me angry, "I'm not a child. I can still take care of myself, I don't need a babysitter."

"Yes, yes you do," Tom disagreed, staring me down.

I pulled my hand away, "Goodnight." I slammed my head down upon the pillow. I was so angry, so helpless. I wanted to be mad at him, slap him in the face, but as he pulled the covers over me to make sure I would be warm, I couldn't help but think of him huffing and puffing as he pushed me through the snow. It was hard to remain mad at him. Instead, I remained mad at myself for being such a burden.

The next morning the snow still blanketed all that I could see, but Fin said that the Bulls could pull the wagon today. He was in a hurry, and with the snow it would make a hard day's ride, harder. Apparently Fin was not here just to get us, or perhaps us at all. His wagon was packed full. Tom made Fin mad, he held him up as Tom reworked the boxes of goods. He created what looked like a fort I used to make as a child. He slid me in and covered the entrance with a blanket so I might not freeze to death.

He felt horrible, "Morgan, sorry I can't ride back here with you, but..."

I finished his sentence for him, "There's not enough room." I smiled, "No this is fine, I'm fine. Plus, I have my book to keep me company."

Tom smiled, "Sure glad you love that book so much."

Fin barked from the front, "For the love of the seven Gods, are you ready yet?"

"Yes," Tom yelled back. With that he gave me a quick smile while sealing me in. Tom and Darrell would have to take turns riding with Fin on the bench of the wagon. The other would have to follow by foot through the snow. Tom started on foot, first. I peeked out my blanket, feeling the cold air bite my nose, Tom followed, hands in pocket, trailing in one of the tracks left by the wagon. His head was looking down, he had a fur hat on, but he was trying to keep the cold wind out of his face.

Every day was another day to watch my brother work overtime, while I was nothing but a burden. A great pain raced through my chest as I looked down upon my book. What if this was all just a story? I mean, how could I have a true magic book? And without this, what use can I possibly be?

It was hard to see, so I thought of trying something simple. I pulled at the blanket just enough to let the light in, freezing air came in with that light, but I needed to see. I picked a stone out of my pocket, it was just an old road stone, round and smooth that fit in the palm of my hand. Taking my steel knife, I carved the symbols into the rock. This was not easy, the cart was bouncing, the stone was hard, and the light was inadequate. Not to mention I only had one hand. The stone had slipped, and almost fell right out of the cart more than once.

After finishing the task I covered the hole back up with the blanket, now I was freezing cold. Holding the rock in my hand, I said the magic words through chattering teeth. Over and over again, pushing my will into it. I could have been wrong, but I swear I could feel my power going to this stone.

If I did the instructions right, I would find out soon enough. I laid the stone right outside of the blanket, so that it was in the sun. Now it was a matter of time. This enchanted rock, if I did it right, if this works, it would not only emit light, but heat. For every twenty minutes of sunlight, I would get three hours of light and heat. I waited for what felt like eternity, then I reached out my hand and pulled the cold rock back in my shelter with me. I looked down at the rock, barely able to make it out in the dark. Teeth chattering, "Please work." Holding the cold rock in my hand, I said the word to activate it, "*Illumination.*"

The Rock burst forth with an amazingly bright light, blinding me. I had to cover it with a piece of my dress so that my eyes might adjust. My heart pounded, and I could barely contain a squeal. The light turned blue, because it was under my blue dress. Then I felt it, not hot, but warm, warm enough to warm my cold hand. I wrapped my fingers around it tighter, trying to drain the heat to my numb limb. I had magic, real magic. I smiled and giggled to myself.

Making my magic rock and playing with it, really made the time go by. Before I knew it, we were stopping for lunch. There would only be one stop, it was an eight hour trip, perhaps longer with the snow covered roads. We would not stop again and Fin had made this crystal clear. I turned off my rock and hid it. I wasn't sure why? One part of me wanted to show Tom and Darrell what I had done, but something held me back.

Tom and Darrell joined me on the back of the wagon to share some cold chicken, bread and water. It wasn't good, but I was starving. Fin had been dealing with the Bulls and checking the rig, he joined us shortly. He was good looking, still, something in those eyes, I didn't trust him. Better make sure no one but my brothers knew about my new found magic book.

It wasn't long before I was bouncing down the road again, holding my rock in my hand letting it warm my fingers. I was tired, not only from the journey and lack of sleep, but enchanting the Rock itself. The book warned that using magic would drain your physical energy. This is why enchanted objects were so coveted, because you charge the item and use it when you wanted. Enchanting would be like exercise, the more you did, the more you could do without becoming tired. I fell asleep, dreaming of a world full of magical items. Everything danced around at my will, lights, furniture, dishes, it was a very happy dream.

I was awoken from my dream by Darrell, I could hear him telling Fin how many miles we traveled and what our average speed was. I could tell Fin was tired of Darrell and fussed at him, "Make yourself useful. Go get your sister's chair and help her in it, then count the strands of hair on her head."

Tom spoke up for Darrell, "Hey, he can't help it."

Fin barked back, "And either can I. It's been a long trip, so help me unload so I might get paid and get on my way."

Tom asked, "You don't live in Backwater?"

Fin laughed, "Hell no, I don't live in this God forsaken place. Just one of my stops. Now stop all the jabbering and get to work."

Tom said something that I couldn't make out, but it didn't sound nice. Darrell raised the blanket, forcing me to close my eyes from the bright light. He asked, "You awake?"

Annoyed, "Yes, help me out of here, I've been back here all day."

Darrell is much smaller than Tom, he almost dropped me trying to get me into my wheelchair. Once seated, and my eyes were looking into the setting sun, I looked around at my new home in Backwater. In a word, ugly. The snow still lay upon the ground, so that part was pretty. Blue trees, evergreens, that were still blue, spotted the land, making it white and blue. The trees were far apart over slowly rolling land. This part was ok, but the town of Backwater, now that didn't look friendly at all. The roads were mud, snow already driven to the side. The buildings were all made of wood, and roughly built. Not one building look like it was made by the same man. A river, ran through the middle of the town. The river was called, the Snow Spring River, and it was one of the cleanest water sources around. A bridge connected both sides of the town, and on one side of the bridge was a dock, where small river boats came and went.

It was a covered bridge and the wood was rougher than even the buildings. I could see men and women moving about, all wearing plain brown working clothes. No fine clothes in this mud hole. I heard the pigs before I saw them, a few of them darting in between buildings. Of course they lived with the pigs.

We had stopped in front of a large wooden building, just outside of town on a hill overlooking the land. The building had a large porch, which Tom and Fin lifted my chair up to. Of course, there was no ramp, and the few steps up to the porch would have been too much for Darrell to carry me up, so Tom would always have to carry me. I sat up on the porch taking it all in, as my brothers and Fin unloaded the goods from the wagon. I noticed a small sign hanging from the edge of the porch, all it said was, General Store. This must be my uncle's place. A chill ran through me, this was my new home.

My uncle walked out from the store, I knew it was him. He was most definitely my father's brother, his height, his build, his nose, mouth and his eyes, but this was certainly not my father. It was what I might imagine if my father was eighty years old. White hair, long and unkempt, thin and balding. His face weathered with deep wrinkles, eyes dark and empty. He appeared to be angry, or unhappy. His back bent, he leaned on a cane that looked old and wicked. The cane was twisted and full of knots, bending at the top where he held his right hand, leaning to support his weight. He wore what looked to be at one time a nice suit. Now it was worn and dusty looking, threads visible around the edges, especially around the cuffs. The old brown and gray suit didn't match the dark black top hat that he was carrying in his left hand.

He said nothing as he stepped, hobbled to the edge of the porch. Placing his hat on his head, he turned and faced me, looking down at me with a sneer. He then produced a pair of glasses, round with a small frame, sliding them on his face and taking me in. Clearing his throat with a deep cough, "You must be Morgan. Take off your goggles, so I might look upon your face girl."

Being outside it is best to always wear your goggles. The air would burn your eyes and affect your vision. I had been wearing my goggles all day and even forgot that they were on. Feeling it was rude of him to ask me to take them off outside I responded with, "Uncle, let's go inside first."

His face became tight, "This is not the fancy Golden Arches. The air is the same inside as outside, you may as we'll get used to it."

I fought my emotions back as I removed my goggles. My eyes itched at once. I blinked, trying not to rub my eyes. "How do you protect yourself from the air?"

He laughed, but it was a dark laugh. "We don't, get used to it. Your life of privilege is over, and it will be hard to find a use for you in your present state." If my eyes hadn't burned so much, I would have cried. I didn't say a word as he turned and hobbled away. I put my goggles back on. I would wear them night and day if I had to, I would not expose myself to more than need be.

My uncle explained to Tom, not only were we all living in the General store, but we were to live in the cold attic. Tom was to carry me up to sleep, and down in the morning. The staircase was narrow and steep, it hadn't been built for anything other than access for storage. The restroom was even worse, it was an outhouse some yards from the General store, over rough ground that my wheelchair would not easily traverse. This meant at night that I had to use a chamber pot, which my brothers were responsible for emptying. I could not get on and off this pot without help, I wanted to cry every time one of my brothers had to help me use the restroom. Meanwhile, my uncle lived in a house some ways off from the general store.

Uncle did not supply us with more than one treatment of Zen. Which Tom thought I should always take, being the weakest. I couldn't stand it, why should only my brothers go without. I hate my uncle. Our parents had left him more than enough money to pay for our treatments. Furthermore, he just treated us like slaves. He was a sick man, and now he had someone to run his store. He fired his one worker, and we became his unpaid workers. Once again, I was little help. All I could do was run the register, while my brothers did all the lifting and cleaning.

I couldn't wait to enchant. Magic was the only thing that gave me hope, or brought a smile to my face. When the sadness threatened to overtake me, I reached down in my pocket and rubbed my enchanted stone. The first few weeks were so exhausting, I couldn't even find the time to try another enchantment. I hate it here, but then again, what else did I deserve after killing my mother.

Chapter 8 The Seven Gods

Tom Jones

It was only March 23rd, eight days, but it felt like much longer. We were working at the store, and uncle had started to leave earlier and earlier. He was wandering around barking orders telling us all what he expected done. He was obviously preparing to leave. He stood there, thinking about God knows what. We all ignored him. I had been told to restock the feed bags, each bag weighed at least eighty pounds.

Walking up to the first bag, I tossed it over my shoulder. Carrying the bag inside, I dropped it onto the shelf. Uncle exploded, "Careful, foolish boy. That shelf could break, or the bag could break. You want to spill my money all over the floor? I will beat you with this cane boy. Do you understand me?"

I answered icily, "Yes."

"Yes, sir," He bellowed.

"Yes, sir," I repeated through gritted teeth.

Uncle pointed his cane at me, "Just watch your step… finish your work. And you'd best take care." He angrily wobbled away, leaving towards his house.

Morgan waited until he was gone, then mumbled under her breath, "We need to get free of him."

I agreed, "Yes, but how?"

Darrell pointed out, "We'll need money."

I was so mad, I snapped at Darrell, "You don't think I know that? You don't think I ask myself, how we might save money? It's not like he is going to pay us."

I went back to work. I was working way too hard for my uncle, but I was angry. Tired and sweaty, I took a seat in one corner of the store. It was dark and Darrell had just locked the door. We would need to make dinner soon, head to bed, then start it all over again in the morning.

I looked down at the floor, lost in thought. A pile of dirt and dust sat in the middle of the room, I had just swept it up, but still needed to take a dustpan to it. I felt like crying, but instead, I sang a song. A song mother used to hum around the house.

I lost my concentration, and stopped in mid verse, I had forgotten the words. Of course that upset me more. I muttered, "Well, that was helpful."

I heard chuckling, Morgan was looking at me from the counter. "Don't get upset, that was great." Then she finished the verse, her voice rang through the shop. She kind of sounds like mother did.

She made me smile, "That was pretty, the first song mother taught me. It's based on the God of wind, or the patron of wind."

Morgan asked, "What God, is the patron of Wind?"

"Let me think, I was never very good with the seven Gods."

Darrell stepped over and took a seat between Morgan and I. He asked, "I don't understand, what does the wind have to do with the seven?"

I laughed, "Something my brother does not know."

Predictably Morgan chastised me, "It's not nice to laugh at someone for not knowing something. Otherwise, we would always be laughing at you Tom."

I snapped back, "The joke was over, after they named you."

Morgan threw a piece of paper at me, I swatted it back at her, the paper went wide. She teased, "Nice try, loser."

Darrell asked, "Are you guys going to tell me?"

I grinned at Morgan, "Yeah, us guys, will. Girls need to be quiet."

Darrell was quick to say, "I didn't mean it like that."

For whatever reasons Morgan never teased Darrell, just me. That didn't bother me because I enjoyed the teasing. Morgan reassured him like she always did, "Don't worry about it Darrell. I'll tell you, do you know about the seven schools of magic?"

Darrell thought for a second, "I know about fire, water, earth and wind."

I finished the list, "There is, also, Conjuring, Charming and Enchanting. Each school of magic has one of the seven Gods as its patron."

Morgan added, "Father once told me how the different schools worked and which God went with which.. Correct me if I'm wrong Tom."

I smiled, "Don't worry, I will." My sister was smiling. I hadn't realized how long it had been since I have seen her truly smile. I realized this was a moment for the three of us. We hadn't really said much to one another since mom and dad died. We all wanted to hear what father had told Morgan.

Morgan stated, "First, the God of Forgiveness looks over the School of Water."

I added, "Also known as the God of Wrath."

"Hey," Morgan complained, "Don't confuse Darrell."

"All I'm saying, is not everyone looks on the seven Gods as good Gods. Some call them, The Two Face Gods, and I'm telling Darrell the other name."

Morgan waved her hand at me, "Fine, where was I?"

Darrell reminded her, "The School of Water."

"Yes, the School of Water. Now that is not just the control of water, because water is hard to move. Rather, most study this magic to learn the art of looking into the future. It's less accurate the further one looks into the future. So looking in the near future is good for fighting, you could use it to dodge a blow. Then there's the God of Empathy, she looks after the School of Wind. Wind is a pretty straight forward type of magic."

I added, "Also, called the God of Envy."

Morgan went on, "You can move things with wind. Next is the School of Fire. The God of Love," before I could say it, she quickly added, "or lust. Fire, seems kind of simple, but father said it truly showed how much power a wizard could produce. Since it took pure energy, powerful wizards could produce lightning. Of course magic items can help with that. Then there is the School of Earth, and its overseen by the God of Harvest."

Darrell added, "Or gluttony."

I laughed, "Very good, you're getting it, but be careful. Believers of the seven will take offense to the second names. Just be careful who you say that in front of."

Morgan continued with her class, "Earth is magic that has anything to do with the physical world. You need to be stronger, faster, lighter or even heal. A lot of warriors practice that magic, or use of enchanted items. In short, Earth power is the physical world in which we live. The living, not the dead.

"The God of Steward or Greed oversees conjuring. That school is neat, but few can do it. Father also said, the best he has ever seen, was a man conjuring a small fire element."

Darrell asked, "Where do the conjured come from? I've heard that wizards can conjure animals and elemental spirits over to fight for them, but I wonder where they come from."

I shrugged my shoulders, "Keep wondering, no one knows and if they do, they're not telling. The textbook answer is, Conjuring is the art of bringing magical creatures from another dimension. What dimension? I don't know."

Morgan went on, "The next God, Determination or Sloth," Then Morgan teased me by saying, "It is the one power that Tom will never have, Charm."

I laughed, "I have plenty of charm. Plus, Father told me that Charm magic is for thieves, and politicians. The only reason upright wizards even study it is, that they need to learn how to fight against it. The monsters that surround the gate can't be charmed. Spells like Fear, Confusion, Sleep, Memory Loss, they only work on the living."

Before Morgan could say the last God, I added. "Personally, my favorite School is Enchanting. The God of Humanity and Pride. It is truly the greatest art and only a few wizards every year are chosen to live in the enchanted Gardens to learn the art. Imagine, casting magic into items. It's not easy, you have to spend years as an apprentice to even do it. Only if we had magic items for sale, then we could leave this place."

Morgan's face changed, she went stiff. Darrell noticed it and asked, "Morgan?"

I added, "Did we upset you… Talking about dad?" She shook her head, I asked her, "What's wrong?"

Morgan smiled mischievously, "I have an idea." Darrell and I looked at my sister in surprise. She motioned for us to come closer. Then in a quiet voice, "Let me show you my rock."

Chapter 9 Enchanted

Morgan Jones

The next couple of days we plotted. Tom was amazed that I could enchant. That rock, he mused, was worth a pretty penny. I could make money from rocks, but there was a problem. If uncle found out, I could become his printing press. Forced to make magical items for him to sell. Selling anything could produce another problem; how could we hide the fact in such a small town? Still, we were working in a storefront. It would take time; time, none of us wanted to spend here.

A few days passed by, and we worked the store during the day and planned at night. I also made a few more rocks and enchanted my pocket watch so that it didn't need to be wound up. Fathers was still broke, stuck at ten, ten. Tom didn't want me to fix it and I didn't ask him why. Now my watch was like my father's watch used to be. I enchanted a shovel for Tom, it almost dug the hole by itself. Tom figured we could make a secret deal with the right person. Uncle would only see a shovel being sold, not the fact it was enchanted.

The customers worried me, they were the one big hole in our plans. First, they were poor, they could barely afford the shovel, let alone the enchantment. Second, they didn't like us, they saw us as being rich spoiled children with nice clothes. A lot of them came in with injuries, and sick from the cough. Worst of all, most couldn't even afford the Zen they needed. How could we make secret deals with people who hated us, and worse, had no money.

Things went from bad to worse. Tom was often sent with an old wagon, attached to an even older donkey, to deliver feed to the farmers. Darrell was little, and struggled to load customers' orders. On such a day, Mrs. Clark and her three inbred boys came in. Her boys were mean, big, and stupid. They could be triplets, and when they spoke it was hard to listen to, let alone understand. All they talked about was their prize winning pigs. Mrs. Clark hated me, and believed me to be useless. I did my best to pretend I didn't hear the nasty things she said about me while shopping. She approached the register, "You have my total yet?"

"Yes, ma'am," I said, trying to sound annoyed.

"How do you plan on having any baby's with one hand and no legs?" She asked, with cruel eyes.

I didn't answer, "Your total is…"

Before I could finish one of her boys said in a very loud voice, "She still has one use." The boys laughed as they eyed me. I felt gross, and sickened. I was only twelve and these guys had to be much older, but I knew what they meant.

Mrs. Clark snarled, "No, she's not even good for that. Look at her with those goggles and fine dress. She thinks she is going to a ball. Maybe she thinks the man will carry her around." They all burst into laughter as if what she said was the funniest thing they had ever heard. The boys now gathering around the counter.

Of course I didn't feel special and my dress was dirty and starting to look worn. At this moment I was feeling awful small. I tried again, "It will be…"

"Little wingless fly,"… "Whore," "Useless freak," were but a few of the things the boys said in between laughing. My eyes betrayed me as tears came out freely. Forcing me to remove my goggles to wipe the tears away. "Oh, look the princess is crying," they teased.

A loud voice came from behind them, "You all need to leave… Get out." They stopped laughing and turned to see Darrell standing behind them, with an anger I had never seen. Never had I seen emotion from him before.

One of the boys challenged him, "And you're going to make us?"

I pleaded to my little brother, "No Darrell."

He ignored me as he produced a wooden dowel. It was only about six inches long, then he pointed it at them, "You're leaving, how do you want to go?"

Mrs. Clark snarled, "You little monster. How dare you? Take care of him boys."

The biggest boy moved towards Darrell first, and to everyone's surprise, Darrell flew into action. He closed the distance with a sudden burst of speed. And with one quick stabbing action the wood dowel slammed the boy's chest, not only knocking him to the ground, but knocking all the air out of him too.

His brothers attacked, but there was not much room between the shelves. Darrell quickly backed into an aisle, forcing the brothers to follow him in single file. The lead boy attacked Darrell with swing after swing, which, Darrell moved around like he knew where each punch was going. With quick movements he beat the much bigger boy's arms, hitting them with his hands and that wooden dowel. The boy cried in pain and when he pulled his arms back Darrell beat him over the head until he fell to the ground.

The other brother grew tired of waiting and ran around the shelves to come at Darrell from his back. Seeing that his brother had already fallen, he picked up a large bag of seed. He was a large boy, like his brothers and hurled the bag like it was nothing. It flew straight at my brother. My brother cart wheeled backwards. Then jumped straight up, with perfect timing he landed on the bag in mid air. This caused the bag of seed to fall straight down, landing on the back of the brother who had been trying to get up.

Darrell wasted no time as he flew at the remaining brother. The first brother had now caught his breath, and with his mother's encouragement, ran to help his remaining brother. What happened next was mind blowing. My brother surrounded by two bigger boys, fought from between them like he was on fire. Breaking free from the brothers, he ran to the wall where we keep all the hardware. Grabbing a hand full of metal nuts, he turned to face all three brothers.

All three brothers were standing now, battered and bruised. They cursed him and threatened his life, they found the courage to attack him again. As they moved forward, Darrell started throwing the nuts. Accurately every nut hit the boys, he first hit their heads, but when they put their hands up to block he would through a nut, right into their nuts. One boy tried to charge him, Darrell whizzed a shot in his knee, the boy fell and before he could right himself another hit to the head, sending him to the ground.

The next boy came at him using a feed bag for a shield. Darrell threw a nut against the shelf behind him, it ricocheted, then hit the boy in the back of the head. He fell forward landing on the feed bag face first and right at Darrell's feet. Darrell kicked at his head until he backed off.

Now the boys backed away and towards the front door. Mrs. Clark was in a rage, she reached over and picked up a heavy glass ink well from one of the counters. She pulled her arm back to throw it at Darrell. Hardly even looking at Mrs. Clark, Darrell sent a nut right to her hand. She squealed in pain, dropping the ink well. It crashed on the floor and shattered, luckily there was no ink in it.

Mrs. Clark yelled, "You monster. You haven't heard the last from us. Come on boys, let's go."

"Ok, mom," One said, another whined, "It's not our fault, he used magic on us."

Mrs. Clark gave us both a dark look, "You'll pay for using your sorcery on us. It's unnatural, you can't go around hurting other's with your dark powers. We may be simple folks, but we know evil when we see it."

Darrell stepped forward. His face was once again that cold, emotionless, mask, "I told you to leave. You chose how. On your feet, or your back, the choice is yours." He came to a stop right before Mrs. Clark, she was cursing under her breath at him, but she retreated with her boys in tow.

I said with a quiet voice, "I hope you don't get in trouble... Thank you."

He nodded, "Trouble, trouble just left."

Trouble came, uncle was furious. He claimed we were running off his customers on purpose. Apparently it was because we were lazy. Tom had a pretty heated argument with him, ending with uncle smacking him. That night we all huddled in anger and frustration on what we might do. The next day was more of the same, bad news. Uncle decided that Darrell could no longer be at the shop. Instead, he sent him to a man up the road, a man named

Forrest. Darrell would work for him, mending fences and working on an old barn.

We were upset by this, not sure how Darrell would be treated. When he came back that afternoon, I didn't even let him speak before I asked, "What happened? Are you ok?"

He gave me a small smile, "Fine, Forrest is a nice man. A lot of work, but I don't mind it."

Tom's face relaxed, "Good. Now we just have one more problem to solve."

A lot of problems crossed my mind, but I wasn't sure which one he was referring to, "And that is?"

"How to protect you when I leave the store," Tom answered as if it were the only problem in the world. Of course that upset me, once again, the need to take care of me.

Darrell spoke, "I have something." Reaching inside his jacket he pulled out a small branch. Thin and slightly curly with broken off shoots. He then produced a small piece of metal. "White oak, copper."

Tom's face filled with confusion, I smiled, then said, "You found them. Forrest had that?"

Darrell said, "He didn't see me take it, but his workshop is full of wood and different kinds of metal hardware. You think this will work?"

"Yes," I responded.

Tom was confused, "Work? What is it for?"

I smiled a wicked grin, "To protect me."

That night I didn't sleep, while Darrell helped me attach the copper tip to the wood. That night I took my enchanting rod and etched the new wand with symbols around its shaft. It took me two days to finish enchanting it.

As we all prepared for sleep Tom announced, "I have to make a delivery tomorrow."

I knew his fear, I could hear it in his voice, "Don't worry brother, I finished it." I produced the wand, "Should we try it out?"

"You two never told me what it does," Tom complained. He had asked a few times, but I wanted to surprise him.

Darrell added, "I never knew. Morgan said it would help her defend herself, I was kind of wondering how?"

I was ecstatic to try out my new wand, "Well, it's supposed to stun someone." I held the wand in my hand and said, "Taz," at the end of the wand, the part made of copper, glowed. It glowed with a blue tint, almost hot looking. I lowered the tip down to my metal cup that sat next to my bed, it still had a half of a cup of water in it. Not sure what would happen, if anything, I touched it to the cup.

A small explosion went off, the cup flew into the air, spraying water over everything, the metal cup bashed against the ceiling and then clattered against the floor. Tom picked up the cup, wiping the water from his face. He lifted the cup, and examined it. There was a hole burnt through its side, the metal was discolored from the heat. Tom whistled low, "Yeah, that will do it."

I didn't end up needing it. Even though Mrs. Clark would stop by time and again, she kept her distance from me. Her children were afraid of our magic, so instead, they just ridiculed us. Days turned into weeks, weeks into months, and we were still Uncle's little workers. Watching him about to cough to death, and watching my brothers look sicker by the day. Being outside, and always giving the only share of Zen to me, it was having its toll on me.

In fact, I felt a little crazy. I remembered seeing a cat on the way here, on the train. It was near the station in Texas, really no big deal. Then I noticed another cat just like it the few nights we stayed in Winterlight. It was orange with white spots and long hair. I swear I've seen the same cat around the store. It's just a cat, but the fact is something about that cat is bothering me.

Chapter 10 Dinner

Tom Jones

The last few months have been hell on me. It was already April 8th, and I felt no closer to escaping from Uncle's. My sister was depressed, and looked sick. I have hardly seen Darrell. Yet, with all this I have been slightly jealous of my siblings. Both of them showed signs of magic. How could that not help them later in life? Of course in our present situation, it might just turn out to be a curse. I concentrated on unloading the latest delivery. If I were going to be having these kinds of thoughts, they should be on how to get out of here.

I finished unloading a delivery. Uncle came in the shop, he was in a surprisingly good mood. He smiled at us, "Tom, when you close the shop, roll your sister up to my house for dinner. I have good news, we must celebrate. Oh, Darrell will be late today, do not wait for him."

Morgan stammered out, "Ok, Uncle."

I was too surprised to say anything. I couldn't imagine what the news was. Later that evening I rolled Morgan's wheelchair towards Uncle's house. My chest hurt, a bad feeling came over me. Morgan told me not to worry, but Darrell not being with us scared me to death. I hadn't been inside Tony's home, it was located some ways away from the store. The path that led to it was narrow, unkempt, and full of potholes. This made the ride difficult, I had to lift the wheelchair whenever one of the wheels fell in a hole, or sank in the sand. The house itself looked like every other building, old wood boards, stained brown, but mostly faded from lack of upkeep. Once inside it was a nice enough looking home, dusty and old, but nicer than the cold attic that we were living in.

Uncle led us through the living room to the dining room. There was a fireplace burning warmly on one wall, and the food was already set out. It was chicken, the smell made my stomach ache in hunger. I spied all the food laid out before me, bread, mashed potatoes, and rice. We had been living off rice and beans, but this looked like fried rice. My mood was lifted, we would eat well tonight, and just perhaps Uncle's news was good for all of us. We sat and ate with Tony and for once it was a good time. The food, Uncle's spirits, he even entertained us with stories of growing up with our father. Of course the way he made it sound, father was somewhat of a jerk. Instead of arguing, Morgan and I just kept eating. We all finished our meal, and our uncle was just finishing a story, "So, you see, that's how your father got away with it. Have to say, clever man, your father."

I asked nicely, "Do you know about what time Darrell might join us?"

Uncle's expression changed, "Let us talk about the good news. In part, the good news is because of your brother." I seen Morgan's eyes narrowed, and my heart sunk, but we did not interrupt as my uncle continued. "Your brother has a gift, and just recently, Forrest explained it to me. Apparently he can measure any object just by looking at… imagine that. He can even do more, he can see angles, determine the movement of an object, he can see the math. No wonder he gave those boys a pounding."

Morgan and I exchanged looks. That explained lots of things about Darrell, and in a way I always knew. I asked, "How is this great news?"

Uncle's face darkened, "It isn't?" He stared at both of us for a minute, then must have decided to come out with it, "I have sold your brother to a man that lives in Carpenterville." We both started to argue, but Uncle yelled over us, "Before you get angry, hear me out. He will be trained to be a craftsman, he will make a fortune. Let us not forget, that with the money I made selling him, I will be able to afford to go to Eden and get my treatments. You do want your uncle to get well? Don't you? Or, perhaps you would like me to remain sick, and die? Are you that eager for your parents money?"

My sister spoke, low and slow, pronouncing each word, "Where, is, our, brother?"

He lifted his right hand from under the table, he was holding a bronze looking tube. It made a snapping noise, two metal bars had popped out from the side. I realized he was holding a small crossbow and was pointing it at me, "Careful boy." I had not realized that I'd risen from my seat, I slowly sat back down.

Morgan quickly added, "Wait, Tony. Give us a chance to buy him."

I snarled, "Don't." She couldn't tell him, no good could come from it.

Uncle spoke without looking away from me, "That's enough from you. Let's hear what you have to offer… Morgan."

She always stored her book under the wheelchair, I had fashioned straps to hold the book below the seat. Using her one hand, she was able to pull out the book. Morgan held it out towards uncle, "It's a magic book, it's priceless."

Uncle stood up with a wicked grin. He warned me, "Don't even move." He stepped over and took the book from her. "So you've all been hiding secrets. Let's find out, shall we?" Without warning, he hurled the book into the fireplace.

Morgan screamed in surprise, then asked in a panicked voice, "What are you doing? Pull it out."

I was half hanging off my seat, eyes switching back and forth from the fire and then to the crossbow. Uncle's voice was full of venom, "You must believe me to be a fool. I may not be a wizard, but I know a few things about magic. If that book is a magic book, it will not burn. No wizard would make a book and not have it enchanted." His eyes flashed to the fireplace, were clearly the book was on fire and burning brightly. "Just as I thought, a trick."

Tears fell from her face, "It was not a trick, it was full of magic spells."

"Liar," He screamed at us.. Then, looking back and forth at both of us, he announced in anger, "I have had enough of the both of you. Not only will you never see your brother again, but you'll never see each other. I will sell you both," Looking at me, "To the iron mines with you. And you, my dear niece, I suppose you could still work in a whore house."

I couldn't stand it, first he took my sisters hope, then he wished her harm. I jumped to my feet, but stopped when uncle aimed his crossbow more sharply at me. "Careful," Uncle warned. I slowly returned to my seat, staring at him with hateful eyes. He laughed at me.

Chapter 11 Thieves & Politicians

Morgan Jones

My brother was close to being shot. I could see the anger in his eyes. I could tell my uncle was pondering if shooting him, was what it would take to stop him. I reached down to the side of my wheelchair. My eyes were full of tears, but my heart was full of anger. I looked up at my uncle who still stood right in front of me, his attention was fully upon my brother. He gave no notice to the crippled girl in the chair, so I slid out my wand.

Without a word I reached out and pressed the wand into the side of Uncle's stomach. He stole a glance, at that moment I caught motion from the edge of my vision, Tom ducked below the table causing uncle to whip his attention back towards Tom. Then I said, "Taz," forcing all my will into my wand.

Uncle's body went rigid as all his muscle bunched up, causing him to pull the trigger on his crossbow, the bolt sailed into the back of Tom's empty chair. Tony's body fell to the ground in convulsions, I followed his fall leaning forward, keeping the wand to his body. He didn't scream, instead he shook around the floor like a fish out of water, foaming at the mouth. His eyes were rolling into the back of his head when I finally pulled my wand back. Tom by this point walked around the table and stood over uncle, who was moaning on the floor.

Uncle coughed, then moaned, then slowly crawled on his stomach away from me. He shook violently as he pulled himself to his feet using his chair. Tom stood next to me staring at uncle with disgust and hate. Tony was leaning heavily against the back of his chair when he slid out a dagger.

Tom stepped forward, unafraid. All this time lifting bags of feed, hauling me around, and for the first time I realized how strong Tom had become. He was taller and looked like my father as he battered the dagger free from uncle's hand. It bounced across the floor. Tom pushed Tony against the wall, then punched him hard in the face, followed by a blow to the ribs. Uncle fell to the ground and began to cough.

Uncle started to cough and the more he coughed, the more blood he coughed up. We both watched quietly, not one word between us, we watched as he coughed and shook, pleading for help with his eyes. We watched him die, and neither of us did anything to help him. After a minute or so, Tom walked slowly over to the dagger and picked it up off the floor. He stuck the dagger into Uncle's skull. He would not rise, he would remain dead. A calm came over me as I stared at his lifeless body. The pool of blood was slowly forming under his head.

We sat there quietly, picking at our food. I felt nothing, not even fear of what the future might hold. Tom broke the silence, "I'm sorry about your book. We'll be ok."

I chuckled darkly, "The local law enforcement will blame us. Nemos, that's where they'll throw us, and throw away the key. Not that it matters, at least we will know where our next meal is coming from."

"That won't happen," is what Tom said, but his tone said otherwise. After a moment he went on, "Maybe it's time I use that enchanted shovel. Uncle was leaving town in a couple of days. Maybe they'll think that he left town, it will give us more time to get away."

"Ok," I answered with a shrug. "I'll be fine, hurry back."

I rolled out to the living room, I was sick of looking at Tony's body. I was sitting there wondering why I had no feelings. Most likely shock, but, I knew that no matter how many days past, I still won't care that he was dead. My brothers, they were all I have. Darrell was gone, and how to find him? How to get away? I had caused all of this. How could I make it up to my brothers?

I looked over and noticed a trunk sitting in the corner, and on top of it was a briefcase. My uncle was all packed up and ready to go. I rolled over, spilling the contents of the case on the ground. Just personal stuff and a book. A big bag fell to the floor as I jostled things around, when it hit the wood floor, it made the unmistakable sound of coins.

I smiled, I found money. Wondering what else he might have, I noticed a book on top of the trunk. I picked it up. It was a Google, my father called them encyclopedias, and Google was everyone's favorite for looking up information. I opened it, and burst into laughter. Inside it, was full of spells. Flipping through the pages, I saw my magic book. It was never the book, it was me! I wondered how this was? Then the image of an angel with glowing eyes flashed in my head. The Angel had a scroll, of words that I could not read. She had said if I didn't sign my father would suffer. I had already killed my mother and left my brothers orphaned. I signed, with the promise of power… and a price to pay.

I shook it off, that was nothing more than a bad dream. Hope filled my mind, along with a plan. I slid my enchanting knife out, there was work to do. I was busy while Tom was gone, emptying Tony's chest of his clothes and scribing my symbols into one of his suits. Tom came into the room with shovel in hand. One look at me and his eyes narrowed in wonder, I smiled back. "What's going on?"

"I have a lot to do. First, I found that the book itself was not magic." Pointing to the Google, "I see the same spells in this. It was never the book, it was me. Also, I came up with a plan. Look at what I found." I lifted a large purse.

Tom took it and dumped out the money on the table, "This must be what he got from our parents… And perhaps selling Darrell. Thirty gold coins, three hundred and four silver pieces, plus a hundred pennies. And to think, my sister has magic to tap into knowledge."

I hadn't thought of my power being that of knowledge, but that made sense. I eyed the pile of money, "I've never seen a gold coin before." Tom tossed one at me, but I missed and it fell to the floor. Tom laughed and handed me another. "How many silver does it take, to make one gold?"

Tom thought, "It depends on the market, but the going rate is a hundred and forty. Takes a thousand pennies to make one silver."

"We're rich," I have never seen this kind of money before.

Tom shook his head, "Not really. I mean we could get by for a while, but we're not rich. This will help us get away, but for how long? It would last long here in outer circle, but where would we go? It would be better to go to Eden if we could get in. The downside being our money won't go as far… I'm not sure."

I laughed, Tom gave me a quizzical look, "I told you I have a plan."

"Do tell," Tom pulled up a seat.

I looked at my brother, I was proud. This time I would save him. "This is what we will do. First, you'll bury Tony Jones. Second, you will become Tony."

"How," Tom wondered, lifting one eyebrow.

I giggled, I loved it when he did that. "Glad you ask. See, I found my magic book and I can once again enchant. Look," I pointed at one of uncles finest suits, which I pulled out of his trunk. It lay draped across the couch where I had been carving small Symbols in the fabric. "I'm enchanting, and when you wear this, you will look and sound like our late uncle Tony. Everyone will see you leave in two days time, no one will be looking for Tony."

I could see Tom working it out in his head. "But how will I take you?"

"Trunk," I answered with a smile. "It will be no ordinary trunk when I'm done with it. I will enchant for comfort. We can take the pass that Tony spent our money buying. Then we will go to Eden. There I can sell my enchanted items, we can make enough money to buy Darrell back."

Tom smiled, "That will work… Wait, what about us? I mean, won't they be looking for us?"

"I'm sure he has told everyone in town that he was on his way to Eden. Everyone will also know that he is leaving us behind. Unless, someone that looks like him, hires someone to run his shop and tells everyone else that he sold us. That way, no one is looking for us."

"That will work," he had a faraway look in his eyes. "I've always wanted to go to the city. Well, I have a hole, to dig, and you have lots of enchanting to do." He got up to leave, then stopped and turned, "One more thing, see if you can't enchant something to hypnotize people with, we might need it."

"Good idea, Charm magic, for thieves, and politicians." I smiled, Tom laughed.

Tom added, "Apparently runaways too."

Chapter 12 Eden

Morgan Jones

I turned to my book and picked a random page, and there was a spell on how I could make a hypnotic item. I smiled, now I understood it. Whatever I wanted to know would be in any book, on whatever page I picked. Lifting up the documents that uncle purchased to enter Eden. I noticed there was a letter showing that he had been accepted into the care of a Dr. Weaver. Well, I might have to drop in, otherwise the good doctor may wonder where his payment is. Tom was right, we'll need a hypnotic device… And more weapons.

The next couple of days went by quickly and what we discovered over the last few days, made any regret of not saving our uncle vanish. My spell on the suit work great, Tom looked like and sounded just like my uncle. Even though he was a little bit shorter, I doubt that anyone noticed. Tom went to town, to try to hire some people to run the store. He was stopped by the local banker, who, had been looking for him and was beside himself that Tony was late. Poor Tom was dragged to the bank, confused and somewhat scared. What he found out, blew our minds.

Tom signed paperwork, then received another fifty gold coins. Tom was smart, he kept coughing while signing so no one would question the signature. As he sat and talked to the banker, it didn't take him long to find out what the money was for. Apparently Tony had already sold his house, and the store. The banker asked if he had sold the rest of the children, which Tom quickly replied, yes. He then made up a story about how a carriage from out of town had already taken us away. Now we knew that our dear uncle had always planned to sell us and take his money to the city.

It all worked in our favor, now no one would be looking for us. It took me up to the last minute, but I finished the trunk. It was now bigger on the inside than the out. Not only that, but it would stay the same temperature, I put my rock in for light. There was enough room for me, a couple bags of our personal belongings. I was in the trunk looking upward at Tom, who at this moment looked like my uncle, "I hate that look."

Tom smiled, "Just until we arrive at the hotel. Will you be alright, in here?"

I reassured him, "I'm fine, better than looking like an old man. It will only be for a few hours."

"Ok, rest, I'll see you soon. By the way, you look good inside a trunk." Tom shut the trunk with a smile.

This would be a two part trip. First, we would travel to the center of Backwater, where Tom would board a ferry. The river would take us to a small town, that was nothing more than a dock, hotel and train station. It lay between our hometown of Taylerville and Eden. That's where we would get a room, the next day we would board a train as father and daughter. I had new disguises, that will change our features. Everyone will have seen Uncle leave, and no one would be looking for him, and in case someone does look for us, no one will have ever laid eyes upon Tom and I.

When Tom was in town, I asked him for two rings that fit his middle fingers. One steel, the other copper, he asked why, but I told him that they were a surprise. With my two rings I would have plenty to do on the first leg of the journey. I had made quite a lot of magical items in the last two days. The clothes that made Tom into Tony, my magic trunk, and two magical bracelets that changed our appearance. I had a knife, a wand and a crossbow. I was thinking of making Tom a weapon, but decided on something else. Something we might need.

The trip went quickly for me, soon as I became comfortable inside my chest, I fell to sleep. All the enchanting had exhausted me. I barely woke up when Tom moved me from the chest to the bed in the hotel room. I woke to Tom gently shaking me, "Get up sleepy head. We need to get ready, I would like to have time to grab breakfast before the train arrives."

I moaned, "I'm up." He laughed because I didn't even move. After a little bit I finally woke up and prepared myself for the journey ahead.

With our new disguises, no one would know who we are. It wasn't major changes, but it was enough. Tom looked older, perhaps forty, with white mixed in his black hair. Face aged, and nose just slightly bigger, he looked like a man. He was what I imagine he might look like when he does turn forty. My disguises are simple, I still looked like a young girl with long black hair, but now I appeared to have both arms and legs. I was still in a wheelchair, and I had a cast for one leg and a sling holding the fake arm. It was all a magical illusion. No one would be looking for a middle aged man and a girl who looked like she fell down a flight of stairs. That would never lead back to our real identities. Tom thought I had gone a little far with it, because he couldn't see how anyone could be looking for us. Better safe than sorry.

We hurried our meal, and boarded the train. This was the first time I would ride in style. We both thought it best to update our seats from Coach to First Class. Instead of being crammed in a cart with many strangers, we would have our own cabin. Less eyes on us the better. Our cabin was nice and adorned with gold and red fabric. Two benches could easily be used for beds. Tom shut the door to our compartment, he closed the drapes so when persons went up or down the hallway they couldn't see in. I sat next to the window, and I watched as the train pulled free from the station and the countryside started to roll slowly by. The train ride itself was only but a few hours.

The closer we traveled to Eden, the more homes, and small towns we passed. The houses were nice, well built and very clean looking. Farms filled the spaces between these small clusters of homes. The trees became more numerous, the closer to Eden, my heart filled with hope, and fear, of the future.

I was watching out the window another small town came into view. This one was different, it had been burned down. A large fire must have happened, not one building stood. Some small trees and bushes had grown back, making me think this fire must have happened some time ago. I noticed the remains of one of the buildings. The building had been made of stone and most likely the roof had been timber. All that remained was the melted walls. How hot would a fire need to be to melt stone? It didn't make any sense.

I said out loud, "What on earth happened here? How could fire do that to stone structures?"

Tom answered, "What do you mean?"

"The stone, look, it's melted."

Tom said in awe, "I see what you mean."

A knock at our cabin door, "Come in."

A young man slid the door open. He was wearing his bright red uniform. The waiter asked, "How are we this evening?"

Tom answered, "Good." Then handed him a piece of paper with our order on it. "We've finished our dinner order."

"Very good, sir. Will there be anything else?"

Tom was saying, "Where good for now." When I blurted out, "What happened to that burned down city we passed?"

The waiter smiled, then leaned in, "You must mean Beaumont. You've never heard of the Dragon of Beaumont?"

"No," both Tom and I said in unison.

"Well, about ten years ago a great dragon burned the city down, no one made it out alive. People on the outskirts of the town claimed to see a giant dragon."

"Truly," I said, amazed. "There really are dragons? What happened to the dragon?"

The boy laughed, "No one knows. The dragon had never been seen before, or sense that fatal day. Perhaps it was magic. I'm afraid will never know."

He slid the door closed as he left. Tom scoffed, "Dragons. Dragons indeed."

I chuckled, "Careful Tom, you never can tell what's real or not."

Tom rolled his eyes, "I'll keep my eyes peeled. Don't want to be burned alive."

I stuck my tongue out at him, "I don't know, I would love to meet a dragon. Perhaps if you were nice, the dragon would be nice too."

Tom laughed, "I'll remember that, just case I ever get a chance to date a dragon." We both laughed.

After dinner Tom helped me open the window, so that I might stick my head out. At first the walls of Eden didn't look big, but as the train kept moving at an even pace, the walls grew taller and taller. The walls were a golden brown, and completely made of stone. Unlike the outer wall, it had been a mixture of stone and wood. I do remember what Darrell had said about Eden, being that it was a smaller length and built long ago, it had also been made stronger. It stood three hundred feet high and fifty feet thick. There were four large gates to enter Eden, but the trains didn't use any of those. All the trains ran under Eden, great round stones would roll out of the way and a section of the track would lower into place allowing the train to enter the tunnels.

The ground started to rise up around the train, as the tracks slopped downwards towards the tunnel entrance. I could barely see ahead, the smoke from the train became trapped between the banks of land. The train slowed down, and soon we entered into the tunnel. The compartment went black as night, Tom turned the knob on the wall lantern and the flame flickered a dim light. The tunnel was dark, only lit by lanterns too far apart, giving the tunnel a eerie glow. The train now moved slowly down the track. "How much longer?" I couldn't wait to see the city.

Tom guessed, "I don't know, about twenty minutes. All the trains unload at Grand Central Station. I hear the station itself is amazing, truly a sight to behold."

"I wish Darrell was with us," thinking about all the facts I was missing out on.

Tom smiled gently, "Soon, we'll get our brother back, soon."

It was hard to hold my excitement, "Where are we staying?"

Tom shrugged his shoulders, "Not sure. Really didn't have time to figure it out. We don't want to go to the hotel that uncle reserved."

"True," I agreed. "We'll figure it out."

After a while, my window filled with light. My eyes widened in wonder, we were now pulling into the main terminal. Our train was moving down one set of tracks and more and more tracks ran alongside. The train slowly made its way between other trains coming to a stop next to platforms on both sides. Trains were stacked next to each other with platform between each one. The place was brightly lit, with hundreds of lanterns, attached to every wall and pillar. Looking up the lanterns dotted the ceiling. There were so many levels hanging above us. Large black steel walkways hung overhead, where hundreds of people moved about. The smoke from the trains seemed to be nowhere, and the air looked clean. Perhaps magic. Everything was so decorative, the stone was all white with swirls of black, the pillars were carved round and with decorative patterns.

It looked like pictures I had seen in a book. I couldn't wait to get out, I hadn't been in Eden for a minute, and I already felt as if there was no other place for me. We unloaded, and because we were First Class it didn't take them long to bring us our trunk and my wheelchair. Tom was able to put the carry-on bags into the trunk, seeing as it had plenty of space. A young man was moving through the crowd with a cart. He eyed us, then pushed his cart over to us. The boy looked about my age, his clothes were brown and plain. He said quickly, "Are looking for a runner? I am the best in Eden, Roger they call me. Let me get that trunk for you good sir." Not waiting for a no, he slid the trunk onto his cart. "You new in town, or getting back from a long trip abroad?"

Tom was a little taken back, I answered for him, "New in town."

"Have a place to stay?"

Tom answered him, "Not yet, have any ideas Roger?"

"You bet, I know every place in Eden, and the fastest way there. How much do you plan on spending?"

Tom thought, "Not too rich, but I don't want to be on the bad side of town."

He started to push the cart, "Right, I know just the place. It's a bit further, but it's clean and not over priced."

I asked, "What's it called?"

Roger smiled, "The Feather Inn."

Tom nodded, "Lead the way… And by the way, what will your service cost?"

Roger grinned, "I'm not a licensed worker, I can't charge you anything…. But, I sure could use a tip."

Tom nodded, "That will work." Then tossed him a silver piece. The boy's eyes widened, apparently no one paid that much. Tom didn't seem surprised by his reaction, he added, "I thought I might tip you a little extra, we might require your services once we settled in. You seem to know your way around this city."

Roger's eyes were ready to please, "My pleasure sir. I didn't catch your names."

"Just Tom and Morgan," Roger nodded, and led us while pushing our trunk, leaving Tom free to push me.

The city was great, equipped with elevators so Tom wasn't forced to carry me up every flight of stairs. I had never ridden in an elevator before, it was fun. The Station was huge, full of restaurants, stores, gift shops and more. The ceiling crested to a giant dome. When I looked up at it, I kind of felt dizzy. There was also so much to take in, smells, sights and sounds. Paintings on the walls and beautifully tiled floors that made me wonder how they kept them so clean. Once out on the street the buildings were tightly packed, and stood at every height imaginable. The streets had people going here and there and everywhere. Large trolleys traveled down the middle of the street, instead of steam, they ran off magic. A lot of younger people were riding bikes. I always wanted to try that, I suppose I never will, but even that thought couldn't bring me down today.

By the time we made it to the Feather Inn, it was twilight, yet the city was still bright as day. Lights were everywhere, light poles were placed on both sides of the street. It was so amazing to see so much light at night. It made me want to run through the well lit streets, that is until I remembered I had no legs.

My room was nice, but not as cheap as we would have liked. Tom pointed out that we would need to find a room to rent, Inns just cost too much. I rolled my chair to the balcony. Our room was on the top floor, three stories high. The Inn itself sat higher on the land than the buildings around it. I could look over the city, glowing in the night, like a carpet of lights.

Tom laid his hand, on my shoulder, "We should try to sleep. Big day tomorrow, lots of stuff to do."

I smiled up at him, "I know, I'm scared, but I'm excited too."

He sighed, "I know what you mean."

Chapter 13 Enchanted Things

Tom Jones

The next couple of days were amazing and exhausting all at the same time. The city was huge, and we went to a few tourist sites. The library was incredible. The Museum of Modern Man was full of strange things. Lost knowledge, we once knew so much more, that's what I got out of it.

It was a beautiful April day, Sunday the 8th, 2604. We just arrived at a park, full of stone walkways and beautiful gardens. I was slowly pushing Morgan through one of the gardens. We hadn't said much, the crowd disappeared and it was now just Morgan and I.

She commented, "That must be a common cat, yellow with white stripes. They're big cats, and I see them everywhere."

I looked, "Where?"

"Next to that tree," She pointed, "Crap, it just went into those bushes. Did you see it?"

I shrugged, "No, but it's just a cat."

"I know that," She sound unnecessarily concerned.

I calmly replied, "I know, you know, but if it's that important to you; I'll try to keep an eye out."

Morgan voice softened, "Sorry, I didn't mean to snap."

I teased, "It's ok... Jerk."

She laughed, "Butt head."

The park lay between the Eden Grand Library and the Dan's Caster school of Magic. Everything here was beautiful and clean. It was a beautiful day, the air was clean enough to take our goggles off. We splurged on some new clothes, I was wearing a fancy black suit that made me feel more like a man. Morgan's new dress was dark blue, with a black corset with blue embroidered flowers on it. I bought her a matching hat, it was a top hat, but somehow it's shape and size gave it a much more feminine look.

We came through the gardens and out of the park. Across the road was a shopping area and our destination. We came to a small shop, called Just the Enchanted Thing. This had been our destination. Roger told us where the best shop for buying and trading enchanted items. I rolled her into the shop. It was filled with all manner of magical stuff. Unlike some of the high-end shops, this place had everything. Clothes that stayed dry and wrinkle free, a never ending bar of soap, clocks of every shape and size. I could stay in here all day, and Morgan could get a million ideas on what people might want enchanted.

A nice middle age woman approached us, "Can I help you?"

"Yes," Morgan and I said in unison.

She chuckled, "Looking for something particular?"

"Not a thing, but rather, selling," I answered.

"Oh, well if you want to sell you'll need to speak with Scott. He only comes in on Mondays, that's when all the purchases are done. He's always on the lookout for something extra special." She said with a wink.

Excited, I told her, "We have rocks, that give out heat and light. They charge by sunlight, twenty minutes for every hour."

Her eyes widened, "You don't say! Now that does sound special, but today is Saturday." I gave her a confused look and she explained. "Even if Scott came to the shop, there would be no way for him to check the registration."

I quickly added, "Well of course. I was just trying to get an idea of value."

She smiled, "I don't know, but I'll tell you, I've been in this business for ten years; and I've never heard of enchanted rocks. What a treasure!"

Morgan started to ask, "What is…" But before she could ask about the registration I loudly interrupted her, "Thank you for all your information. Tell Scott, we will see him on Monday."

The lady smiled brightly, "Oh, I forgot. I didn't get your names."

I had already started to roll Morgan out, "Monday, see you soon." She was telling us to have a nice day as the door shut behind us. I hurried us down the sidewalk.

Morgan asked with concern, "What was that about?"

I answered in a stiff voice, "We're going to the library. She said registration, they register magic items."

"So," she snapped, not seeing the problem.

"So, if our magic items have not been registered, they'll believe them stolen. If we ask too many strange questions…"

"Oh," I could hear the defeat. Then she asked, "What now?"

My mind raced, we had little money left. Everything in the city was so expensive. We knew we couldn't stay at the Feather Inn forever, so I put some money down on a small apartment. It was one expense after another, dishes, towels, beds and some new clothes. We had money for a few months, but our plan all along was to sell Morgan's enchanted items.

Morgan spoke, trying to sound upbeat, "We'll figure it out. We can go to the library, I'm sure that there will be books on how we might get our magic items registered. I bet it's just a matter of a fee or something."

I nodded in agreement, but I had a bad feeling that this was not going to be simple. A few hours later, I found out how right I was. Apparently enchanted items were only made in the Summer's Tower, located in the enchanted garden. Since no one, but the enchanters had enchanting rods, and the knowledge on how to make the rods had been lost. Therefore, no one should be able to make magical items. The cheaper items were created by apprentices, the greater the enchanter, the greater the price. Of course, some of the items blew my mind, like the anti-gravity crystals that were used in the giant air ships. Without them the balloons could never lift such huge boats and cargo into the air.

Every enchanted item received a letter, telling you who made it and when. Then this item was logged in the city deeds and records building. Every time a magic item was sold, the record was updated and this office was closed on the weekends. That is why Scott could not buy on a Saturday, in fact, we couldn't have purchased anything ourselves. To top it all off, there was jail time for selling stolen magical items. If we came forward about her ability, it would lead to a lot of questions. Where we were from? How did we get here? We might not go to jail for stolen items, but we would for murder and stealing. We left the library and headed back to our apartment building. My mind spun, I pushed her along in silence. What to do?

Chapter 14 Meeting Dr. Weaver

Morgan Jones

It was a few days later, April eleventh. Tom had been quiet, reading the paper, looking for a job. We both knew he didn't have working papers. I was cleaning out my bag that hung from the side of my wheelchair. Throwing most of the stuff in the trash, when something caught my eye. I reached down and pulled out one of the brochures, it was from the university. It was a call for Doctors. I had picked it up at the library with other free fliers.

Not any doctor, but magicians who could heal. They were looking for people who possess healing magic. They offered a full ride through college, room, board, the works. I opened and read through it, there were really only three requirements. One, you were under twenty-five, two, you show basic magic ability in healing. Lastly, you have a signed referral from a licensed doctor to vouch for you.

Tom was young enough. He had no magic, well that we knew of… I thought about the rings I made. The rings were for healing, this would give any user the magical ability required. They would believe he was a natural healer. I had never heard of a set of enchanted healing rings, and could find none in the registry list in the library. In fact, healing items were extremely rare. I wasn't worried about Tom using them in front of others. No, they would never guess the power was from the rings, the big problem was finding a licensed Doctor that would give him a reference letter.

I pulled out my watch and looked at it. My brother had told me that I should make a hypnotic item, so, I had enchanted my father's broken watch. The hands of the watch stuck at the moment he died, ten, ten. My mind then slipped to a name, a doctor. Dr. Weaver, the one uncle was supposed to see.

I had worried, when I realized that uncle had an appointment with him, but Tom had thought it best if uncle never arrived. That way they won't look for him in the city. Still, I had done some research on the doc. Seems that he was somewhat of a quack. Ran a clinic from his home, and was estranged from his two children. Apparently he was once one of the leading doctors in Eden, and still sat on a small fortune. I couldn't help but wonder. I rolled my chair over to the phone. I picked up the earpiece and tapped on the button and the front desk answered. "How may I direct your call?" The nasally voice asked.

"Please connect me, to a Dr. Weaver."

After a few minutes the phone rang, and the old man answered, "Dr. Weaver, what can I do for you?"

He sounded drunk, I looked up at the clock, it was only two in the afternoon. I smiled, "Yes, I need to make an appointment to see the doctor."

He grumbled, "Have you money?"

"Oh, yes sir, plenty. Can I come straight away?"

A long pause, "Yes, of course… Who is this?"

"Morgan, I'll be there in two hours. Will that be ok with you?"

"Sure, come on by, I'll see you then," after a short pause, he added, "Bring money." Without another word, the line went dead.

Perfect I thought. I yelled to Tom, "Get ready, we're going out."

Tom yelled back, "Where?"

"Time to see a doctor," I replied.

Tom was confused as he joined me, "Doctor?"

I handed Tom a small box, "Happy Birthday Tom."

Tom smiled, "It's not my birthday yet." He opened the box and took out the two rings. "Aren't these the rings you had me buy?"

"They're enchanted now, and now they'll give you the power to heal. Hurry, we only have a couple of hours to get across town to see the doc."

"And why are we going to see a doctor? Is there something wrong?" His face was suddenly filled with panic.

Realizing that he was coming to the wrong conclusions I laughed, "No, nothing like that. Let's just say that I may have figured out a new way to make a living."

Tom calmed, "Well, I'll get ready. I can't wait to hear what you've come up with this time."

On the way to Dr. Weaver's office, we rode one of the magic street trolleys. It clattered down the tracks. The trolley was much quieter then the steam power ones back in the Golden Arches, but it still was a noisy ride with the sound of the city playing in the background. People yelling, machines working; they were building, street repair, moving people here and there. The machines worked tirelessly day and night. I watched as a giant machine arm reached into the earth, a bucket for a hand, it lifted out a mighty pile of dirt. An idea came to me, but it seemed unlikely. Could I build an arm, with machine parts? I laughed at the idea. Still?

I concentrated on the task at hand. My brother was full of questions. I told him to give me time to work out the details, and now that I have, I knew that I was out of time to explain my entire plan. Once the trolley stopped, it was only a few blocks. The sky darkened and it looked like it might rain. Tom helped me with my goggles and hat, and made sure I was covered properly just in case. We hadn't traveled far from the trolley stop, when Tom asked, "So, what are we doing? I hope it's not illegal."

I was careful, "Illegal, yes, but, we need to survive. You'll just have to trust me on this."

He was indignant, "What! Why can't I know what we're doing?"

I chuckled, "Chill bro, mostly because we're there, and we're out of time. No worries, just follow along."

He mumbled, "Just great, my sister the con artist."

We were now standing out front of Dr. Weaver's home. It was big, and took up more than its fair share of space. It was crammed between other buildings. All the other structures in this area had a similar look, with roughly the same kind of buildings and streets, but not this house. Here stood a beautifully designed home, with large white stone making up the outer walls. Large arches sat over the giant windows. Truly a great house, but it also appeared to need some care. Around the sides weeds lined the ground and it had been some time since someone had bothered to clean the stones. A sign, once again fancy, but also faded, stood above the front door, Dr. Weaver Medical Center. Tom snorted, and I asked, "What's so funny?"

He responded, "This place. No wheel chair ramp."

Sure enough, there were four large steps to the front door, and there appeared to be no more entrances. Maybe around back, I thought, "It doesn't matter, let's go in."

Once Tom finagled my wheelchair to the front door, he found the door was ajar. Pushing me inside, we found ourselves in a very large entryway. The place had tables against every wall, and papers piled everywhere. Tom whistled, "This place is something."

I hushed him, then yelled out, "Dr. Weaver? Anyone here? It's Morgan, I'm here for my appointment."

A few minutes later an old man came out, leaning against a cane, hair as white as snow. He looked disheveled, even his bow tie was crooked. His face was full of big wrinkles and cheeks were bright red. He looked pretty healthy for a man his age, and that was rare nowadays. I could smell the whiskey, which made me wonder if he even needed the cane. He spoke way too loud, "No need to yell, not deaf you know."

I replied, "Ok."

The doctor then turned his head, "Speak up girl, ears aren't what they used to be."

I laughed, Tom pointed out, "Just thought you told us you weren't deaf."

The old man spoke animatedly, "That's right, not deaf, just hard of hearing. Bet your ears won't be so good when you're as old as me. Just turned eighty-three, and still as fit as a fiddle. It's why all my grandchildren hate me, haven't died and left them anything yet." He ended it with a big laugh.

I asked, "What about your children? I'm sure they don't want you gone."

He shook his head, "Out lived all my children, nothing but useless grandchildren now. So, let's take a look at you, follow me back to my exam room."

"Sure," I answered. Tom pushed me slowly behind the old man. I had to wonder how I might make my makeshift plan work, but it was like the Seven Gods were looking out for me. The old Doctors back story would work nicely, couldn't have planned it better.

Tom whispered in my ear, "Are you sure about this?"

I smiled and whispered back, "Oh, yes… Definitely."

Once in the exam room, I could see why he was known as a nutter. At one time Dr. Weaver was one of the leading doctors in Eden. His exam office was full of equipment, most of it looked old and out of use. Covered in dust with stacks of books and papers strewn everywhere. In the center there was an exam table, one that needed clean sheets. I almost laughed as the crazy old doctor pretended to be looking for something, but was just sneaking a quick drink from a hidden bottle. He turned to me, "Well, let's see… What seems to be the problem?"

"My hand, my only hand, let me show you." I pulled out my pocket watch and let it swing back and forth. "See, see how it moves? Look at the swinging, the swinging watch. Do you see what time it is?"

Dr. Weaver's eyes glazed over as he repeated, "The swinging watch. Why it's ten ten."

"Yes, ten, ten and now it is time to relax. Relax… you're feeling good. No worries, just relax. How do you feel?"

The doctor and Tom both said, "Relaxed."

I hated this part of the plan, but Tom could not be my caretaker. He was only fifteen, and taking care of his twelve year old sister would only hold him back. The thing I was about to do, would be the hardest thing I have ever done. I took a deep breath, calling the doctor by his first name, "Whyte, you forgot about me moving in."

He looked confused, "I did?"

"Yes, you did. Your nephew, Tom Weaver brought me. Tom, remember how happy you are to see your uncle." Weaver looked mad, realizing he didn't get along with his family I quickly added, "No, this is your favorite nephew, he's the one you love, and adore, and you've been waiting to see."

Dr. Weaver broke into a big smile, "It's good to see you Tom."

"And you as well," Tom said joyfully.

"What brings you to Eden, Nephew?"

Tom paused, unsure of how to answer the question. I answered for him, "He's here going to school. You were about to write him a letter, so that he would get a scholarship."

Dr. Weaver shook his head like it was all coming back to him, "Oh my, how forgetful. It's hard to remember, when your eighty three, bet your memory won't be so good when you're my age. Just give me a minute."

He left the room, to write the letter that Tom needed to be a doctor. Tom was not completely under my spell, and now that the doctor had left, he hissed in my ear, "What do you think you're doing? I can't leave you here, I can't be Tom Weaver."

I swung my watch, "Yes, yes you can. You will not worry about me, you will live your life and become successful no matter what. It's ten, ten, time to be free of my burden."

His eyes fought my power, "This isn't fair. This is my choice."

I held back my tears, "You would have never stopped caring for me. We would live poor and on the run. We would be lucky not to end up in Nemos, and perhaps we still will. I love you brother, and it's because I love you so much, that you have to go. You cannot live your life… as my caretaker."

Tom was crying, "What about you? How will this work?"

With tears now falling freely from my face, I said,"Easy, I'm wheelchair bound, with lots of medical problems. I'll make him think that I have rich benefactors paying for my room and board. The doctor has plenty of money, I will manage him. You see, no one can know about us. So, your Tom Weaver, I'll be Morgan… whatever name I want. When you come to visit your uncle, you will secretly be visiting me." I handed him my watch, the one I had enchanted. "This never needs to be wound, and when you open it a picture of whoever you wish to see will appear on the inside lid. You can see me, or our parents, whenever you wish."

He took the watch, then Tom wiped his face. "I'll become the greatest doctor, I swear it. When I have enough money, you will live with me."

I smiled, "Yes, I would like that." I knew he could leave now, he would succeed better off without me. I held up father's watch, "It's ten, ten, and time to leave."

Chapter 15 Alan Walker

Alan Walker

I hate running the Mill. I walked slowly through, eyeing my workers. The workers sweated like beasts in the field. The place stunk like cotton and sweat, and blood. They hid their faces from me as I walked by. Everyone working as hard as they could, hoping, I would take no notice of them.

Tim was falling down the staircase trying to speak to me. Apparently he was not capable of walking and talking at the same time. I kept the fool because he was good with numbers, but his age and his eyes had begun to fail him. I had been forced to buy a boy… I mean hire, a boy. I smiled at the thought, the difference between slaves and workers… small. I looked across the field of employees sweating at their weaving machines, making clothes for almost nothing. How many would count themselves free? I wonder.

Tim had been trying to tell me something, but between the noise in the shop and his banging into everything, while he tried to walk over, I couldn't understand him. "Calm yourself old man." He now stood there, saying nothing. I barked, "So, what was so important that you felt the need to fall down the staircase to tell me?"

"Oh, yes sir. Well, you see, the boy you hired."

"Yes," I urged impatiently. He was promised to be gifted, I had my doubts.

The old man fumbled with his words. "Well, you told me to tell you, if he couldn't do it, or, if there was anything else wrong with the boy."

I knew it, the child was useless, "What is wrong with him? Spit it out for the love of seven Gods." I had been ripped off, someone was about to die.

The old man had trouble looking at me when he spoke. It was hard not to throttle him, but my impatience was worsening the situation. He finally gathered his thoughts, "It's not that there's something wrong. Rather, to say it bluntly, he is extremely gifted. He can do more than calculate numbers, he can see them. There is nothing he cannot do. Numbers are just the beginning. His mind has more gears and cogs in it than any clock."

I smiled at him, "That is the best news I've heard in a while." I started to dismiss him, then thought to ask, "Music? Do you think it can be applied to music?"

The old man nodded with a grin, "I can't see why not. If you play it by the numbers." He said with a wink.

"You've done well, expect a little something extra in your pay."

"Oh, thank you, sir, thank you." The old man smiled a toothless grin as he hurried off.

My mind wandered, for all things I could do with the boy? What couldn't I do? I wanted to create music, and get away from this mill. I was nothing more than a slave here, just like the workers. I may be the big fish in this pond, but I yearned for a life in the city. It would take five or so years, but I would be free of this wretched place.

With two magical children it should be easy to get into the Caster School of Magic. That might find us a place in the city. Still, I need to insure *my* place in the city. I loved music, and just perhaps I could make it in the city as an entertainer. That reminded me, I should check on Evie and perhaps introduce her to the boy.

I headed to the top of the mill, where my quarters were located. Walking into my large office, I found my daughter where I had left her. Evie was playing with her dolls. The funny thing was, Evie looked like a doll. Her round face and big brown curls, she was cute beyond measure. Movement in the corner of my eye, I paused. Something else was in the room. I asked, "Who is here?"

No reply. I turned to look. Whoever it was, whatever it was, was about to find out what it was like to mess with Alan Walker. A growl came from the corner of my office, from behind my couch. Evie was like the boy, gifted. That was the reason I adopted her. Of course, there was an issue with raising gifted children. The creature growled again, this time more menacing. Great. What did that girl summon this time?

Book 2

Six Years Later

Chapter 1 Dr. Weaver

Tom Jones

I woke in a great mood. I received my grades yesterday, top of the class. Quickly dressing, I checked myself in the full length mirror. Nice white pressed shirt, black trousers and matching vest, I straightened my bow tie. I said out loud to no one, "What a handsome man you are Tom Weaver, or perhaps I should say... Dr. Weaver."

My roommate Percy, popped his head out of his covers. In an annoying voice chimed in; "Perhaps you should call yourself, Dr. Asshat."

I laughed, "So jealous, we can't all be me."

"Ha!" He yelled through his blanket. "Go be you, somewhere else."

I slipped on my long black coat, then I grabbed my walking cane and top hat. My goggles were wrapped around the dome of the hat. I checked my pockets, making sure my papers, money and watch were all in their proper place. With a triumphant voice I boomed, "Indeed, I will be off! Good day to you good sir!" I could hear Percy cursing as I slammed the door harder than necessary. He was a good roommate, but somewhat of a pansy. I would miss my friend, but I would not miss this small, smelly, dormitory. I headed downstairs and out the front door.

Rain was falling, I slipped on my goggles, spinning my cane around in my hand and saying the word, "Umbrella." The walking cane magically unfolded into an umbrella. I double checked to make sure no one saw me. I forgot, I should never let anyone see me using one of Morgan's enchanted items. Which also reminded me, I would need to go see her tonight. Had to make sure she received an invitation to my graduation. Six years of medical school, finally, I would be a doctor!

Walking down the street, passing all the other umbrellas, I couldn't help but feel pride at my height and build. Standing six feet two, I was now taller than my father. The women I passed, their eyes followed me. My eyes landed on Tiffany, but her look was one of pure hate. I walked on as if I had not noticed her. I have broken some hearts, sure, but who could blame me. The crowd was mostly students, younger classmates on the way to their next class. A pretty little thing caught my eye, and she noticed me looking at her. I gave her a smile, which was returned. My heart sank in disappointment as I kept walking. I had to meet my girlfriend, and I had promised myself to keep my hands off of the other ladies. It would be dreadful if Vicky found out about any of my extra activities.

Vicky Webb, the "love of my life." I chuckled at the thought. I wondered what others thought of our relationship? Perhaps it was her looks, if you found chunky boys attractive. Perhaps her face is tolerable, in the right lighting, or no light at all. I could tell others it was her laugh, tell them how much I love her screeching at my jokes. Maybe they will buy that I was in love with her mind. I could tell them I loved how she prattled on about nonsense all day, often repeating herself. At first, I believed she thought no one could understand her simple ideas, and repeating them might be necessary. Now I knew, she subconsciously understood that no one was paying her idiocy any attention.

No, they wouldn't buy any of that. They would suspect why I dated Vicky Webb. Her father, Marvin Webb, Dr. Marvin Webb, of Webb's family practice. The top clinic in all of Eden, and the most successful Doctor I'd ever heard of. It didn't matter if she wasn't beautiful, or talented, or interesting. I could make this girl love me. I dreamed of my life in a few years, a big home with the finest furniture and the best and newest clothing available. Yes, I could love Vicky, or at least love what she can do for me and my career.

Under the veranda, Vicky sat with her two friends Michelle and Donna. Donna was in love with me, a true nerd, big glasses, her hair and clothes appeared to have been slept in. She was nice enough, it was Michelle I could not stand. Pretty, with sharp features and a sharp wit to boot. She saw straight through me, and never missed an opportunity to point out what a terrible person I was. The only ace up my sleeve with her, was the fact I had sex with her. She was a true friend to Vicky, they grew up together, and it was her biggest fear that Vicky would find out. Of course I questioned what kind of friend she was, then I found out her parents worked for the Webb family practice. Perhaps her fears of Vicky finding out about her betrayal, were well founded.

They were enjoying some afternoon tea, enjoying a day outside. These days seemed further apart for some reason, but then again, I could hardly recall one when I lived out in the outer gate. I wondered why, but my thought was interrupted by Vicky standing up and shrieking, "You're here. How long do you plan on keeping a girl waiting?"

I teased, "Just long enough to feel wanted, but not too long let such a beauty as you escape."

Michelle rolled her eyes from behind Vicky. Vicky was all smiles as she yelled out much too loud, "Hurry my love, my arms long to hold you!"

Ugh, it took will power not to roll my own eyes. Tipping my hat, I headed towards the door to the Bitten Apple. This was truly my favorite diner, filled with things from a forgotten age. What they were, we might never know. They hung from every wall, shiny and white, with black glass, all with the same symbol of the Bitten Apple. I went through the front door, nodding my head to the staff who all knew me by sight. Vicky tackled me with a hug. By now she had the entire crowd giving us sideways glances. I said, "Sweetheart, we're still in public."

She laughed and gave me a big smile, "I don't care, let them eat their hearts out. Let them see love, and wish they had but a drop of it."

"A poet, I never knew it." I held her seat for her while she sat. Donna quickly gave up her chair so that I might sit next to her. "Why thank you my dear," giving Donna a big smile, watching her face turn red. Turning back to Vicky, "My dear, I will not be able to stay long. I need to stop by and visit my uncle." Really, I needed to visit my sister Morgan, but no one knew that she existed.

Michelle made some underhanded remark, "Sure, right, your uncle."

Loudly I asked Michelle, "What was that?"

With a tight lipped smile, "Nothing."

Vicky laughed, Michelle had done this so often that Vicky just thought she was joking. She believed it was a game between us, and in a way she was right. Vicky scolded, "You two, stop it. Tea time is a peaceful time, not a time for your Tom foolery." She then laughed loudly at her own joke, "See what I did there?"

"So witty dear," I tried to smile, and not to look half as bored as she made me feel.

"Well, I won't hold you up." She must have plans with the girls. She hated to be alone for any amount of time.

My heart jumped with happiness, she wasn't going to make me sit here for twenty minutes and listen to her go on about nothing. "I will see you for dinner then," giving her my best smile.

Vicky frowned, "No my Peachoums," It took all my will power not to flinch as she used my horrible nickname in public. She went on, "I will not be joining you tonight, my father wishes to have dinner with you, and you alone." She was holding back a smile as she said this, her smile broke free. "This can only be good news. Never has my father wanted to talk one on one with my suitor." Quickly adding, "Not, that there has been many." This was true, in fact, I had only heard of Shane. She was rejected, and heartbroken for months.

I was nervous enough knowing that I would be eating with her father tonight. I had only met the man a handful of times. He always made me feel like I was ten, and I had a sneaky suspicion that this may not be a good thing. I answered with false excitement, "Well, I look forward to it. The only bad thing is... That it will be that much longer before I am able to see you again, my love."

She beamed, "I know, but I'm sure it will be worth it. Call me tonight, no matter how late. I simply must know how your dinner goes with father."

"I will, and good day to you ladies," Donna gave me a heartfelt goodbye as Michelle pretended not to hear me. I headed out of the Bitten Apple and towards the trolley station. My head swam, what could Dr. Webb want? Or better yet, what does he know? I would ask Morgan, she was a genius at these things.

It would have taken me twenty minutes to get to my uncle's, if I had taken the trolley or a rickshaw. Days like this are few, so instead I walked. Lost in thought, I arrived at my uncle's faster than I believed possible. Checking my watch, it had taken me forty or so minutes to get here. I must be nervous about dinner with Marvin.

I looked at the line of people standing in front of Dr. Weaver's residence. The place was completely remodeled, wheelchair ramp included. I remembered what it looked like when Morgan and I first arrived here some six years ago. That reminds me, Morgan's eighteenth birthday was right around the corner. I was proud of my sister. No one knew she was my sister, but I was proud. She had turned Dr. Weaver around, controlling his drinking; well to a degree, and putting his practice back on the map. She manages everything for that man, and he loved her for it. Morgan no longer needed to put a spell on him, he adores her.

Of course, when Morgan first planned on staying with the old doctor, she thought him to be rich. It hadn't taken long to realize that the old man had made many bad investments and lost most of his money. That's when he decided to become a full time alcoholic. Morgan had not only repaired his business, but she had given him hope again.

I walked past the house, then down an alley. Busy days it was easier to use the back entrance. The back entrance still looked very much unkempt. Slipping inside, I had to give the door a hard yank to open it. Hanging my hat and coat on the familiar hooks, I moved down the hallway. I could hear the nurse calling in the clients. I shook my head in wonder, how my sister turned this back into a successful clinic? It was truly miraculous. Checking to make sure the coast was clear, I pulled the candle stick holder attached to the wall. It moved ever so slightly as I said the magic key word, "Tinker." A part of the wall slid away, revealing a passageway. As soon as I entered the door slid tightly behind me and I descended downwards on a twisted staircase.

On the way down my hand slid down the smooth hand railing, the same magical handrail that would carry my sister's wheelchair to the top. Arriving at the bottom I enter into Morgan's workshop. Surrounded by what appeared to be junk.

I knew all this stuff was not junk. A pair of boots, you could walk on walls. Several pairs of goggles, each with different ways of seeing the world. Last she told me she was working on one that could change by the flip of a button. You can even see at night.

I spotted a large glass bottle full of marbles. I had picked one up once, Morgan tried to warn me, she was too late and I dropped the marble. The world plunged into darkness. This was no normal darkness, for not even light itself could pierce it. All we could do is wait until the spell wore off. I found later how lucky I was, some of the marbles were designed to explode.

I notice a box marked, anti-vampire, what on earth does she need that for. Then again I had heard that some of the night, police were vampires. I hope Morgan didn't plan on running a criminal empire.

I headed through the maze of shelves. My sister sat hunched in her wheelchair, half asleep. Head over her workbench, she appeared to be working on something metal that I could not make it out.

Morgan looked awful, she had gained a lot of weight. She was always in pain from sitting all the time, but the extra weight was not helping. I announced my arrival, "Morgan, are you sleeping?"

Her head snapped up, and she answered with a yawn, "Wide awake."

We both laughed as I pulled a chair up and joined her. "What would you like for your birthday? I was going to surprise you, but to tell you the truth, I have no idea what to get you."

She smiled, "Don't get me anything. Instead, do something for me."

"Well, I'm kind of busy, that's a lot to ask." I said this with a wink.

She had a tired look in her eyes, "Go over there, to that table. Pull off the sheet and take a look."

Getting to my feet I headed over to a large table sitting in the corner of the room. I had seen this dark brown sheet laying over this table, covering something oddly shaped. I had never even wondered what was under the sheet, but now that Morgan had pointed it out, I was curious. Pulling off the old dirty sheet, my eyes took in the sight before me. I looked at the object before me, not sure what it was, but yet I knew, my mind started to put it together.

It was a metal spine that shined like gold, each vertebra linked together by pins. The spine attached to what appeared to be hips, leading to legs of mechanical design. The top of the spine attached to shoulders, with one mechanical left arm. The right arm looked incomplete, it appeared to be wires and other mechanical parts, but not a full arm. The closer I examined the spine, the more detail became evident, small wires coiled around and through the spine. They had loose ends, waiting to be attached, and it all reminded me of the hundreds of nerve endings that traveled down a human spine. I spoke without thinking, "You would never survive the surgery."

Her voice full of pain, "I won't survive without it... And if I do, it will be mimicking a fat slug. My one good arm is dying. I'd rather be dead, than alive like this. You must do this for me Tom."

I closed my eyes tight, and took some breaths. Opening my eyes to my sister's greatest creation, then to her and back again. "It can't be done... You are asking a lot of me." She eyed me and said nothing. I huffed, "It cannot be done all at once."

Her face brightened, "Of course, whatever you say."

I went on, "This will take dozen of surgeries, and quite possibly years to complete. The pain will be great, you might die." I paused, "but you might live. I don't know about this... maybe."

Her eyes shone with tears of joy, "Thank you Tom, brother. You will not regret it, and you watch, I won't die... I will walk again, no... I will run."

"Into a tree," I jest.

She laughed, "I would be glad of it, as long as I was running."

Chapter 2 Dinner and Blackmail

Dr. Weaver

I had a good visit with my sister, but I had to cut it off or I would late for dinner with Vicky's father. I could have stayed all night talking over the plans for replacing a good portion of her body with mechanical parts. I left with enough time to walk to the restaurant where we were eating. Much as I tried to prepare my mind for the meeting with Marvin, all I could think of was Morgan's new spine.

Before I knew it, I was being seated by the host, Marvin had arrived before me. He had a scowl on his face, I greeted him pleasantly, "Good evening."

"You're late," He replied abruptly and none too pleased.

Looking at the large clock in the dinning room, and comparing to my pocket watch, "Five till…"

He interrupted me, "Early is on time, on time is late, and late is unacceptable. No matter, you are here now."

Luckily the waiter came for our drink order so I didn't have to answer the man. My mind spun. He was already hostile, he was probably making his move to get rid of me. I would have to be careful, if I planned on winning this man over. Arguing over the fact I was early would get me nowhere fast. We waited in silence for our drinks, and I mentally prepared for the duel of words.

I did not have to wait long, after the drinks arrived, Marvin asked, "So, Tom, let's cut to the chase. No need to order, this won't take long. I see how my daughter is smitten with you. I realize you just graduated top of your class… Of course that was because you were able to pay with the city scholar program. I can't help, but be curious, why are you with Vicky?"

Clearing my throat, I began in with my well rehearsed lines, "Well, sir, I find that Vicky is the second half of me. Together we make…"

Marvin burst into a laugh, quickly stopping and giving me a menacing glare. "I love my daughter, but I know what she is. I see no reason for *you* to be with *her*, well, except for her money and an opportunity she might provide."

Caught off guard I stuttered, "I graduated top of my class. I can make a great living… I don't, I mean, I will not require her money. Furthermore, I can find work in any hospital."

He glared at me, "Stop the games Tom. You're a smart lad, you know there's no money in other practices. Well, no money like working in my practice. We serve the elite, the Enchanted Garden and its residents. Have you ever been in the Garden?" I shook my head, "I thought not, few have. Someone from your background wouldn't even be allowed in. I hate to inform you, this will not happen. I will make you an offer instead."

My mind quickened, this was a trap. It was hard not to squirm in my seat under the man's gaze. I made up my mind, I would fight this man. "I'm sorry, sir, but my mind is made up. I love your daughter."

He ignored me and went on with his offer, "Tom, my offer will also include a good place of employment. Without me, you'll be working at clinic patching up soldiers on the outer wall."

This angered me on so many levels. I straightened my shoulders, "Wait, wait. You are going about this in the wrong way, that's not even what we're here to discuss."

I waited for his reply, his face a twist of anger and confusion. "Excuse me?"

I went on, "We are here to discuss that I have five other offers, from great clinics. Being that I am top in my class. Now we both know what a great asset I would make to the Webb family practice. What is your offer?"

He burst into a chuckle, "You're bold." He went on, getting angrier with every word, "As if, I, have no offer to make you… to work for me. My offer is to help see you off."

I countered, "I have five other offers, but there are negatives. None of them are in the city of Eden."

He had the look of victory, "Well, I guess you will be leaving."

"I suppose so, I will be traveling to far off lands. Even dangerous places, like the wall." I smiled a wicked grin.

His face hardened again, he took a slight pause. He was working out my game in his head. He burst out in anger, "And you believe that my daughter... Would go with you?"

He was smart, it hadn't taken him a second to understand my threat. Keeping my face as neutral as possible, "Won't she?"

With a growl, "You would blackmail me?"

"Negotiations," I replied.

Before he could say another word, the waiter interrupted to see if we needed anything. I found this was a good time to have him refill our glasses. Then I picked up the menu and began to order. The waiter turned to Marvin and asked, "And what would you be having this evening?"

Marvin about bit the waiter's head off, "I have lost my appetite." He hurried away for his own safety as Marvin and I went back to our death staring contest.

After a little bit I said, "Webb and Weaver, Family Medicine Practice, it has a good sound to it."

His eyes tried to bore a hole through me, "There is no way, you are getting a partnership."

"There is no way, I'm not."

Minutes clicked by, Webb stopped the waiter and ordered dinner, "I may as well eat; since you are determined to waste my time." The food came, and we ate and drank, neither breaking the silence between us. The waiter had just asked if we would like a dessert, and topped off our glasses. Marvin broke the silence, "Even at the cost of my daughter, I could not just give you a partnership.

You haven't even graduated, let alone had any time in the field. Perhaps, I could find a position for you."

I had realized that when I asked for a partnership, there was no way I would get it. How could Marvin give a kid with no experience a partnership? There were plenty of doctors working in Webb practice, and a few partners. I would have to prove myself, "You are right. I said that in anger. I just know, that no matter where I go, I will make a great doctor in time."

Satisfied with my response, Marvin gave me a tight smile, "Good, I hate unreasonable people. Let me make you a real offer."

"Thank you," I responded, keeping my face as neutral as possible. I felt like I had won, but I was not about to let my guard down.

Marvin announced his offer, "First, you will serve a five year apprenticeship, and not one year less. After that we will talk about what kind of doctor you have proven to be. You will be reviewed under my board." Then he added with authority, "There will be no favoritism."

I nodded, "I won't need it."

He grinned at my remark, "Good. Secondly, you will marry my daughter."

To my own amazement, I held a straight face, "I had planned on it."

"It is the envy of every doctor in town to work for my practice. We normally don't accept students straight from school, but I will be making an exception. Do not expect any more. Thirdly, more important than how you perform in my office… The happiness of my daughter will be your greatest concern. If, she is ever to be found heartbroken, or I find out you are cheating on my little angel; not only will I fire you." His face narrowed, and using his eyes like spears, "I assure you, I will ruin you, and the only place you'll practice is in the mines of Nemos. Do you understand?"

"Yes… Yes, sir," I stuttered out.

This was truly a dangerous game, no one can know the truth. I will become the lie, and my life will be that lie, and once I get what I need, I will be able to become what I want to be.

Chapter 3 A New Friend

Morgan Jones

It had been good to see my brother yesterday. It lifted my spirits that he was willing to help with my surgeries. I originally thought Dr. Weaver could do the surgery and not tell Tom. Weaver would not work, I could not trust the old doctor. He was showing early signs of the cough, worse, he had found the bottle again. After talking to Tom he explained that installing my robotic spine could not be done in one surgery. No matter what, I couldn't have done this without him.

I was grateful beyond words that Tom was going to do this for me. I looked around me, a room full of my inventions, a lonely room. I was in isolation, with no one but an old bitter man to keep me company. I've been watching my brother live the life as a college student. As much as his stories of adventure bothered me, I could not wait for him to visit and tell me all about what he had done. I deserved my isolation, for it was I who killed our mother. I had no idea where Darrell was, it all made me feel like a failure.

Being alone was my choice. Whenever I ventured out, people would look upon me with pity in their eyes. I could not stand it, yet, I didn't want them to remember my face. One day I'll walk, and when that happens, they will not remember the legless girl in a wheelchair. I was finally ready for the last step, the surgery to install my creation. It could take years, but I would walk.

I caught a tear running down my face. Why do I cry? I deserve no one's pity, not even my own.

I had enchanted my wheelchair and with the smallest of movement from my hand, it would zip across the floor. I needed fresh air. It was late and dark out, less chance of people, and no chance of them seeing my face. I worked in the basement, it would have cost a pretty penny to have an elevator installed, so I enchanted the railing on the staircase. My wheelchair would float next to the railing, gliding in the air just a few inches from the stairs. I had paid workers to put in ramps, both in front of the house and back. It only took me a few minutes before I was free of the house and taking in the cool night air. My chair bounced down the alley, emerging onto the main street. From there it was only a few hundred yards to a small park planted between the many homes.

It was a dark night and the park was not lit up like the streets. My goggles were enchanted to see at night, so I knew the park lay empty. I like it here, at night, the dark kept the honest people away. Every once in a while, some young men would enter the park, but I had a way to deal with them. I enchanted my chair with many different abilities. I had been working on creating illusions of evil spirits, with haunting sounds and ghostly images flying through the trees. I really enjoyed watching them run for their lives. Of course it had been many nights, and the park remains empty. I mean, who wants to go to a haunted park anyway?

I caught movement out of the corner of my eye. I turned quickly, but it was only a cat, "You scared me kitten." The cat just stared at me. "Come here kitty. Come here sweet kitty." The cat meowed at me, but didn't come any closer. I frowned, "You probably have friends." I turned from the cat. A chill ran through me, it was much cooler now. I was full of emptiness, I was truly hoping someone would be out tonight so that I might scare them, but I wasn't sure if that would even make me feel better.

I was startled when the cat landed in my lap. I yelped, but the cat just meowed at my face. "Well, maybe you don't have any friends. Good, I need company." I talked to the cat, patting it with my one good hand. It purred. Such a large cat, it was the size of a small dog. And as it sat in my lap its head was even with mine. I couldn't help it, a wave of nervousness washed through me. Was this a wild cat? It appeared to be friendly. It was happy enough to be on my lap sharing my warmth, perhaps it was someone's pet. If so, they were foolish not to put a collar on it. The night guard killed wild animals, and I might steal it.

I stared at the cat and realized something. There were a lot of yellow and white cats in Eden. Large cats too, unless this was the same cat. I think I will steal this cat. I then announced, "I will call you Mittens." At last, I had a friend.

That night had been special to me, for finding the cat helped with my loneliness. My cat kept me busy, and time went by quickly with her company. It was hard to believe I found the cat a week ago, and now it was time for the first of my surgeries. Tom had arrived an hour ago, the old doctor and he prepped the surgery room for the first of my surgeries.

I was nervous, Tom hadn't seen me naked since I was a little girl. Could you die of embarrassment? Tom came to me, to help me out of my chair and onto the operating table. He first helped me out of my nightgown. His eyes never changed. I stopped worrying about being au natural, almost immediately. Tom made me feel so loved, and I was only a little surprised at how comfortable I was around him. He smiled as he lifted me up and commented, "Amazing, you didn't gain a pound."

I accused, "You're stronger."

He gently slid me onto the table, "Perhaps." He laid me on my stomach, there was a hole in the table for my face. I was now looking upon the floor. He asked me, "Are you comfortable?"

"Yes," of course I wasn't really comfortable. "Thank you brother, for everything."

He was putting my hair up, "It's not too late to change your mind."

"It's not too late to get a personality." I shot back at him.

He teased back, "Personalities are over rated. Especially when you have a charm like mine."

I turned serious, "I can't turn back, I'm ready to live, or ready to die." I was so nervous, but I had to do this.

He was quiet for a minute, "I know. I should have never left you, not for my false life. It would have been better to live a lie with you."

That upset me, "Tom, no regrets… You hear me. Even if I die, you live. Promise me!" I owe him so much more.

His voice was soft, "Promise, Morgan, but you're not going to die, so it's an easy promise. Are you ready?"

I tried to sound confident, "Yes." Noticing the cat, I asked, "Is it ok to have the cat in here?"

"What cat?" Tom barked.

I complained, "I can't see her anymore, limited eye and head movement here."

Tom grunted as he looked around the room for the cat. "It must have left, I didn't even know you had a cat."

I barked back, "Well dad, I must have forgot to tell you."

Tom huffed, "I'll shut the door, we don't need animals in here during a surgery. Let's begin before the dogs arrive."

This was the first, and perhaps the most dangerous of my surgeries. Tom and Weaver would have to cut open my back, from my butt to my neck. Then metal plates fitted over each spinal disk, each metal piece would be attached by steel pins. Through the use of magic, thousands of little wires would bore their way into my spine. Attaching themselves to my nervous system.

If I survived, it would be a miracle.

Chapter 4 Four Years Later

Tom March 8th, 2613

Why am I having such a hard time finishing my paperwork? I feel like life has no meaning, an emptiness in my chest that consumes my mind. I squeezed my fingers to my temples, trying to understand this depression that comes more often than not. Not that anyone would know it, I was an actor… more than a doctor. No one knew how I felt, or what I thought of them.

A nurse interrupted my thoughts, "Working late?"

Forcing a smile on my face, "No, I'm heading out shortly."

Her smile was good natured, "Don't stay too late." Her face disappeared from my door. I couldn't help but think, perhaps I won't have to stay late, if others would stop interrupting me?

I looked up at the grandfather clock, it really was getting late. I would need to get home, my wife would not like it if I kept her waiting. My wife, it was still strange to call Vicky my wife. Her happiness was my happiness. Four years working for my father-in-law, and I was a shoe in for a partner. Not only did I turn out to be a great doctor, but thanks to my sister's rings, I was one of the best. Marvin and I turned out to be great friends, his daughter was in love with me a little bit more each day.

My mother-in-law, Jennifer, at times acted as if she would like to steal me away from her daughter. It didn't take me long to see where Vicky received her personality from. What she did not receive, was her mother's looks. Her mother is gorgeous, even for a woman half her age. I never really took into account what Marvin looked like, but I have had time to reflect. Vicky had received both of their shortcomings, her mom's oddness and foolishness, and her father's looks. I shook my head, it would be worth it for a good career and safe life within Eden's wall.

Most importantly, my sister was doing well, she may not require any more of me. Four years of surgery, and Morgan can walk. The very thought gave me chills. She looked good, lost weight, and her color returned along with her smile. Both arms working, and her legs have moved from walking to running. She was a work of art.

Tomorrow was Tuesday, on Tuesday I leave early from work, to head over to my uncle's. At first my father-in-law was sure there was another woman. I remember the day he burst into my uncle's house and demand to see me. I had just finished a three hour surgery on Morgan and was covered with blood. Exhausted, I sat on a chair next to the operating table. Marvin burst into the room, yelling, "Caught you red handed. You thought you were fooling me… Oh, Dr. Weaver, what is going on?" At that moment Marvin realized what was going on. He started to stutter, "Surgery, of course, inside an upstairs bedroom."

The old Doctor replied, "We make do with what space I have. I hadn't expected you Dr. Webb, Tom never mentioned your visit."

I had to keep from laughing, "I would have been glad of your assistance, but we are quite finished for the evening."

Dr. Weaver was eager to drink, "Let's all journey downstairs and have a toast."

Marvin started to stammer, "Well, I hadn't really planned on staying."

I quickly added, "We don't have a nurse right now, I must stay and monitor my patient."

Dr. Weaver was downtrodden, but Marvin was happy for an excuse to leave. He hadn't understood what, or who, I was operating on. He had busted in believing that I was cheating on his daughter. He was so embarrassed he never questioned me again. Which was good, because he might come to realize that I was always operating on the same girl.

I felt like crying, why was I so miserable? I felt as if happiness was but around the corner. Maybe, if I reached my goals, became a partner, realized my potential. Perhaps then I would be content. Clenching my teeth, there it was again, the nagging feeling that my wife held me back. Then again, if it wasn't for her I never would have been hired by her father. We live well beyond my salary. It was her need that bothered me, always demanding, always needing more of me. It was like filling a tank with water when there was an obvious hole in the bottom of it. No matter how much you added, it just poured right out. Vicky was a bottomless pit, draining me of my life.

I must be careful with this line of thinking, I must make her feel loved. Her happiness was my happiness, because her father could make or break my career. Marvin was more impressed by the smile on his daughters face; than the leaps that I made in medicine. No, I was stuck in this lie…. My life, not until I had enough success to be free of the wretched woman.

I had enough of this thinking. Time to go home, dinner will be waiting. As I closed the door and headed down the corridor, Marvin stepped out of his office, "My boy, you're still here, I need to see you."

Intrigued, I replied, "Of course."

"Not that I want to keep you from your love." He said this with a very sincere smile, which made my stomach turn. Still, my face revealed, nothing. "I think you are ready my dear man." He said with a grin.

"Ready, for what?" I questioned.

He smiled, "The Enchanted Garden." I was speechless, and knew my mouth must just be hanging wide open. "Normally only partners, and our top doctors see patients within the Gardens, but something has come up."

It was hard to hide my excitement, "What happened?"

His eyes looked around the room, as if there might be ears, "There is a very special patient. She's finicky, she only allows Dr. Cambridge to tend to her, but as you well know, the poor man is on his death bed with the cough. Every day he took his Zen, the best you can buy, still, sixty-eight is too young. Better than most, especially in the outer ring, if you know what I mean."

Skeptical I asked, "And she wants me to tend to her?"

Marvin tilted his head, "Not really. She doesn't like any of the other doctors that serve the Gardens. Mostly due to the other patients that they serve. It's a long story, but her family is the oldest and a very influential family in Eden. She doesn't want doctors, who have anything to do with… How would I say this?"

I offered, "Rivals?"

"Yes, my boy… rivals. You're new, and have no clients within the Garden. Understand this Tom, it is very important that she is satisfied, this is not a client that I can afford to lose."

I straightened up, "You can count on me, sir."

Marvin patted me on my back, "I know, or I wouldn't even ask you. You better hurry off to your wife. Thursday morning I'll take you into the Gardens and introduce you officially to your new patient."

As I hurried off, my mind raced. Finally a chance to work with real clients! Then it hit me, he didn't even tell me who I was going to be working with. I wondered if that was on purpose, oh well, it didn't matter. This was turning out to be a glorious day, and tomorrow I would be able to tell Morgan all about it. With my spirits lifted, I hurried home, and for once I didn't even mind talking with my wife.

It had been a mistake, telling Vicky about my invite into the Enchanted Garden. She was full of excitement, well that was until she figured out that there was no way I could take her with me. Then I had to hear a full twenty minutes of why it was not fair, and how come she couldn't go? Apparently, she had never been, and that little information made me feel just a wee bit better about her annoying me so late in the evening.

Falling asleep proved to be difficult. At first I was just too keyed up to sleep, but after a while my mind started to succumb to my need to rest. Then Vicky started with her ridiculous questions. "Are you asleep yet?" She would ask.

"No, dear," I answered as nicely as possible. When I was sure she was done talking, I would close my eyes, only to be asked another unimportant question. As nicely as I could, "Dear, please, I'm tired and tomorrow is a big day."

"Of course it is, the Enchanted Garden. I knew that you would rise up to be one of the great doctors of Eden. My father couldn't see it, but now he can." She almost sounded as if she were done when she asked, "Are you sure... You mean to tell me there is no way I can go?"

"If only my love," Why had I told her?

Chapter 5 Steam Power

Morgan Jones

I awoke to perform my morning diagnosis. I looked at the calendar, March 8th, 2613, only five months and I would be twenty four. Yet I felt much younger, I felt as if years of my youth had been taken from me. This didn't bother me, since I was about to take them back. It was my punishment for my sin.

My legs were fast, I found it hard to walk when I wanted to run. I dressed like a young boy, ladies didn't run down the street, but the runners did. Young boys, and sometimes girls, would often take jobs as runners to earn money. It was easy, you just picked up the packages and delivered them. The more you delivered, the more money you could make.

I loved running, the money wasn't great, but the wind in my face was. Most of the boys who lived on the street, or in the orphanage ran. They all had single names that were found on artifacts from Modern Man. An older boy named Amazon had seen me running and convinced me that I could make good money as a runner. Since Dr. Weaver's practice was not going so hot, I had taken up this job under the false name of Samsung. It didn't take long before everyone just called me Sung. At first, I received most of my work through Amazon, but in time I learned my way around the city and had no trouble finding a job.

Arriving at a small warehouse behind the bakery, I went to find Amazon. He had work for me. The other runners were there picking up packages for delivery. I passed by my fellow runners, giving a small head nod to them as I passed. Sun-drop, one of the few female runners yelled at me, "Hey, Sung, over here."

"What's up Sun-drop?" I headed over to her. She was leaning against a table covered in sweat, she must have just returned from a run. When she saw me heading her way she turned and waved for me to follow. "Hey, I'm looking for Amazon."

"I know," She waited for me to catch up before saying more, "Just follow me, ok?" It wasn't long before she led me to the far side of the warehouse, out of sight from everyone. She stopped and turned to me, "Amazon told me to catch you when you came in. He has a job for you, pays good. Take this box, to this address... This is the important part, don't let anyone stop you, and don't let anyone see you enter the building. And when I say; don't let anyone stop you; I mean the law."

I looked at her suspiciously, "What are you talking about?"

"More money, that's if you're up to it."

I wasn't sure, "Why don't you do it? If it pays so well."

"I do," She lowered her voice and looked around to make sure no one overheard us. "Look, Amazon has some sweet deals going on, but it's not for everyone. If you don't want to, that's cool."

I wondered, "Why trust me?"

She smiled, "Because, you're a girl pretending to be a boy." She must have seen the surprise on my face. She laughed, "Please, you can fool the boys around here, but not these eyes, sweetheart. Look, Amazon and I figure you have your reason, but you are no cop. Hell, I'm not even sure where you're from, but undercover try too hard to blend in. You in, or no?"

I looked at the small box, "Yes, how much more for the delivery?"

"Double, sometimes more," she winked and handed me the box. "Don't be late."

I nodded as I took off for the door. I was not sure if this was a good idea, or if I needed the money that bad, but the whole idea excited me. Before I could think about it, I was running. I was sure I knew this area of town well enough to be out before anyone took notice of me.

My legs moved me along much faster than anyone else could run. I had to pay attention, if anyone was to close I had to slow it down. I couldn't afford being seen running this fast, but when I could, I love to let loose. The wind in my hair and the rush of objects and buildings flying by. The sweat poured off, it was effort to run, but not like having legs. It hadn't taken long before everyone, not only realized I was the fastest runner in town, but I could run all day. After people started talking, I took less work. It was important that I didn't draw too much attention to myself.

Maybe because I was nervous I hadn't paid attention to my overall speed. I arrived at my destination a little too quickly. I was only a few houses down when I stopped running and checked my watch. No one could have gotten here this fast, I would have to waste some time. I moved off the quiet street and into a very small alley between some buildings. I looked up, perhaps on the roofs of the buildings I might get a clear view of the house I was to deliver to. That seemed like a good idea, seeing as no one could see me enter.

The alley was only wide enough for one person. Looking back and forth I made sure the coast was clear. With the strength of my arms and legs, it was no problem for me to scale the walls by pushing from one wall to the other. I was on the roof in a moment. The roof had many angles, and steep inclines, but I moved across the different surfaces like a spider.

It didn't take me long to find a nice resting spot between two sharp angles in a roof line. It was dark, the sun never found this spot. Overlooking the house I was to deliver to, I decided to rest. I hadn't been there for ten minutes when I noticed a man standing across the far side of the road. At first, I thought nothing of the man until I realized he was watching the house I was supposed to deliver to. He had found a corner between two buildings across the street, from up here it was easy enough to see him, but from street level, you wouldn't have seen him until you were directly out front of the delivery location.

Taking my time looking around I spotted a second man at the rear of the building. Unlike the first man, this man appeared to be working on some pipes. He wore a blue work uniform with tools hanging off a brown belt. After watching him for a few minutes, I could tell he was just pretending to work and his head kept moving over to the house checking on the back door. My heart pounded in my chest, should I just leave?

She had told me not to be seen entering the house, but she hadn't said what to do if the house was being guarded. Perhaps it was a trap, maybe the house was already full of police. I took a deep breath, and seeing that neither man had seen me, I decided to calm down and think about it.

After a bit, I came up with a plan. Why should I even bother to deliver this stupid box? I knew why, because I loved the challenge of it. It was a good twenty feet from the roof I was on, to the roof of the house I need to get to. Also the roof I was on was a solid two stories higher. I moved quickly back the way I came, and out of sight of the two men watching. It didn't take me long to gather some wire from one of the roof tops. The owners would notice that the radio no longer picked up anything.

Tearing off some metal edging from the roof, I bent it into a makeshift hook. From there it was an easy toss with my left arm. The hook sailed through the air, landing with a clang. I spied on both the watchers, but neither reacted. They must not of heard it down on the street, I had been counting on that. I slowly pulled the cable. I could see the hook sliding across the roof of the other house. It grabbed the ledge, I tugged hard until it became tight. I said to myself, "Got it."

Once I secured the cable, it was easy enough to slide across. I watched carefully to make sure the men were not looking, then off I went. The hardest part was not to yell out, "Weeee." I landed on the roof and went into a body roll, then back onto my feet. Nice landing, if I do say so myself. The only part that went wrong was I had dropped the box on the landing, it came precariously close to falling off the roof, but luck was on my side.

Once on the roof, I had no problem slipping down the side of the wall and onto a small ledge. My luck was still holding because one of the upper windows had been left open. I quickly slid in. Once inside, I found myself in a small bedroom. It looked to be set up for guest perhaps, nothing made me think an individual lived here. As I moved to the door, I could hear voices filtering up from the lower level.

One voice was clearly Amazon's. "Sung should have been here by now. I had high hopes."

The other voice was female, older, "Give the boy some time. Maybe he is smarter than the others, perhaps he has seen the guards and is trying to figure out how to deliver."

Amazon huffed in disbelief, "No, probably got scared and turned back. Still, Sung's fast, you think I would have heard from Sun-Drop. I really was hoping Sung would work out, I need another runner. And the city has been putting on a lot of heat with stolen enchanted items."

The woman was calm, "Yes, but that also drives the prices up."

Amazon agreed, "True, Linda, but we still need to move this stuff."

So that's the game. This is a test to see how I might do, and the job is to move stolen enchanted items. A light went off in my head, an idea, I could be a straw person. I could get involved, then pretend to know a seller of stolen items. Selling my enchanted items would give me the income I needed.

After a moment I made a move, I burst into the room where Amazon and Linda had been talking. Tossing the package to Amazon he almost dropped it. I flipped open my watch, "Five minutes late, it took me a while to get here from the roof top. Don't worry, no one saw me come in, and no one will see me leave."

A smile, danced upon the lips of the woman. She was middle aged, thin, and quite the looker. Her face was rough, something about her let you know she lived a hard life. As pretty as she was now, she must have been gorgeous when she was younger. I was jealous, I would never look like that. She introduced herself, "I'm Linda, you must be Sung."

"Yes, ma'am," I reached to shake her hand. She smiled, but she didn't shake my hand. "It's been good meeting you." I turned to leave.

Amazon spoke, "Hold up Sung. Stay awhile, this was a test and you passed with flying colors. Let's talk about the future."

I smiled, at last, a future for selling my enchanted items. "Sounds good."

Chapter 6 Enchanted Garden

Tom Weaver

It was a restless night, partly because Vicky kept me up, but also because I was excited about my journey to the Enchanted Gardens. I picked up the paper, March 9th, I tried my hardest to read the stories. The morning just dragged. At last I joined Marvin on the seat of the rickshaw. Today we wore our dark gray suits with overcoats. Both with the same style of top hat and our goggles on, it would be hard to tell us apart from most men on the street.

The day was gloomy and looked like it might rain at any moment, but the rickshaw had a cover and we would not get wet. Couldn't say the same of the man who pulled us. We moved up around the streets and past the Caster School of Magic, which lay close to the northern entrance.

The large white walls stood so tall they appeared to touch the sky. I hadn't been this close to the walls that surrounded the Enchanted Garden. Castle White stood within these walls. I could barely make out the tall towers standing above the Great Wall. The towers appeared to stretch into the heavens as the tops were hidden by the gloom and mist. Soon we were too close to the walls to see the castle towers within its confines.

The rickshaw dropped us off near the gates. There stood enormous white doors, in the shape of a Roman arch. Twenty men abreast, standing forty feet tall, could pass through, if the gate were open. Inside one of the great doors, was a smaller door, only wide enough for a wagon. Two soldiers stood guard in front of it. One was a female and another male. They were intimidating in their shiny black armor with symbols of the crested moon on each shoulder.

We approached the gate, the women spoke harshly, "Stop, name yourself and your business in the Garden."

Marvin cleared is throat, "Dr. Webb, and Dr. Weaver, we are here to see Lady Lily Green, of the house Dare."

The man looked at us with a bored, unconcerned look, while the female looked at like us like we had just told her a lie. After a few tense seconds, she finally answered, "You're expected."

We passed through the gate and into the Enchanted Garden. I was about to ask Marvin if the guards were always so harsh, but the question never left my lips as my mind and eyes took in the sight before me. Marvin at times seemed able to read my mind, "My boy, you'll get used to the guards, but you'll never get used to the Gardens."

I could barely answer him with a, "You don't say."

He laughed, "Our appointment isn't until this afternoon. I thought you might like some time in the Garden. Plus, I have some general information I need to share with you about our client. I dare not speak of it outside of these walls."

That caught my attention, "Why?"

"There are always forces looking for information. You never know who might be eavesdropping, and by what means. There are places to go, to whisper secrets. But all that is for later today. For now, you should enjoy the sights, let's walk."

"Good idea," Was all I could say as I matched pace next to Marvin.

I had never seen so much green. Even the trees were green, I couldn't make out one blue tree or plant anywhere. The buildings were covered in plants from head to toe. Marvin pointed out that I would never need my goggles here, the magic filtered the air. I took them off, and took a deep breath, the air smelled clean and did not burn my lungs. Everything felt so alive here. Cables ran across the sky, from wall to wall, far above the buildings. Carts with people glided across the air, on their way to some place unknown to me. The buildings were designed so differently, great detail in each stone. Shops and carts dotted the landscape which appeared on many different levels. In the distance I could make out beautiful parks, and magic was everywhere. A man tossed his trash on the ground, only to have it scooped up by a trash can.

I wondered out loud, "Where are all the smoke stacks for the steam engines?"

Marvin answered me, "Hardly any steam is used within the Gardens. Everything here runs off magic, much cleaner… of course that magic comes at a price. Only the rich and powerful live here."

I corrected him, "Well, let's not forget the soldiers and workers."

Marvin chuckled, "We would be the only ones remembering them." I thought about that, it was cold, but perhaps he was right. Did these people ever take notice of their subordinates? He added, "Few of the soldiers or workers here, are human."

At first I thought he meant magic, but something in his tone told me something else. Something more, ominous. I figured that was a story for another time, I was too caught up in the enchantment of the Enchanted Gardens. Morgan would be in love, enchantments everywhere. And there standing on the far wall, Castle White. A dozen beautiful round white towers sprouted out of the middle, each one taller than the next. A part of the castle was built right into the wall, or perhaps the wall was built off the castle. Castle White is the oldest human settlement since the fall of Man. It was some ways off, it was a huge structure. That's where the Court of Dolls, and the law of the land was administered from. The largest ruling party of Eden lived there. Managing everything from the law, commerce, and the army.

Marvin pointed out a large building near to us. Tall and spooky looking, it was completely covered in plant life. There stood a giant crescent moon above the front entrances. I knew what this was, the Crescent House. This was the place that administered, airships, the prison, wall construction, and secret police. Local law was governed by local authorities, but if the leaders of Eden wanted to get involved you could be visited by men with crescent moon on their jackets. My father hated them, calling them the dark force within a great military. I never knew why he said this.

The multi level city buzzed with activity. A crowd gathered on the street, near the Crescent house. The buildings were stacked next to each other sharing their outer walls and covered in green vines. Trees lined the street, some so big it made it hard to see around them. The more you walked, the more of this great city would pop out from behind the greenery. I noticed the building we headed towards had a large arched opening, with people moving in and out. Chairs and tables lined this part of the street, people of all kinds sat, eating and drinking, or just talking amongst each other. There was only a small sidewalk, the rest of the Gardens were covered with dirt and leaves. It was like walking through the forest with buildings in it.

We entered into the archway and inside was a giant café, that's when I noticed it. "This is just like the café near the school, the Bitten Apple. I love that place. Of course the one at the school is not half the size… Or half as green."

Marvin informed me, "The man who owned that, owns this one too. He calls this the Bitten Apple as well. I'm not sure how many he owns."

Marvin asked a host to please seat us where we might speak in private. The host led us over to a booth. It had curtains and sat against a wall, the benches had sheltered backs. I figured it was enchanted, or else I could not see how this could be a private conversation. We both ordered sandwiches and coffee.

Our order arrived shortly, the host inquired if we needed anything else. The server closed the curtains. Marvin said, "Enchanted booth, we can say anything, and no one will hear us in here my boy." He took up his sandwich and began to eat.

I thought that might be the case. Out of the hundred of questions that was filling my mind about the Garden, I asked, the one that bothered me the most. "Why no blue trees?" Everything had been so green, not a single color of green, but every shade of green I could have ever imagined.

After swallowing, he answered, "Funny question. You must be the first person to ask me that." I must have made a face, "I didn't mean it like that, my boy. It is a good question, a great question… just funny it was the first you asked. Few notice that detail with all the wonders of the Garden. The answer is easy enough. The blue, is a kind of magic, or science they use on the trees so that they might grow outside of the Garden. Apparently, many types of trees just die because of the pollution outside of this place."

I was surprised, "Is there no pollution inside the Garden? How is that possible? I thought modern man destroyed the world. It's just hard to imagine that much magic in one place."

Marvin finished washing back another bite before answering, "Very little, and the reason why, is that it is protected by magic. The further away from the castle, the less protection. This is why life is so hard in the outer circle. Lucky for us, we've never had to go there."

If he had only known, "Yes, lucky."

Marvin's face was serious, "We have some important business to cover. I've picked you for this job, and not for the fact you're my son-in-law. You have proven what kind of man, and doctor you are. You have loved my daughter, and for a while I didn't believe it. I had you followed, I was sure you would be caught in a brothel. You never went, nor did you cheat on my daughter." He laughed, obviously remembering something funny, "And that time I busted in on you at your uncle's office. I was sure that you devised the visit to see another woman. No, you've proven to be my son, more than my actual son." He quickly added, "In a way."

It was an act to make sure my face held the right amount of admiration. I had learned to like Marvin as a person, but I didn't think him my equal. Over the years I pretended to look up to him, and he liked that. I didn't love his daughter, and his son was an idiot. He was an only child, and was working for the practice before I arrived. It didn't take long before I out shined his son Devon, in every way. That wasn't a big feat, for his son was incompetent. All I could say was, "Thank you, you honor me."

Marvin went on, "It's no honor, you deserve it. This is a job for someone I trust, someone who I know comes from a good family. With no questionable background. I need that, for whoever takes this job will inherit secrets, secrets that not only could get him killed, but me as well. Now let's eat, and after we're done, if you still want to know more, I'll tell you. I just need you to know what I'm getting you into my boy."

I nodded, "Ok." Even as my teeth barely took their first bite, I already knew my answer. I must know, for secrets influence others. I waited until we were both done eating. I didn't want to act as if I made the decision to quickly and have him think me too rash. I lay my half empty glass before me, "I want to know more."

He gave me a devilish grin, "I figured as much." He stifled a yawn, "Men of my age do not have the energy that we used to. Well, let's see, where to begin? Everyone knows that Governor Cooper is no more than a figurehead. Yes the people voted for him, and he does wield power, but he is not in charge. The man in charge lives in Castle White, and before you say it, most people realize that. What they don't know is his name."

In astonishment, I asked, "And you do?"

He smiled with pride, "I do, Jeffery Dare. There is more to it than just a name. First, let me be clear, I've never met the man and doubt I ever will. Still, knowing about him is one thing, but knowing about his family… Is another. One of his granddaughters, Cindy, is very sick and Dr. Cambridge was treating her. She is the patient you will take on, so you see, just how important this will be for your career. Let us also not forget how important it could be to your very life."

I nodded, "I understand."

Understand is what I said, but deep down I was sorry I agreed to this. If they were to find out about my true background, both Morgan and I would be in great danger. Yet, I could think of nothing to say to stop the chain of events, without creating the very questions I feared. No, I must go forward, my lies devouring me whole.

Marvin gave me a minute, then his face went blank, "There is more. Believe me, the rest is hard to… Well, to believe." He paused, but I said nothing before he went on. "Have you ever heard of vampires?"

I almost chuckled, "Yes, I hear that is what most of the secret police are. Blood sucking creatures who swoop in at night and prey upon the weak. I figured they were nothing more than scary stories."

"They're real my dear boy." He chuckled darkly.

I took a small drink, "Really not that hard to believe. Look at the monsters that live outside the gate. Look at the magic in this city, and the wizards."

Marvin nodded, "Good, it's better that you believe without me having to go on and on."

I inquired, "What I have heard about vampires, would make me believe that medical care was one thing they could do without. So I'm guessing I don't need to deal with them."

"Not exactly," he answered. "But, there is more than one kind. The first is like the boogie man we have come to hear about. Men and women, changed, normally early in life. Once turned they are stronger and faster than any human, and only become stronger as the years go by. Early on, they made deals with our forefathers, to protect them at night in exchange for blood. I hear their blood is flammable, either by fire or sunlight. Their blood defines everything about them, it holds their memories, and repairs their body to the precise copy of what they were when they died."

I had no idea, "That explains a lot. The blood is what they are, it just uses the flesh to get what it needs. It needs others life force? Perhaps that is their true need of blood."

Marvin chuckled darkly, "That is correct. Don't ask me what all their strengths and weakness are, because I don't know. In fact, what I've come to understand, that it's best not to know."

"I bet. What is the second kind?"

Marvin finished his drink, "The second kind we call, The Noble Dead, or some call them the Fallen. Not created, but born. They live a human life at first, and from a medical standpoint they are nothing special. When they die, they rise again, only more powerful. What I understand is a new born fallen, has the power that can match a hundred year old vampire. And with time they become even more powerful."

I took a guess, "Let me guess, Jeffery is a Noble Dead."

Marvin smiled, "You catch on fast my boy, but there is more to it than that, he is the father of their house. He was the one who established Castle White. He has reigned for a long time, back before the fall of Man."

I whistled, "That old."

"Yes, he's that old," Marvin paused. "I believe you should understand this. The Noble Dead are trying to maintain control, they are under pressure from many different factions. The Dare family through the years has shrunk away to almost nothing. See, first you must live a human life long enough to have children, then once you've done that, you may die. If you are lucky, in seven days… to seven years, you will rise again. Some do not. They have lost family members to wars, or they haven't changed, and even more lately, to sickness."

I understood. "Cindy is a noble dead, and she is sick. If she doesn't live she won't be able to have children to keep the line alive."

Marvin corrected me, "Not exactly. Yes, they need her to bear young, but more importantly, they need her to die and rise again. They never rise, if they die before puberty or are too ill. Our patient is only fifteen, she's old enough, but too sick. What I've come to understand, is that the change is more successful at the ages closer to twenty, but I doubt Cindy will live that long."

I realized this was not the opportunity I had hoped for. There was a high chance of failure. I smiled, hiding my concerns, "I hope I can change all that."

Marvin nodded. With doubt he added, "We will see."

Chapter 7 Cupid

Morgan Jones

I wish I could say that I was not jealous of my brother's adventure to the Enchanted Gardens, but I was. He told me all about it just a few days ago and I couldn't get it off my mind. I want to go.

I looked into the mirror, my mechanical arm and legs were nothing short of a miracle, but still, it was hard to look upon my scarred body. Not to mention my left hand was nothing but a machine. My right arm was full of scars, with mechanical pieces poking out. I was stronger than any man, but I looked like a freak.

When I ran as Sung I wore long sleeves and gloves. No one could see my hands nor my arms, my face was the only part of me not scarred. I could hardly stand to look at my back. Parts of my metal spine still were exposed, surrounded by red flesh and scar tissue.

I dressed in a beautiful green dress, with a black corset. The dress was open in the front, and I wore dark stockings and tall boots that laced all the way up to my knees. My arms were visible from the elbow down, but thanks to some magic and rubber, they looked real and free of scars. They even felt real.

I looked into the mirror, then twirled around. There in front of me was a pretty girl, with a smile. Today was a day of adventure, who knows where I might end up, perhaps in the Enchanted Garden itself.

It hadn't taken me long to find myself in the heart of Time Square. A large clock was set in the middle of a small park and around it were five roads intersecting and circling around the park. On one side of the road was a bridge over the Blue River. The river cuts through Eden, the people just strolled hand in hand down the side of its banks.

There were lots of bars, restaurants, and dance clubs located all around. The area is lit up by millions of lights and full of art, statues and small gardens. This is where the city came to party, and tonight was going to be my first time joining them.

It didn't take me long to find a young man who was willing to dance with me. He didn't catch my fancy, so during a song I slipped away. I moved from one place to the next. Taking in the people around me, I listened to the laughter, hoping to find a friend. Of course I found trouble first. He grabbed me by the arm and pulled me towards him. The man was big and drunk, "Hey sweetheart, you alone?"

With little effort I wrenched my arm free, when he went to grab me, I smacked away his arm with more force than necessary. He yelled out in pain and stepped back in surprise. In anger, the man lunged at me, I sidestepped and with the power of my left arm I shoved the drunk down. He crashed against the ground, sliding on his face. He almost knocked a few pedestrians down. I used this moment and quickly moved through the crowd and away from the man.

What a way to ruin a good evening. I slipped out of the crowd and towards the banks of the river. Loneliness threatened to wash me away faster than the river. I hadn't heard the man yelling. Or perhaps, I hadn't realized he was yelling at me, "Miss, Miss. Are you ok?"

A young man came up behind me, a group of friends followed him. Three couples, plus the young man now surrounded me, the woman's eyes full of concern. They were all young, my age. One of the girls, "We saw that guy grab you, he was huge. Are you ok?"

I realized that this group had witnessed the exchange I had with the man and were coming to my rescue. One of the others asked, "Are you alone?"

Before I could answer one of the girls said, "It takes some kind of something for a lady to brave these streets without an escort." She added with a look of awe, "Then again, you seem to know how to handle yourself."

The young man who seemed to be without a date declared, "Well, she's not alone now. My name is Sam, short for Samuel. You are?"

Without even thinking, "Sung, Sung Weaver."

"Well Sung, these are my friends…" He named off each one and I forgot their names as quickly as he told them, but I couldn't take my eyes off him. He was a good looking man, with dark brown hair that hung loosely around his face. His dark brown eyes were bright and focused, but what really caught my attention was his high energy level. His body couldn't stand still, he was alive with passion that came through his voice and body. I liked him at once.

I realized he was awaiting a response, he smiled, "I know, I'm overwhelming you. Sorry, I don't mean to be overbearing…"

I interrupt him, "No, it's fine. You were asking if I would like to hang with you? I would."

His face lit up, "Great, let's go. Wait, where do you want to go?" His friends laughed.

The laughter was infectious, "Anywhere we can dance."

He smiled slyly. "We, we could dance right here. Still, I think I know a place." He then announces to the group, "Let's all go to JD's, what do you say?"

They all hooped and hollered in agreement.

The night was amazing, and I hated to say goodnight to Sam, but my spells would not last forever. Nor would the magic that powered my robotics. I went home with a smile on my face. Half way home I noticed Mittens, that cat followed me everywhere.

I may have not gone to the Enchanted Gardens, but it was one of the happiest nights of my life. I hurried home, thinking about Cinderella, when her spell ended, so did her night. I only hope that my happy ending is right around the corner… perhaps Sam was my Prince Charming.

Chapter 8 Cindy Dare

Tom Weaver

We arrived at Castle White. There we entered another set of huge doors, with more guards. We were led into a garden, once inside I found myself surrounded by every color imaginable. Everything was wet, and the air was a thick warm mist. The flowers stood open, inviting, with their smells and brightly colored petals. We passed through and emerged to find a great door, standing open with two silent guards on either side. We walked through without a word, the place was huge. The ceiling reached the sky, giant white pillars stood far apart. There was so much to take in, it made my head spin.

I could barely take in the detail of the beautiful marble floor, with swirling patterns of black and white. Tapestries hung from the walls, with pictures of battles, and places I have never seen before, woven in great detail. The room was so large, I would have needed hours to take in half the details this great room had to offer. Statues, white, beautifully carved, stood everywhere and of every size. Some were maidens, others where animals, or magical creatures. A large statue stood at the far side of the room, of a knight upon a horse. Of course, there were no horses now, but I have read books and seen pictures of the animals. Yet another thing lost to the past.

We passed through quickly, and down a large corridor. Marvin turned and led me into another great room, and I knew at once that we had entered the chapel. Standing near the front of the church, right below the pulpit, a man with white robes awaited us.

The inside of the church was like the rest of the place, full of decorations, paintings, carved wood, and colorful glass that allowed the light of the sky in. I was unsure of this place, my father had never believed in the Seven Gods. The most striking thing about the church was the seven statues standing behind the pulpit. Forty feet tall, and made of white marble, their faces staring down at us, with judging eyes. The seven Gods, or as some called them, the seven Two Faced Gods.

Stopping in front of the holy man, Marvin took the man's hand and lifted it to his face, then kissed the back of his hand. I have never seen this before, but I realized with Marvin's sideways glance that he expects the same of me. I did the same and Marvin spoke, "Father Thomas, so good to see you. Have you been well?"

The man eyed me, "As well as an old man can be nowadays. I find my job to be… tiresome, with all the demands of the flock. I see you have brought your doctor. He's awfully young."

Marvin answered quickly, "Yes, but he is a wonder with his craft."

Raising one eyebrow the holy man questioned, "Truly? I do hope so. Much rides on the girls' health."

Before Marvin could respond, I spoke up, "I could tell you what a great doctor I am, but I rather show you."

"Bold," the holy man said with a half smile. "We will see, let's waste no time. Dr. Webb, I'm sure you know the way, and may the Seven Gods smile upon you."

Marvin gave a small head bow to the man, "Thank you for the blessing."

I quickly added, "The pleasure has been mine."

Marvin led me away quickly. Once in the hall, Marvin had explained that it was best not to speak to the man if it could be avoided. He hadn't needed to tell me that, I knew the minute I met him. The castle was so huge, and the more we traveled within it, the more I realized just how big this place must be. Heading up a winding staircase, wide enough for four men abreast, we worked our way upward. I stopped to look out one of the few windows that lined the wall. I could see we were in a tower, overlooking some of the lower towers. Each tower was huge, they didn't appear half as big from below. The top of the towers was topped with an egg shaped dome made of glass. From the bottom, the glass structures were hard to make out. Each was filled with trees, flowers, and all kinds of plants. I knew that hundreds of years ago, man used these greenhouses to plant food. Now all the farming was done outside of

Eden, in the outer circle. Now the greenhouses were nothing more than giant gardens for royalty.

Marvin walked up next to me and said, "Beautiful, but wait until you see the inside of one of these great gardens."

"What do they call them?" I wondered out loud.

"They each have a name, but most of us just refer to them as the hanging gardens. I should learn what their names are. Interesting fact, each one represents a different place on earth. The one we travel to, is called the Savannah, Cindy's home is right below. Speaking of Cindy, we should try not to be late."

"Yes," I replied with a nod. We began to climb the steps again, and as my legs burned, I couldn't help but think; Is there no other way up?

After what felt like a lifetime, we reached a great landing. The floor was a white marble with black swirl patterns. Richly decorated, the round room had many wooden doors, located around the walls. We were surrounded by doors, it felt like a maze. Each with different carvings and symbols. It felt like it could take a lifetime to explore this castle. Then again, immortals lived here, perhaps the place felt smaller from their perspective.

A door opened from across the room, and a woman swept in. She wore an emerald green dress, the fabric looked like it shined as she crossed the floor. Her hair hung loose, long, and so black it appeared to have strands of violet. Her face was an olive color, with soft rounded features, she was truly breathtaking. As she closed the distance I could see she had the greenest eyes, the eyes seemed to swallow me in. Unblinking, I was trapped within her gaze. She broke the spell with her voice, "Welcome."

"It is truly wonderful to see you again Lily," Marvin answered. "This is Dr. Weaver."

I smiled, "Thank you, it is a pleasure to be welcomed by such a lovely lady."

She replied with a tone that bordered on nasty. "Your words are kind. Everyone here calls me Green-e, because of my eyes." Her tone changed as she turned to speak with Marvin, she sounded very pleased he was here. "Dr. Webb, it's been too long."

Marvin winked at me, "I like Lily, what can I say."

She gave him a little smile before her face became serious again, "I don't mean to be short, but let me get to the point."

"Of course," I agreed eagerly.

Her eyes narrowed, "Cindy is not well. Dr. Cambridge did her no favors by leaving when he did. I am Cindy's Lady in Waiting, and I have been waiting long enough for your office to send a replacement. I truly hope that this doctor…"

I filled in my name for her, "Weaver."

Her eyes were challenging, "Yes, Weaver, let's see what you can do. Shall we?"

Marvin started to say, "Dr. Weaver is young, but you will find him…"

I finished his sentence, "More than capable. Take me to the patient, and let's see if I cannot help her more than Dr. Cambridge?"

Marvin shot me a dirty look, and Green-e huffed, then turned, "Follow me then."

I knew that Marvin would not like it that I was coming off as if I might be better than Dr. Cambridge. After all, he was one of the best in his practice. Still, I knew this was my chance to shine and I had a power that none of them did. I just hoped by using this power it was not my undoing.

We followed her back through the door through which she came. I found myself climbing more stairs. Luckily we hadn't climbed for long, my legs were about to give out on me. Arriving at the top I once again found my eyes, overwhelmed by the complexity of the decoration. We stood in a giant room, filled with beautiful furniture. Dark wood with brightly painted borders filled the room. Gold and copper ran along the walls, statues of all shapes and sizes lined the upper part of the walls. The statues were painted, and lifelike. There were dolls, and dollhouses throughout the room. Dresses hung across one side of the room, each a work of art in its own right. A gigantic four poster bed dominated the room, the posts almost hitting the ceiling. Once my eyes found the ceiling, it was hard to look away, it was painted like the sky with white clouds, on one side of the room it appeared to be a storm was coming. The more I looked, the more the clouds appeared to be moving. I realized with a start, they were. The ceiling must have been enchanted.

The far side of the room was a giant glass wall, in the center of the wall a large glass door that led out to the balcony. The doors were shut, but the light shined through illuminating the entire room. On the edge of the bed sat a girl in a plain pink gown. I froze a few feet in front of her, taking in the Lady Cindy. She looked at me with a shy, nervous face, but that wasn't what took me off guard. I had heard about people with golden hair, my father had once told me that it was once called, blonde. Yet I have never seen it until now, long yellow hair flowed from the girl's head, her skin was white as the marble statues. Her blue eyes were like the sky. I realized that I had been staring too long without saying anything. I quickly bowed my head, "I'm Dr. Weaver. It is truly a pleasure to meet you, and to serve you."

She smiled shyly, "Nice to meet you as well. It is good to see you again Dr. Webb."

Webb stepped forward, took one of the girls' hands, then kissed the back of it. He simply replied, "My lady, the pleasure is all mine."

Out of the corner of my eye I could see Green-e looking on impatiently. She barked, "I have a full list of the medications that Dr. Cambridge has prescribed. I do feel that they are ineffective, Cindy is sick, and hardly eats."

The girl stiffened, "I do eat." Her voice softened, "It's not that bad."

Green-e quickly disagreed, "It is bad. She is sick all the time, and in pain."

I decided to control the situation, "Let me see the list?" I asked with a smile. She handed the list over to me. I looked it up and down, "Let's see here." On the list were herbs and medicine for bowel issues. I looked up, "I will need some privacy with this patient."

Marvin and Green-e both started in with their disagreements. Marvin wanted to make sure that I didn't screw this up, and Green-e did not trust me. She did not use these words, but I could read into the situation. I declared my need to work with my new patient. They stood still, silently defying me, and right when I thought that they might never leave, Cindy spoke, "If you two might give the doctor a chance."

Her big blue eyes looked at me with nothing short of hope. Green-e and Marvin left, with only the smallest amount of dirty looks. I looked at the girl, "I need you to trust me." She nodded her head. "Lay on your back, I have great magic. I will heal you, it will take more than one time, but I know that I can."

She looked at me confused, "Dr. Cambridge said that I was beyond magic, and only medicine could help."

I spoke softly, "You are beyond *his* magic, and the medication he has given you is just masking the problem. Lay back my dear, and let me try."

The girl lay down. I found a small chair in front of her powder mirror and moved it, so that I might sit down next to her. Laying my hands upon her stomach, I chanted, using the two rings. These rings Morgan had made, would allow me to find the problem and determine what it was. I could see it in my mind, her bowels, sick and full of disease. She was dying a slow and painful death. I could heal her, but it would take many treatments to undo what the disease had done.

I changed my chant, and now used the power of the two rings that I wore on my middle fingers. I reached deep within me, I reached for that manna, and the power poured up through me. I felt it race through my body down my arms and in my hands. The rings fed upon the power like hungry gators, then they changed the power, using it to heal her body. It not only fed upon my manna, but hers as well. It was unexpected, but helpful. This girl had magic, deep within her, untapped power. It made me wonder, just for a second, then I forced my attention on my current task. I would not be able to heal her, not in one sitting. Over time, yes, overtime I could heal her completely.

Once I finished, I slumped in exhaustion. Cindy lay there breathing heavy. Her hands felt around her lower belly, where my hands had been just a moment ago. She sat up slowly and I warned her, "Careful dear. This is draining, let me get you some water."

She shook her head, "No, rest doctor. I can see this has tired you." She then turned her head towards the door that Green-e and Marvin had just left. It was a big room, so I would have expected her to yell, but instead she said in a small voice, almost a whisper, "Green-e, water please. Some for Dr. Weaver, if you would be so kind?"

A few seconds later the door swung open and Green-e swooshed into the room, her dress trailing behind her quick steps. She carried a glass of water in each hand, Marvin hurried behind her trying to keep up. She offered Cindy her glass first and she drank it up greedily. I took the glass she offered with a "Thanks," and took a long, deep drink, almost finishing the glass.

After some small talk, I gave Green-e a list of medications. Green-e asked, "What about her diet?"

Cindy protested loudly, "All I get are bland foods and vegetables. What's the use of living, if you don't get to live?"

I laughed, "I couldn't agree more. Eat what you like."

The girl jumped up and threw her arms around me. I was taken wholly by surprise, "Thank you, thank you so much. I shall have cake, pie..."

I interrupted her list with a laugh. Spying Green-e's angry face, her green eyes staring at me like daggers. I quickly started talking, "But, you didn't let me finish."

Cindy's smile dropped, she gave me an over exaggerated pouty face. I smiled, "You may have what you like, but it still needs to be a sensible diet. Green-e will know best, you may have some sweets, but within reason and only once a day."

Cindy smiled again, "I can do that." She said it with such excitement and joy, it filled the room with smiles.

Green-e accompanied Marvin and I from Cindy room to the round room with many doors. She was giving me a strange look, "I have not seen her that happy in some time. She is always in pain, and I am spellbound to know that. I can feel what she feels and know her needs. I know that she is not in pain, not since you worked your magic on her. I could feel your magic I had no idea Marvin that you had this kind of magician on your staff."

I guess that explains how she knew that Cindy needed water. This also meant the cat was out of the bag about my abilities to heal. Marvin patted me on my back, "That's my boy, a real talent."

She nodded, but her eyes were filled with doubt, "We'll see. If you can keep her well, you will be rewarded. I don't think I have to tell you what might happen if you are faking this."

I smiled, not missing the threat or the fact she couldn't believe what I had done. I might have gone too far, but I could not afford to hold back, not with this girl. "Don't you worry, I'm full of surprises. I look forward to my next visit. I will see you in a week."

She nodded, Marvin bid her good evening and we headed back down the long staircase. Marvin said nothing to me until we were boarding a rickshaw and being pulled away from Castle White. "What did you do?" His tone was blank, his voice was cold.

I answered him indifferently, "I healed the girl, or started the process of it. What did you want me to do in there?"

He looked at me, hard, then he said in an even voice, "You better be. This better not be a trick. The power you showed today... I had no idea you could do that."

I had over done it. I tried to play it off, "I heal lots of little people, all day long, every day. Why do you think I'm so far ahead of the other doctors? You seldom give me a big case, or the very sick. So, how would you know what I could, or could not do?"

Marvin looked thoughtful, then with a kinder tone, "You're right. You keep up the good work, I'm really losing my touch. Having such a great talent in my office, and not even realizing it."

The lie grows yet another inch. "Thank you, you're too kind."

"I'm not, truly." He paused, unsure if he would finish saying what he thought. "Perhaps it's because of my daughter."

"What do you mean?" I tried my best to look surprised, but I knew what he was about to say.

"Well, I hope you forgive an old man. You see, I love my daughter, but on the outside, she not the… Well you know. Still, she pretty enough, but you, you're what my wife would call a looker. I'm ashamed that I thought you might be a gold digger." I laughed, then he chuckled, "Ok, it wasn't much of an admission."

I realized that I missed the chance of seeing one of the hanging gardens. With everything that happened, I forgot to go to the Savannah greenhouse that was right above Cindy's tower. "We still have some time, how about you make it up to me? Show me some more of this Enchanted Garden."

Marvin grinned, "Now that my boy, I can do."

Chapter 9 Green-e

Tom Jones

"The Gardens are like nothing I've experienced." Green-e smiled at me as we walked through hanging garden. They called this garden the Rain Forest, from a place far away and long ago. Perched on the second largest tower on Castle White, the views were astonishing.

She smiled at me, "I'm glad you appreciate its beauty. Some men… Miss it, I'm afraid."

Eyeing a bench overlooking a small valley, I motioned for us to take a seat. "After you my lady."

"Why thank you," slightly lifting her pretty green dress, Green-e glided onto the bench.

I sat next to her, unable to stifle a yawn. My eyes took in what was before me. A world of green and water. The mist fell from the sky, and already it had rained on us. We both wore enchanted clothes, so the water just beaded off. My top hat protected my head, and a small umbrella did the same for the lady.

A small valley lay before us, complete with trees hanging off sharp rocky inclines. Waterfalls roared from different heights, falling down to the bottom. Many small rainbows appeared in the spray of the waterfalls, disappearing when dark clouds passed by. It was strange seeing clouds from inside the glass dome, but also amazing.

Green-e observed and whispered, "You must be tired. That was quite the healing you did today. What does that make this? The third healing."

I was coming every four days to monitor her medicine. My time here had become so important to me. I thought about it and answered, "It's May the 2nd, so yes, I believe you're right. She is becoming stronger. I truly feel that I can heal Cindy, given enough time."

Green-e was beautiful, and my eyes were suddenly trapped within her green gaze. A tense moment passed, her cheeks flushed. A bird swooped by, allowing Green-e to break the stare. I could tell she wanted to look back, but dared not, instead she preoccupied herself with bird watching. "I worry about you, Tom. You must not push too hard, you can hurt yourself. Don't rush this. I know you can do it."

I smiled at her concern, "I can feel her healing, and I will accomplish it as soon as possible."

Her eyes found me again, but this time they were full of disapproval, "That's what I worry about. I have never seen, nor heard of a man with your ability. Yet, even you must know not to push your power too far. You can damage yourself. If you do that, *who* would heal Cindy?"

I conceded, "You do have a point. I do not mean to worry you, nor is my goal to cause myself harm."

She countered, "But you push yourself to the very edge."

I respond, "I do, but I feel it necessary."

Her eyes narrowed, "And why is that? To hurry your fame and fortune?"

I looked away, hurt. I replied, "You wound me. Is that what you think of me, a gold digger of sorts? Use a dying girl to further my own career?"

She snapped back, "Not completely. There are just things about you, I cannot interpret. I see you with Cindy, and I can see your heart for her. I know you wish her true health to return. Still, something about you…"

I softened my tone, "What can I do? To convince the Lady Green-e to believe that I am not a villain. What words could I say to make you feel my heart's truth?"

She sat quietly for a moment, she gazed at me with wonder. I was dying to know what she thought. After a moment she took a breath, "I feel that my question, may damage our relationship. Some things are best, unasked."

I tossed my hands up, "You cannot do this. Do not hang this over my head, let me know what vexes you. I promise to answer honestly. I will listen with an open mind."

She grinned, "Ok, fine. Let's see that heart of yours, and what lies in it. I have but one question for *you*."

I turned my shoulders towards her and took her eyes into mine. "Ask your question."

She stared at me, taking me in. "Do you love your wife?"

My mind reeled in panic. I answered defensively, "Why would you ask this?"

She shot back, "That is not an answer, that is a *question*."

I fought my emotional outburst. Then I did what I do best; I lied, "Of course I do."

She narrowed her eyes in disbelief, "Do what?"

I shook my head and stood, "This is inappropriate. Good day." I started to walk off, stopped, turned around and looked at her. Her face was oddly sad, I had proven her correct. She could see right through me. "Sorry my lady, if I have been rude. I'm afraid my exhaustion has gotten the better of me. Let us talk of this another time."

I gestured a tip of the hat and turned to leave. I was not sure, but I thought I heard her say, "I understand." I was too ashamed to find out.

It was the very next night. I was sitting at the dinner table, surrounded by guests who I could not care less about. My wife was busy talking about nothing, in great detail. I sat quietly, pretending to listen, but really thinking about Green-e. I had woken up in a sweat, a nightmare, and the only part I remembered was Green-e asking, do you love her? Of course I don't! I despise her. No one can know that, yet Green-e knows that. I couldn't do it, lie to her face. I had convinced everyone that I loved my wife. I couldn't put on the show for Green-e, so now she knows the truth. Ever since my first success with Cindy, things had changed at blinding speed. Almost every day I was in the Garden. Either at the castle, or a very rich resident's home. My abilities were well sought after by the rich and powerful.

Unofficially Green-e had become my contact and guide. I think partly to make sure I kept Cindy's confidence. Every day we met up and talked. She was not only breathtaking, but smart. Time flew by when I was with her, and there were countless conversations that I could not wait to have with her. Her background was like mine. Born poor, she had been a daughter of a Baker. Some kind of trouble had led her to serve in the Dare house. Green-e wouldn't share what trouble, but she had lived in the outer circle, not in Eden. Her beauty and grace, plus a chance meeting with a high lord had found her in the service of the castle. Soon she was a lady, for the Princess Cindy.

I don't know when it happened, I couldn't put my mind at the exact moment, but I had fallen in love with her. That was what really bothered me... Yes, that is what it was, the way she had looked at me when I was unable to answer her question. A gold digger, a fake, a liar, the true me. My life was nothing but a lie. She had thought of me, as a man born into privilege. What would she think if she knew I was like her, starting from nothing, yet, instead of earning my life, I stole it.

Chapter 10 Late Night

Morgan Jones

The room spun as he twirled me around in his arms. The music filled every inch of my body, the thrum of sound made my body move. It made me twist around, my hips led, and my legs followed. Sam pulled me back to him, I spun around landing in his arms. The adjustments I had done to my hands kept me from crushing his as our fingers laced together. My eyes burned as salty sweat dripped from my head to my eyes, but it mattered not, I was absorbed in sound and movement.

The band stood above us, playing on instruments that powered off steam, every note filled the room with a blast of hot white steam. Every note, filled my head and made my passions come to life. I loved the sensation of foot pain as my feet pounded on the floor. I knew it was not real, for my legs were driven by magic, but my spine made it all possible. Through my spine I could feel and control my limbs. Robot and human, I was a cyborg. Sam worked us to the edge of the dance floor, "Come on baby, I can't hardly stand."

I smiled and let him lead me to a table, I bounced behind him holding one of his hands. "Too much for you?"

Sam turned back and yelled, "No doubt."

We took a seat and joined some friends. We both picked up our half empty drinks, and finished them. Sam waved at the server for more. I hardly knew the other young adults sitting at the table. I called them my friends, hugged them when we came together, but in truth, they were Sam's friends. I had been dating Sam for some time now, and we were together every weekend, sometimes more. I was his girlfriend, so by default I was accepted in the group. I led a life of secrets, and at first, this did not bother Sam. His friends, especially Jill, had more questions than I was willing to answer. At first he protected me from her constant probing.

Sam had become tired of protecting me, only to have me blow him off. I told him that I could change, be less secretive. Tonight was going to be another night of me blowing him off. I think he could see it, he eyed me, "You still going?"

It had been in the plans for a week. Sam and his friends wanted to go see the animals and have a picnic at the park. Even the weather looked to be cooperating. "I can't see why not?" I was a terrible liar, and his face darkened with my answer.

He was smart enough to wait until later that night, we had separated from his friends. We walked hand in hand. It was a dark night, but the roads were well lit with tall street lanterns. The wind blew gently, making flames dance in the lanterns giving the shadows a life. It was slightly eerie as I listened to the wind whistle between the buildings and wondering what might lie within the darkness. Sam read my mind, he pulled me closer, squeezing me.

"Why aren't you coming tomorrow?" He asked suddenly.

Shucks, I was really hoping he wasn't going to bring it up tonight. "Who said I wasn't going?" He huffed. I added quickly, "My plan is to make it. Perhaps I'll just be late."

He was trying not to sound mad, "I thought you were going to let me know this morning. Now you *may* make it later… Or not at all. When were you going to tell me?"

"You know I can't tell you," We have been over this before. My life has secrets, and if he wanted to be with me he needed to not worry about it.

He was now mad and pulled away, it hurt, "I wasn't asking why, of course I *should* ask why, but that's against the rules. I asked, when you were going to tell me, tonight, tomorrow morning, the next day? Of course I could also ask, when did you know you might not make it? Or is that a secret too?"

We took a few more steps in silence. I could hear the defeat in my voice, "I planned on telling you tonight. I was just waiting because I knew that it would upset you and I wanted to have a nice time with you."

"How selfish of you," he spit the words out. After a tense moment of silence; his voice softened, "I'm sorry, I didn't mean it. I know you have your other life. I might not be in… I'll take what I can get." He sounded defeated, I couldn't blame him.

My heart sank, "For how much longer?"

He shrugged, then I pulled him back to me. We didn't say anything as we arrived at our meeting spot under a great blue oak. A lovely wooden bench rested at the foot of the tree, and the tree was shoved between two small buildings. It easily towered over both the buildings. We sat on the bench, he held me and warmed me. I couldn't help but think, how much longer could I get away with this? He didn't even know where I lived, he thought my name was Sung. My heart hurts at the thought of losing this boy, but I feared letting him in. What would he think if he knew I was half machine?

Sam Carver was not a rich boy, but he came from a middle class family. They were hard working, and ran a wood shop. They did everything you could imagine. Sam was a true talent, I could feel his strong hands in my mind. He had kept inviting me to his house to meet his family, but I haven't even given him that much. I could not keep this valley between us forever. I made up my mind, "Sam?"

He answered with all the anger washed free from his voice, "Yes my sweet?"

"One month, perhaps a little longer. Give me that time to get my affairs in order. I will come to you, I will tell you everything. Then we'll… We'll see, perhaps." Perhaps he would run away screaming.

He squeezed me harder and even though I could not see his excitement, I could feel it. He kissed the top of my head, "That would be truly wonderful. I don't know your secret, but I'm sure I can accept it. It will be ok, you will see."

Panic shot through me as I wondered if I made the right decision. I didn't want to burst his bubble with my doubt. Lifting my head, I took his face in hand and looked into his eyes, "We'll see." Before he could reply, I kissed him.

That night I used the back way into Weaver estate. I could have gone straight to my lab in the basement, but instead I thought it might be a good idea to check on the old man. There he lay, in a puddle of his own puke. The smell filled my nostrils and I gagged. I shook my head in disgust.

It was easy to be mad at him as I cleaned up the mess and tore off the soiled clothes from the old doctor. I easily carried the man to his bed, laying him gently with just his underpants on. I would have to wash the rest. I looked down at him, listening to his heavy breathing, every other breath sounded as if he fought to breathe.

It was hard to stay mad at him, the man who had taken care of me, housed me, and helped my brother in so many operations to make me whole again. For a time he was happier. I made his business a success, and I was the daughter he never had. After a while he thought of Tom as his real nephew, even though he figured out the truth. Tom never knew, but it didn't matter because the old man kept our secrets. Still, the time of his happiness was too short. Not long after I could walk, Dr. Weaver was sued. He was suffering from a common problem, old age. He had made a lot of mistakes, also drinking heavily again. So here we were, broke, drunk and back to the same place I found the old man in the first place.

There was only one way to pay the monthly bills now that the clinic was closed, I sold my enchanted items to Amazon. Tonight I had a big order, fifty gold pieces for a clock that could tell when someone was telling a lie. Imagine how handy that could be in an office. It was a custom order and I was to meet up with Amazon tonight. With that much money I would be set for some time, and perhaps I could figure out another way to survive.

Deciding not to dwell on the problem. I went downstairs to get ready. Tonight I would not be Morgan the girl, but rather Samsung, the young boy. Taking off my dress I stared into the mirror. There stood a beautiful girl, perfect in most every detail. I flipped a switch on my arm and the illusion magic turned off, and now the mirror showed the true me. I looked more machine than girl, the metal for my legs started at my hips, cutting through the flesh down towards my knees. A few inches above my knees there was no flesh to be found, just metal. My left arm started in my shoulder, and even my right arm was full of exposed metal as I reinforced my right arm with a machine. My back was the worst, and at least I couldn't see it easily. A robotic spine ran exposed the entire length of my back, with wires running from the spine diving below the flesh. My whole body except my face was covered with scars. How could Sam love me? How could he accept me? How could he even look at me?

I turned from the mirror and took a seat, I plugged a hose into my side. The steam from the home's boiler would run a generator and charge the magic that ran my body. The generator itself was located in my side. I had just finished it, I would need it soon. I still planned on leaving the city at some point to find Darrell. I could go all day without a charge… Well, I could go all day if I didn't use the illusion magic. With that I only had six hours, then not only would Sam see me for what I was, but he would have to carry me home as well. I did a full body shutter at the thought.

As the steam whistled out an exhaust port on my spine, I slid my wand out to work some magic. The wand slid out of my right hand, hidden inside my flesh between the radius and ulna in my forearm. This way I would never lose it. It was made of White Oak, with a real silver tip, it had cost me a fortune to have it made. It even took longer to enchant it. It was so much more capable than my first attempt of making a wand.

Not long after my charge, I dressed. I stood in the mirror and looked at the young boy, the boy looked back at me. I wore pants, with tall boots laced up over my pants and ending right below my knees. My shirt and light jacket were too big and stained with a black soot. I slipped a leather aviator hat on my head, wrapping my goggles over my head in the ready to pull down. The hat was all the rage with young boys on the street. A new type of plane had been invented. Not a glider, but a plane that could take off and fly by the power of steam. This invention had captured their imagination. Every once in a while I would see a steam plane fly across the sky, leaving a white exhaust cloud behind it.

I would be meeting up with Amazon and Jeep. I hadn't known Jeep for long, but he was Amazon's friend, or perhaps his thug. No matter, I like him well enough. My cat Mittens rubbed against my leg, purring all the while. Tossing the backpack on with the clock, I was ready to go. The clock was much heavier than I had thought. Not a problem for my legs or back, but the shoulders reminded me that some parts of me were still human enough.

I moved swiftly and quietly out the back door and down an alley. Mittens followed me, she normally did. This was my last night, after this I would be free of this life for a while. Hopefully I will come up with a better plan on how to survive and how to be with Sam.

I moved down alleyways and wound my way through the city. Passing through a lively marketplace, I moved through the crowd like a breeze. Swiped an apple off a vendor table right before dodging down another alley. Jumping a gate with an apple in my mouth, took a bite and slipped out onto a dark street. Without a sound, the cat followed behind me. I glanced back to make sure no one was following. I never worried about Mittens keeping up, she might be big, but she moved like the wind. I walked into a small park, it was pitch black as I moved through the dark shadows. The black spots were trees, it was too dark to see without light, but my goggles could cut through the darkness.

On the far side of the park, stood an old playground. A light flickered from a burning barrel casting long shadows. I knew the two shapes who stood over the barrel. I came out of the trees with my cat in tow. "Hey guys."

"You're late," Amazon replied. I was still walking towards him and the shadows hid one half of his face, the other half glowed dimly from the light of the fire. Amazon was a tall boy, dark of skin with large black curls that he tried to keep imprisoned in his hat. No matter what the long curls escaped and hung randomly around his head. His partner Jeep, which I had the pleasure of meeting a few months ago, was much shorter. He shoulders appeared to be as wide as he was tall. Covered in muscles, he kept his black hair shaved, but his face bearded. Jeep grunted, "Hey Sung."

I was only a few feet away, something was wrong. Jeep, was always rude, always a nasty remark. I stopped short of them, "Damn Jeep, shower much?"

He almost sounded nervous, "Yes… it's not me." Jeep was the rudest man alive, not defensive.

Amazon chuckled, "I don't smell it." He suddenly changed the subject, "So, let's see it."

I turn and ran, Jeep yelled out, "Good luck man." It only took seconds and I was crashing through the trees. Bursting out of the woods and onto the street, I only had a few different options. Without time to think I ran into the alley. A few feet into the alley, I slid to a stop. There, standing in my way was a man with a large top hat and long coat. "Where are you going in such a hurry?"

I was breathing too hard to answer, it didn't matter, I didn't have anything to say. I was about to turn and run back out of the alley when I heard the sound of boots. Lots of men were now coming at me, they must have been stationed all around. There was no way out, and now they all were closing in on me. My only chance was to run past this man. Without a word I leapt forward, falling into a run straight at the man. He leaned forward with a smirk on his face, ready for my arrival.

At the last minute I dodged to the right, but the man was in front of me faster than I could blink. Slamming into him, I believe my speed would knock him off balance. No luck, the man was like a wall, and with one hand around my jacket and shirt he lifted me off my feet. Now that I was closer I could see the man more clearly. He was a handsome man, dark features, long black straight hair and the longest teeth I had ever seen. My heart felt as if it might jump out of my chest as I realized what kind of monster this might be.

His large brown eyes, much too big to be human, narrowed as he glared at me. "Thought you were going somewhere? Sorry boy, your coming with me."

His grip was like a clamp, there was no way I was stronger or faster than this man. I calmed my mind as he lowered me to my feet, confident that I was not going anywhere. He was awaiting the group of men that were now walking instead of running. No one was in a hurry, they could see the monster had caught me, and how could a boy get away?

I grabbed the vampire's arm with my left arm, of course he took no notice of this. I whispered a word and an electrical blast burst from my arm. The vampire let go and fell to his knees shaking uncontrollably. I had hoped that vampires still used their human muscle, this would not kill him, but it would buy me a few seconds to get away. I used my strong arm to lift the surprised vampire off the ground and toss him into the alley wall. Without a backward glance, I ran.

I could hear the screams, "He's getting away." The yell was followed by pursuing footsteps. I also knew that it would only take the vampire seconds to recover and he would be with me before I knew it. Reaching into my coat I pulled out a marble, an enchanted marble. "Shadow," I yellowed tossing the marble behind me. The world fell into utter darkness, as if light itself could not see through the inky gloom.

I reached up and touched my goggles, and once again I could see perfectly. Stopping I looked back, the men had stopped running and instead were searching blindly down the alley with their hands out in front of them. Some of them lit small lanterns, but they did nothing in the darkness. The darkness ate the light. Then I saw the vampire, he was walking past the men, anger in his eyes. He couldn't see me, but he walked down the alley straight for me. He was smelling the air. With no time to lose, I touched the side of each boot saying, "Stick." Then I turned to run, but this time not down the alley, but rather, straight up the wall.

I ran three stories straight up, I then stopped and looked down upon the vampire searching for me in the alley. Taking no time at all, I pulled out an enchanted ring. I whispered, "Silence," then slid the ring onto my finger. The ring hummed, followed by a slight popping noise. Now no one could hear me within a two foot circle. Letting out a breath, I gasped for air as if I had been drowning. All that running up the wall, yet I was afraid to make a sound knowing how well a vampire could hear.

Last but not least I reached into my coat and pulled out another enchanted marble. Holding it between my fingers and out before me, I started to run. "Garlic pop," was the command word for the enchanted marble, it exploded between my fingers and turned to a white dust. I ran through the cloud, my body was covered with powder. Now I would smell of garlic, and vampires could not smell garlic. A form of protection, ever since Tom told me about the secret police being vampires, I had prepared.

I ran along the wall, then down, jumping into the street and merging free from the alley. I wasted no time as I ran across the square. Five streets met here, and a large fountain marked the center. I had to make it to the far side of the square, down Baker Street to another alley. There I knew a way to lose them. Not halfway across the square I broke free of the wall of ink. I hadn't even realized that spell effected such a large area.

Men must have been stationed up on the rooftops, they had been looking down into the alley only to see a cloud of darkness. One of the men must have seen me break free, yelling, "There he goes!" His voice was followed up by the sound of steam rifles firing through the air. I could hear the balls of lead whizzing all around me as I rounded the corner and out of the line of fire.

I made it to the alley, without a moment to lose, I pulled a metal disk out. Throwing it like a Frisbee, the enchanted disk stopped in mid air about six feet off the ground. Acting as a magnet, the manhole cover that it floated above flew up into the air, making a metallic clunk when the two pieces collided. Sliding to a stop just a step before the hole I tossed my backpack onto the ground. The clock clanged with an off tune bell as the clock and bag hit the ground. Pulling off my jacket I held it out, before myself. Using the magical command, "Showtime," the jacket came to life.

Now a young man, looking the same as me, stood before me. Hearing the sound of men and footsteps, I dropped down into the open sewage pipe. It was a good six feet before my legs found the bottom. The next noise I heard was the manhole cover falling into place. I then sat quiet, listening. The men must have poured into the alley, at this point the illusion would pull out a gun. The sound of gunfire filled the air, followed by an explosion. The jacket exploded, it would take them some time to figure it out it was nothing but a trick.

The sewage pipe was small and dark. I flipped another button on my goggles and my night vision turned on. I could now see the copper pipe half filled with debris and rotting water. Taking out a knife I ripped my pants at the knees. Wheels came out of my knees. Dropping down onto all fours, before I was shooting down the sewer pipe at break neck speeds. Let's see them catch me now.

My goggles mapped my way, showing me which way to turn. It was a maze of pipes. Finally, I dropped down, below the underground train lines. Emerging from the pipe into a large tunnel, wide enough for two people, and tall enough to stand. The ceiling was arched and the entire tunnel was made of a flat gray stone. A stone path followed along the left side, and to the right was a flow of water that you never wanted to fall into. It was hard enough just to smell it, but fortunately enough for me, I had enchantment for that. The sweet smell of roses. Of course that was my leather nose guard, it was enchanted to do that. I had made a killing selling them to the men who worked at the sewage plant.

Falling to one knee, I stifled a cry as I face planted on the stone path. My legs had stopped moving. I struggled to my feet. I looked over at my robot arm, lifting a small metal plate my heart sank; my power meter was at zero. How, how could I have run out of power so quickly?

As I tried not to panic I finally noticed the problem. There on my right leg, in the back, right above the knee, a small hole. It was leaking a dark liquid, not just any liquid, but the enchanted liquid that held the power to run my robotics. Apparently one of the shots had been closer than I thought. I had little movement left, I was rapidly fading, unable to move my legs or my left arm. My right arm still moved as I pushed myself up, but even that arm was weak without the its robotic assistance.

I lay there, breathing, then crying. I was forced to remove my goggles because of the tears, only to be swallowed into darkness.

Chapter 11 A Lovely Shade of Green

Tom Weaver

I found myself thinking of Morgan. I want to take care of my sister, but how? Funneling money to her would surely get the attention of my wife. Which could lead to an investigation by her father. No, it can't be done. Not as long as I'm married to Vicky. I needed to get going, I had a client in the Garden.

I couldn't help think, will Green-e be there today? What does she think of me now? It was a long trip to the new client's house, worrying the entire trip about how Green-e perceived me. When I arrived at the estate it was already past lunch. Covered in green, the estate was in the shadow of Castle White. It was a very Gothic style home with a large property. Most houses were built wall to wall, with very little to no property. Land within the Enchanted Garden was a premium. I couldn't imagine what kind of money and power my new client must have. All I knew was the name, Lady Gaven. Afterward, I planned on checking up on Cindy and a few new clients. Except for Mrs. Triviai, most of my patients had minor cuts and bruises. A cold here and there, but Mrs. Triviai has the early signs of the cough. For whatever reason, not even my magic could cure it. I could delay it, and lessen the symptoms. Still, that was more than most doctors could do. I hadn't been told what I was needed for here.

As I entered the front gate, passing through a small garden with a large fountain in the middle, I couldn't help but feel depressed. I had so hoped that Green-e would be here. On the other hand, if her attitude had soured towards me, perhaps it's for the best. Greeted by one of the servants, I was led into a parlor and told to wait. The inside was magnificent as the castle itself, full of art and wall paintings. Every inch of the wall and ceiling was decorated, gold leaf ran inside the wall like a lightning.

I was taking in one of the paintings when I heard someone enter the room. Turning to greet, what I believed to my client, I came face to face with Green-e. There she stood, a testament to beauty. For the first time not wearing green, instead her dress was white and brown. Dark brown thread stitching, made a scene of a forest, woven in the corset. It showed her curves. Her face was soft, with hair in a braid. My mouth betrayed me, "You are breath taking... its good to see you."

She smiled, I could not read her. It appeared she was plotting something. She must have built up the courage. "Sit," she demanded while pointing to a small couch.

"I would love to, but I'm afraid that a patient is awaiting my good care."

The look she gave was most definitely devious, "I called you. There is no one here that needs a doctor. In fact, this area is private for us, this home is used by the royals to wine and dine guest from all over the region. There are lots of rooms, and plenty of places for guests. I have use of it when I have the need."

"I see," I took a seat. I was nervous, my mind raced with confusing thoughts and many questions.

She sat next to me, and once again I was locked with her eyes. She spoke, as if she were embarrassed. "Our last conversation came undone. I spoke out of turn... I've come to realize that your friendship means a lot to me. Not just what you do for Cindy, but... well... I just wish to keep our friendship. I was rude, and pried much further into your personal life than I should have. I guess... I'm asking for your forgiveness." My mind was spinning, she wasn't mad. She still wants to be friends, but is that what I wanted? Her face started to melt, turning into despair as my internal debate kept my answer at bay. She blinked, eyes wetting, "I see, I understand."

But she didn't, she didn't understand at all. I couldn't lose her, I must speak. *Subconsciously*, was a word I didn't believe in. I am a man of intellect, my body does what my mind tells it to. That is what I believed, but only the word *subconsciously*, explains my hand on her face. Pulling her eyes back to mine, our shoulders coming together. Finally are necks giving up the last few inches. Then the world was dark as my eyes closed, the world disappeared, except for one feeling. A feeling emanating from my lips, heat, taste, smell, and most of all pleasure. Lips slowly parting, tongues exploring. A hum

169

of pleasure, I was not even sure who was humming. In that moment I realized, I had never kissed a woman before. What made it different? Her beauty, or dare I say… love?

Her eyes were a mix of shock and confusion. I stuttered, "I'm truly sorry, I… Well," She tried to speak, but I held a finger to her lips. "Earlier you challenged me, and I failed, you must think me a scoundrel."

She shook her head and gently moved my finger away, "No. I am the one who overstepped. I had no right to ask about your wife, or judge you so harshly. I know why I did? And now I believe you feel the same about me."

I knew I shouldn't say it, but I couldn't help myself. I wanted her, if anyone, to know the truth, "How do you see me? And, what if you judge me right? What then?"

Her eyes searched me, "I judge you a cheat. A man willing to take advantage of others for personal gain. Is that what you are? Is that how you want me to see you?"

I was lost, "I do not want you to see me badly. I don't want you to see my lie's, but the lie has become my life."

Her eyes filled with confusion. She asked, "Then how? How do I see you if my accusations are true? How do I make sense… of this?"

Despair rushed over me, "I don't know how, I just want you… I just want you to see me. For what I am, and that scares me." I turned my head away from her. I felt the tears, but I didn't want them. I couldn't love her, not in my life.

She gently took my face and turned it back to her, "I do see you. I can even understand you, I just don't want it to be true. I want to love a good man, *not* a man like you."

I became defensive, "I am a good man." Then I realized how silly that sounded, with a much calmer voice, "I'm a good man that has done horrible things." I chuckled darkly at my ironic statement.

I could see the struggle within her, she shook her head, "I know. I can tell a good man can be capable of acts of evil. There's so much more to this, your wife, my position as lady of the house of Dare. You are not what you say, but who you are you? It scares me, it scares me because… I don't care, I just don't care. What does that say about me? That your lies, are they for me as well?"

I pulled her to me, she didn't fight me. Before I could find any self control, we were kissing again. This time she did not hold back. Kissing her was unlike any women before, the world fell away, it was just me, and her. Some time shortly afterwards my mind stopped, and my heart took over.

As we separated, I fought to take control of my senses. Her eyes once again were locked into mine, and this time I understood exactly how she felt; because I felt that way too. She whispered, "It will be ok, don't worry, it will be ok."

"Yes," is what I said, but I could feel the panic. I knew that after this, I would want this angel, wherever she goes, and damn the consequences.

Chapter 12 Lost in Darkness

Morgan Jones

Hopeless, that was the situation I found myself in. Before someone found my corpse, I would die slowly in the dark. Maybe, eaten to death by sewer rats? They were huge, just the thought of them made me shudder. I even thought perhaps I heard one. My goggles would not work forever, and soon I would be lost in darkness. I had my wand, but what could I do with that. Enchanting took time and care, neither I would find down here.

I heard it again, the sound of small footprints. My heart pounded, would the dirty rats attack me before I died? The sound came again, it was coming from behind me. Soft footsteps, I could barely hear them over my own breathing. A light filled the tunnel from where I had just come from, panic sets in, this was no rat. Unable to set up, I twisted my neck around to see who was coming. My mind filled with a vision of the beautiful vampire. Perhaps the garlic had not covered my scent.

I saw the outline of a person come up behind me. I readied the only weapon I had, a small dagger. In my weakened condition it was folly. The dagger was enchanted, but only to unlock doors or locks. Tom had teased me, saying that it was made to unlock treasures, or the heart of men who hid them. Even if I could kill a person, I was unable to kill a vampire.

The unknown person came close enough to see. Then she said, "Don't stab me... Ok?"

"Who are you?" I demanded. I could see her clearly now that she stood over me. It was a young girl! Maybe thirteen or fifteen, long wavy hair. My night vision goggles gave everything a green tint, so it was hard to make out the color, but like everyone it was either black or brown. She wore what I guessed to be rags, covering just the basic. She didn't even appear to have shoes on. What on earth could she be doing down here?

She answered my question, "I'm Sonja."

"Samsung," I replied.

She giggled, "You look more like a Morgan to me."

I froze, I could hear my heart pounding in my chest. I couldn't figure out how anyone who knew me, would know to find me here. I demanded, holding my knife out before me, "How do you know me?"

The girl put her hands up, "Woah there, I'm a friend. Look at me closely."

She moved towards me, bending down almost in reach of my knife. I pushed the panic inside me down, forcing myself to stay calm. I looked at her closely. At first I saw nothing, expecting to recognize her from someone I knew. Then I notice her ears, they weren't human ears. Long and furry they came out from between her long hair. Her eyes, that starred down at me with an almost loving feel, they were slanted and inhuman. It was the eyes and ears of a cat. The flicker of motion. She had a tail, and honest to goodness tail, and it seemed to have a mind of its own. The tail, the eyes and the ears, "Mittens?"

She smiled, "Your ever faithful cat."

I put my knife away hesitantly, but my choice was limited. Pulling me up and wrapping my good arm around her shoulder, she complained, "Damn, you're heavy."

"Half robot, what did you expect?"

She mused, "Let's go fatty."

"I'm not fat," I declared, she just laughed in response.

Ten minutes later and she was covered in sweat. I informed her, "You only need to get me up one level, where the train runs. There I will find steam lines, and I can repair and recharge.

Panting from the effort, Sonja said contemptuous, "Just one level."

Five minutes later she dropped against the wall. I let out a "Owe."

Next to me a metal ladder ran up the wall and into a round shaft on the roof. Sonja declared, "I can hear the trains and smell the oil. This leads to the train tunnels."

I question her, "You can hear and smell all that?"

"How do you think I found you?" She sat down next to me, catching her breath. "I can smell garlic. I was right behind you, until you did that little show. Hell, I would have thought you blew up, if I hadn't seen you go into the sewer first. I was not fast enough to follow, and afterwards the place was crawling with police. I found another way into the sewers, then followed your scent. How you move so fast is beyond me."

"Wheels in my knees," I told her. Then added, "Wait, you still haven't explained why you're not a cat, or the fact you haven't told me… that you're not a cat?"

She laughed, then ignored my question, "You're like Batgirl, the wheels in your knees, that's cool."

"Who?"

"Batgirl, or batman, never heard of them?"

I shook my head, "Afraid not. Do they turn into bats? Like you turn into a cat?"

She laughed, "No, they are comic book characters. I had a lot of brothers and sister when I grew up. We lived in a library, and when we weren't hunting for mice or rats we read comics. That's what the modern humans called it, before the end of the world. They were paper books, filled with paintings of super heroes. They had words above each painting to tell you what the character was saying. You've never seen those before?"

I shrugged, "Sounds familiar, but I can't say I've ever heard of Batman."

"In the stories, there was a Catwoman. I kind of thought she might be like my people, but she never turned into a cat. Also, I read one about a cyborg. Half man, half machine. Kind of like you, but I think he was a bad guy."

I chuckled, "Sounds like me alright."

She narrowed her eyes, "You're not bad." I shrugged, I didn't want to argue with someone who was saving me. She looked up at the passageway again. "I can't see how I can pull you up that. It's only wide enough for one person. Perhaps I can go up and find some rope."

I reached across me and with some trouble pulled out a pouch from my pocket. Then slide out a bundle of string. "Here," Then I handed it to her.

She laughed, "What's this? Even if you didn't weigh a ton, this won't hold you."

I informed her, "It's enchanted silly. When you get up to the top, let it fall down. While it's in your hand, say the magic word, *rope.*"

"You are Batgirl."

I retorted, "And I don't weigh a ton." She just laughed.

After a terrible bit of pulling, she managed to get me up the shaft. Sonja dragged me for what felt like miles. We finally found a steam pipe I was able to tap into. I made temporary repairs. With a little bit of time I would have enough charge to run under my own power. I became busy with the repairs, so I hadn't even noticed that Sonja was now a cat again.

Unsure of what to think of my new friend, or rather what she was hiding from me, I decided on not dealing with it tonight. I was tired after all. I smiled at the cat, "Thanks Mittens." She hissed, "Ok, thanks Sonja." Guess she hadn't liked my name. I asked her, "So why haven't you turned into a girl before now?" She didn't answer, she just meowed. Of course she couldn't speak as a cat. Rubbing her face against my hand, she purred. I was somewhat annoyed with this. After a time, I was ready to leave, and like so many times before, she followed me home.

Once we both got home, we had crashed. I couldn't remember the last time I was that tired. It was the early hours of the morning when we returned, and now I've slept the whole day away. Sam would be so disappointed, I hadn't made it.

Tossing my clothes around I hurried to dress. Sonja yawned, "What's the emergency?" Once again a now pale girl was before me. Now I was able to take Sonja in with color. Her hair had color patterns just like when she was a cat. I huffed, "I need to meet up with Sam."

"I don't think he's right for you." She said while yawning.

I chuckled, "I think I like you better as a cat. What makes you say that?"

She challenged me, "Show him the true you. Let him see what you look like. He's a middle class ass, trust me. All he is worried about is moving up in society."

Aggravated at her, I turned to look at her. I was saying, "What do you know about him?" I realized she was turning into a cat. Before my very eyes, she shrunk and sprouted hair. Before I knew it the big cat was walking out of the blanket. Realizing she could not answer, I guess our conversation was over, I added, "I'll show you. Tonight, I will show him tonight. He loves me, you'll see."

Sonja followed me as always, but stayed much further away. Good, she knew I was still upset at her. What did she know about Sam? Sam lived in a nice neighborhood not too far from my home. His house was large and attached to the family wood shop. The store front met right on the corner. The lower floor of the building was the showroom, full of furniture and all manner of woodwork. The sales staff was waiting and willing, either to sell what they had or make a custom order.

I knew that Sam's family was large, but I had only met one of his sisters and only one time. She seemed very concerned about my family status. I knew that Sonja was right on one level, Sam's family seemed very concerned on their status. Taking a long hard look I realized another thing. His family was much more than middle class, the building, the house, and the workers in the upper floors of the mill. Even more men working out back, smaller buildings lined the rear of the property, filled with different kinds of raw wood.

I recalled Sam telling me on several occasions, that he was going across town to oversee projects. Some projects were too big to be built on the site. He went to oversee, not to do the work. He was no mere worker. Would he be happy with me when he found out about my poor background? I know that he believed I was from wealth. The way I dressed, I always had money. Perhaps the secrets made him think I was too rich to date him. In truth, I would have nothing to offer, not even a family history. It was time to find out how he will accept the real me.

It didn't take me long to find him. I had barely been standing there, thinking, when I noticed him getting out of a rickshaw in front of his home. He must have just returned from the outing, the same outing that I slept through.

Crossing the street I caught his attention with a wave, "Hey Sam."

He turned and walked towards me, with a very disappointed look, "We missed you today... and when I say we, I mean, me."

I hugged him and gave him a quick peck on the check. "Good news, no more secrets."

His eyes narrowed, "Truly."

"Hey, I keep secrets, not tell tales. In fact, I think it's time I show you something." I grabbed his hand and pulled him into motion. "Come on, follow me."

He laughed, his mood lifted, "Yes, ma'am. This day may have started poorly, but it's all about the finish."

I agreed, and wondered why it had taken me so long to come to this conclusion. I loved Sam, and if I wanted our relationship to go to the next level, he had to know the truth. He matched my pace as I lead him down the road. Soon I slipped down a small alleyway to the rear of some buildings. Across a dry flood channel, we arrived at my destination. An old building stood before us, it used to be apartments. It's four stories high, made of red brick that had turned black from coal dust.

Pushing back the bared door it screeched in protest. Sam laugh nervously, "What on earth do you want to show me?"

"Come on," I encouraged.

"Really, in this place."

I pulled him through the door. Sam hadn't even realized how much strength it took to break that old door open. It was dark, I pulled out a thin piece of wood, a torch, "Illuminated." The hall filled with light as I pulled Sam down it. "Come on scaredy pants."

The place was empty, the floor was down to the base wood. The walls looked to be water damaged, and being made of wood, much of it was rotten. The walls had been painted white once, but very little of the original white remained. Finally, I found a dry, rather clean looking room and pulled him in. He looked around the empty room as I shut the door. "Well, this place is truly something. Sure glad you showed me." I held the torch against the wall. It stuck, it was enchanted with that in mind. Sam asked, "Nice torch, where did you get it?"

"That doesn't matter… I think the best place to start with, is the real me." My dress was enchanted so the buttons came undone with a brush of my fingers. I slide the dress over my head. Sam's eyes stared as he quietly watched me fold up my dress and carefully lay it down, trying not to get it too dirty. I was in my undergarments, it was white and still covered most of me. It hung just below my waist only my underwear was slightly visible.

Sam and I had not gone beyond kissing, not that I hadn't wanted to, but the realization that the illusion spell only hid my metal body parts from the eyes. I had gone so far as wearing a special rubber glove so that no one would realize my left hand was steel. Of course they were enchanted, not only to feel like skin, but to produce heat. Sam looked at me, his eyes full of hunger. One look and I knew he liked what he could see. He nervously said, "Hold on, you don't have to do this. You are beautiful."

I stepped towards him, "Listen."

He smiled, putting his hands out before him like he was surrendering. "Ok, ok, no reason to rush it. So, what is this, *real* you... I mean, I can see you just fine. I love you, the real you. You don't have to prove it, not like this, not here. What you don't have you make up in beauty and style."

"It's not that, well it is that, but there is more. I want you to see the truth. I'm from the Outer circle, and not Eden." I took a breath, tried my hardest to be brave. Sam took me in his arms and pulled me to him. He held me tight, and at this moment I had time to reflect on his words. *What you don't have, you make up in beauty and style.* I couldn't show him, I couldn't lose him. Who else did I have? My brother barely had time for me and the doctor was about to die.

"You're from the outer rings," Sam was looking at me strangely. "How did you get in the city? They aren't letting the poor folks in from the outer rings. What I'm trying to say is, you have the finest of clothes. My friends and I have lost track of how many enchanted items you have. You may be from the outer circle, but you are obviously from a rich family. You have nothing to be ashamed about.

"Let me be honest with you. My father was nothing but a poor woodworker, he has made us rich from hard work. So see, we didn't come from money, but were not poor either. We are slowly, but surely working our family name into the elite families of Eden, and before long we could be invited into the Enchanted Gardens. You don't have to worry about your family roots, with wealth like yours."

I realized, I can't do this. I couldn't show him my secrets yet, he thought I was someone else. He wasn't ready for the truth, and worst of all, he wouldn't accept me. "But I'm not from a rich family. I snuck into the city of Eden. I'm poor, but is that not enough?"

"Ok, I thought we were past secrets, and stories." He was very demanding. He almost looked mad, or upset. "This is hard to follow Sung. First you drag me into this desolate place, then you take off half your clothes and tell me your from the outer rings and you snuck in... and your poor. How is it that you have all these... things? Enchanted things even. You're obviously not poor. Now you just lie to me?"

This was not going the way I'd hoped. I was confusing him or he was confusing me. Was this about money? It would be too hard to explain my story to him without showing him that I was a cyborg. I hadn't even showed him how ugly I was, or told him how I killed my family. "I'm sorry, this isn't how I wanted to tell you." I was now on the verge of tears. "I have some stuff, true, but I tell you I'm broke and have no family to speak of."

His voice sounded strained, "Enough of this. Get dressed, we'll figure this out. I care about you, and if you care about someone, then you can always find a way to make it work." His eyes and tone said otherwise. He couldn't wait to get away from me.

I pulled out my watch. "Do you know what time it is?"

He asked on the verge of anger, "What does it matter?"

I held the watch out in front of me, "It's ten, ten…"

He would not remember meeting up with me, in fact, all he'll remember is that I had stood him up. He stumbled out of the room confused. I couldn't let him leave, talking about his girlfriend from the outer ring. No, Sonja was right, he was a jerk; he was dating me thinking I was rich.

I couldn't help but laugh. I snuck a look down the hall, my eyes filled with tears. I watched Sam stumble out of the building and towards the street. He would soon come to his senses, then go home, and forget he ever spoke to me. His last memory would be of me standing him up.

I could finally see it. He thought I was some rich girl sneaking out and dating below her status. I never thought about that, but I had nice clothes and lots of enchanted items. Enchanted items cost lots of money, I'm stupid for not seeing this before. To think, this whole time I thought he would find me to ugly to date, not too poor. I was both.

I slid down the wall, and pulled my knees to my chest to cry, but I was not alone. A big cat forced itself between my legs and purred into my chest. I cried, but not alone.

Chapter 13 The Death of Dr. Weaver

Tom Weaver

I took one last look at her. She was perfect in every detail. Being a doctor and a good looking man, I have seen beautiful women before, but nothing like this. Then again, it could be in my head, the way Green-e made me feel, overriding any imperfections on her body or face. Her teeth weren't straight, still it was cute on her… Yes, she was perfect, perfect to me.

I was just lacing up my boots when I heard Green-e's groggy voice, "You need to leave?"

I could not hide my regret, "Yes my love."

She could not hide her sadness, "Home?"

I knew what she meant, my wife, "Yes my love."

"Will I see you over the weekend?" Her voice was cold, "I'm sorry, I know you cannot. Either can I for that matter. I cannot be seen with a married man, not in my position in the castle." She could not hide the bitterness.

"Both of us have much to lose. It was a risk for us both to make excuses for last night. Seldom do I not make it home, and I'm sure you rarely miss your duties." She nodded, my words were true, but they brought no response. "I will figure out a way to see you this weekend."

Green-e sounded almost hopeful, "You think… You could?"

I smiled, and tried to reassure her, "I don't know if I can, but I can try. I have never wanted anything more than you." Green-e came to me across the bed on her knees. Pulling me to her, I would be late, I didn't care.

The ride home was torturous, being pulled away from my love only to shower fake love upon my wife. Arriving home much later than usual, I had pre-prepared my excuses. My home was empty, except for our housekeeper. Vicky arrived hours later with a row of servants carrying boxes. I had forgotten, she had a shopping trip planned with some of her girlfriends. Usually on days like this I came home early, knowing that I would have the house to myself.

With all my new appointments at the Garden my work hours had become erratic. Everyone trusted me, so I truly doubted that anyone would wonder about last night. It had not been my first overnight in the Garden, it was a long trip and the Garden shut its gates after dark. Truly, I had nothing to fear, but I was worried, no, guilty.

Vicky welcomed me with a hug, kiss and a smile, "How was your day dear? Or should I say night?"

I smiled, "Good, and yours?"

"Great," She then turned her attention to the men, "Just stack the boxes in the living room."

It looked like it would be a long night of listening to Vicky tell me about her shopping trip, followed by her showing me everything she bought. I poured a tall glass of Brandy. I always hated my evenings with Vicky, but tonight would be unbearable. My heart felt like it was broken just being away from Green-e. How much longer could I live this lie?

The butler interrupted my thoughts, "Sir, you have a call."

"Who is it?" I snapped. The poor butler did not deserve my short temper.

The butler remained professional, like a robot he said, "She says she's one of your Uncle servants, but she didn't give a name."

Vicky chimed in, "How strange?"

I waved it off, "It's probably nothing. My uncle has become eccentric, he probably told his servant not to give his name. Let me talk to her, I'll find out what the fuss is about." I walked towards the phone, trying to stay calm, but deep down I was in a panic. I knew it was Morgan, and she has never called me at home before. I picked up the phone, well aware of the fact that Vicky was ease dropping. "Hello."

Morgan's voice sounded as if she was crying, "He's dead."

"Who?" I asked, but I knew who.

"Dr. Weaver is dead, I don't know what I should do." She sniffled loudly in my ear.

She sounded so small, and a million emotions leaped through my head, but my face, body and voice hid them all. I was a master of lies, I was the lie. I answered her calmly. "Don't do anything, I'll be right there."

I barely hung up the phone when Vicky asked in a panicked voice, "What's going on, where are you going?"

"My uncle, he needs me, don't wait up."

Vicky never really thought much of my uncle, then again, she never really thought much of anyone beside herself. She whined, "At this hour. Can't one of the on duty doctors take care of it. You were already gone last night."

I kissed her on the cheek, "Like I said, don't wait up."

Grabbing my jacket and umbrella I headed towards the door. Vicky tried to sound supportive, but she was a terrible liar, "If you have to go… Be back soon. You know I don't like to sleep alone, and I have lots of clothes to show you. You need to not be gone for two nights."

I shut the door without a response to her contemptible behavior. Vicky might not think outside of her own wants and needs, but she did love me. Or, perhaps, she just needed me, to make her feel wanted and loved. Loving her was like filling a tank, with a hole in the bottom. I felt bad for her sometimes, without me no one would love her except her father. Hell, she didn't even love herself. Perhaps I was being mean, for my need to get free of her. None of that mattered, only Morgan mattered tonight. Morgan needed me, and I didn't do near enough for my sister. She was the only person outside of Green-e who I truly loved, and truly loved me.

I arrived at Dr. Weaver's place and let myself in. I found my sister, dressed as a boy. She looked like she'd been fighting, clothes filthy and torn. She stood still, as she stared down at the Doctor's dead body. He lay dead in a pile of his own vomit. His body was still, it was Morgan tears that made my stomach twist.

I hugged her tightly and asked, "How are you holding up?"

"Like shit," She begin to weep in my arms. "Will it cause you problems coming over here like this?"

I chuckled darkly, "No, no, don't you worry about me. Are you sure he's dead?"

Between tears she answered, "He's dead. On second thought, perhaps you should take a look. I couldn't bring myself to touch him."

I sat Morgan on the couch, then left to inspect the doctor. He was dead alright. I took a seat next to my sister, and asked, "What else is going on? Why do you look and smell as if you've been running through the sewers?"

Morgan then told me about the nights little adventure. She had a close call with the law. Apparently she had been selling her Enchanted items on the street. I could feel the color drain from my face as she told me how close the vampire had come to catching her. "This is not good, " I said multiple times through her tail.

I handed her my handkerchief. She said after blowing her nose. "I've screwed up. I should have not sold my stuff, but I didn't know what to do. I know it is hard to sneak me money… I didn't tell you because I didn't want to cause you any trouble. Don't worry, I won't sell my stuff anymore."

Her voice was small, in my mind, she was a little girl again. My voice was strained, "I should have known. I haven't been paying enough attention to my baby sister. I'm afraid it might be worse than you know."

She looked at me confused and scared, "Why?"

I thought about the many conversions I had been having over the last few weeks. My time at the Garden had been so impressive, I had forgotten about the well being of Morgan. I told her, "Well, enchanted items are only made by the enchanters who live in the enchanted gardens. I know you know this, but, what you may not have realized, or perhaps not considered, is that they keep a record of everything they enchant. Now this is different from the registration, that just proves you didn't steal it. You have been enchanting items, stuff made here in Eden, things never seen or heard of before."

Her eyes open wide as she put the words together. She moaned, "Oh no. I've let them know that someone else in the city can enchant."

"Yes," Was all I could say. We both sat in silence. My rings, her body, all gains of her enchanting. I had thought about this before, but hadn't thought that Morgan might sell her Enchanted items. I said, "I've thought about coming out, telling the truth."

Morgan agreed, "So have I. I mean they might understand what happened to uncle. Plus, with my power I could get a job in the enchant garden."

My voice was grave, "You can't."

She didn't understand, "Why, what else can I do?"

"I don't know," I admitted. "But, you can't be found. At first we hid like children, because of our part in our uncle's death. Then we impersonated Weaver's nephew to get schooling. We sold stolen enchanted items, and I married the rich doctor's only daughter. None of these things are why you cannot get caught."

She didn't understand and asked, "What is then?"

I explained further, "With my new position in the castle, I've become aware of a secret war. It involves the vampires and the church. I'm not even sure who is who, but I will tell you this, if they find out about your power and what you can do, you will either be locked away to make weapons, or killed to keep you from making weapons. There is about to be a shift in power, we are on our own."

"It figures," Hopelessness washed over Morgan face. She asked, "What if I get caught?"

I thought for a minute, "Pretend you work for, or have been cursed by the enchanter. Don't let them know you are the enchanter. Trust no one… but me."

She sat quiet for a few seconds. A look came over her face, a look I knew too well, she had a plan. She looked up at me and announced, "You better go home. Tell the wife that your uncle was looking better when you left."

Tom looked confused, "What... Why?"

She jumped to her feet. "I need to burn this house down, there are way too many enchanted items to hide. In fact, some of the house itself is enchant. I don't own this house, and either will you when the debt collectors come for his estate."

I pulled her to me and hugged her tight. I handed her my purse, "This is all I have on me, I'll get you more soon."

She shook her head, "You don't have to do that." I narrowed my eyes, Morgan knew she could not return it, "Thanks bro."

We made plans to meet at the park in one week's time. Morgan promised me that she had enough money to find a hotel to stay until then. It wasn't the truth, it was not enough. I had been a fool, unable to take care of, or be with, the girls I loved. My lie, is my life, and it had no room for anything I cared about. I left home to Vicky... and deep down I knew that I had made a choice. I should have never left her.

Three days after visiting my sister, I was called back to my uncle's home by the authorities. The ceiling had caved in, the house was a pile of ash and black smoke still rose around from what remained of the walls. I knew that Dr. Weaver's body would be found. It was not unknown, that he had a drinking problem, so the authority would find no reason to waste much of my time with questions.

The next day I planned his funeral. It was easy, he had no money to leave and spent most of his life drunk. His body had already been burned, and few showed up for his wake. My sister showed, but I was unable to speak with her. My wife and her parents' attended the event with me. I gave a small speech to mostly empty seats. In the end, this was best, if the man had been loved, someone might have realized that I was not his nephew.

I was tired, every day the same. Worried about my sister, followed by, how I might sneak away to see Green-e. The weekend passed quickly, and the week was a heartache. I was busy, therefore I was only able to sneak away to be with Green-e once. We did see each other every day, and we talked often, but it was different when we were alone, and holding each other. I long for that, I long for the freedom to do that every day. It was already Friday, and I had patients who needed tending to, that did not live in the Enchanted Garden. It ruined my day when I realized I would not see her. It soured my mood even more when I realized I would not see her the entire weekend. I would be spending that time with my wife, Vicky. My stomach hurt, when I remind myself I left my sister to fend for herself.

I had a secret meeting with my sister. We had planned to meet secretly at the park on the 12th. I left plenty of time between appointments this afternoon. I missed her, and I worried about her. Clutching the bag of gold in my jacket pocket, it made me think about how dangerous it would be to take this money out of the bank. Vicky might notice, but damn her, Morgan needed it. I could not have my own sister living on the street. I gritted my teeth, it would be so much easier if I didn't have so much to fear. I've been married to her… Forever, and she has no reason to doubt me, for I spent every day showering her with false love. To give her doubt now, that could be dangerous, because for the first time I was unfaithful. I could not dwell on this, I had appointments to attend.

I was heading out of the office when Marvin popped his head out. "Tom, come and see me."

What do you want? Is what I wanted to say, but with a nice tone I informed him, "I have some appointments."

Marvin smiled, waving me in his office, "Yes, yes, I know. I only need you for a minute."

After shutting the door behind me Marvin waved towards a seat in front of his large desk. Marvin set down, beaming, I knew this look, it meant good news. "Good news?"

Marvin rubbed his hands together in excitement, "I should wait, but I can't." Marvin's office was beautiful, decorated by one of the city finest interior designers. It hadn't taken me a minute to notice that there was a wooden box laying on the desk. Marvin's office never really looked like anyone worked in here, and the most I would normally see is paperwork laying about. The box was thin, but it was at least two foot square. Marvin pointed at the box, "Guess what's in the box?"

I shrugged, "I have no idea."

"Guess," he insisted.

I was a little annoyed, I was in no mood for games today, "X-ray machine. I don't know, Marvin I do not wish to be late."

Marvin laughed, "What did I expect from the hardest working doctor in this practice? Let's just open and see, shall we?"

Marvin lifted the wooded lid off. It had already been opened. It was a sign, it looked just like the sign outside of our practice. Same size, same coloring, green with the same gold print font, but what it said, now that was different. The sign out front said, Dr. Webb family Medical Practice. This sign said, Dr. Webb and Dr. Weaver, family Medical Practice. I fell into a seat in shock. I whispered, "Partner."

Marvin laughed loudly and shoved his hand in mine, "Partner." He pulled me up to my feet and hugged me. "You deserve this, I've never met a more honest man."

I had to hurry to my appointment, and lucky for me it was not a long visit. It gave me the extra time I needed to get to the park. I was still in shock, sitting on the park bench waiting for Morgan. And the thought of Marvin's last words repeated themselves in my head, "I've never met a more honest man." A funny thought passed through my head as I thought of the sign, Dr. Webb and Dr. Weaver, family Medical Practice. The Webb's we Weave, when we Practice to deceive. I chuckled to myself quietly, that fits my life well.

My eyes darted around the park nervously, I hated to be seen meeting a young woman at the park. I was keeping my eye out for Morgan when an old woman sat down next to me. I turned to her and smiled, "How are you today?" I did my best to hide the annoyance, I had been saving the seat for Morgan.

She laughed, in a young girl voice she replied, "Fine, and you Tom?"

I stiffened in surprise and the old lady laughed harder, "Morgan I'll never get used to your disguises."

"With a little bit of magic, you can be anyone."

"How are you doing?" She smiled, but her eyes revealed the truth. "How are you really doing?"

She shrugged, "Good… It's been good."

I huffed, "I may be good at lying, but you're not. Where have you been?" Morgan turned her head and mumbled something. "You have been staying somewhere?" I could not hide the anger, "You've been living on the street." I accused.

She shook her head, "No, not really." I eyed her, "Ok, a little bit, I didn't have enough money to stay in a hotel every night, and eat."

I handed her the purse of gold coins, "This should hold you over for a few months."

She looked down in the bag, "So much. Can you give me this much?"

"Of course I can, I'm rich," she narrowed her eyes. We both knew that's not what she meant. "You're worried, that she might notice."

"And if she does?" Morgan wondered with concern.

I laughed, "So, you think I should let my baby sister live on the street because my wife might find out about the money."

Morgan's voice was soft, it reminded me of my mothers. "You told me about Green-e. You still… with her?"

"Yes," I admitted.

Her voice held no judgement, "Is it serious?"

I nodded, "Yes."

"Well, then you have a lot to lose. She will notice this much money missing, and you are having an affair." She took a few coins out of the purse, then handed it back to me. "You would be surprised at how resourceful I've become. We need to figure out something that doesn't end up with you being thrown out on the street… Or worse, in Nemos."

"I was promoted to partner today," my voice was hollow.

She was cheerful, "Well… That's good, congratulations."

We sat in silence for a few minutes, "I know something that would solve both our problems."

The old lady's face lit up, "What? Tell me."

I thought of it every day, and lately every hour, but saying it made it real, "We could kill my wife."

Chapter 14 Dreams of Murder

Morgan Jones

The rain was heavy. My old lady disguise wore off hours ago. Finally, I found a dry spot under an old bridge. A small creek ran under the bridge, the brown and green water swirled around. There was enough bank for Sonja and I to huddle up together. Sonja was still a cat, I didn't blame her the rain was cold. With no fire all I could do was sit and shiver. I had enchanted my clothes to be rain proof, tomorrow I would make them warm. Why hadn't I thought of that before now? Maybe because I had a warm house to live in. It was May 12th, so the weather would warm soon enough.

My mind wandered back to Tom and my conversation only a few hours ago. Kill his wife. He would be free to date Green-e. Without his wife looking over his back, he could give me as much money as he wanted to. Enough to buy a home of my own. Enough to go to school and get my own education, and a job that didn't require breaking the law.

Kill Vicky? I killed my uncle, but that was different, he was going to do us harm. What he did to Darrell. Darrell, I would have the money and the freedom to find my brother. Kill Vicky? What had she ever done to me? This would be in cold blood. Tom could not help, he would have to be above all suspicion. What if I got caught? What if I don't do it? My left robotic arm hurt, I need new parts. I needed a blacksmith to make the right parts in the first place.

I could go to school for that. Metal work, was very interesting to me. I imagined all the things I could do. Enchanted hammers to make myself better arms and legs. I could make a living working with metal. I could build a forge on to the side of my house. I could live anywhere, in the country where no one would bother me. All I had to do, was kill someone. No, not someone, Tom's revolting wife.

I could not wrap my head around it, the idea of killing anyone, or the fact that I need to. Being outside made it hard to think. The rain was now coming down so hard that it was a roar of noise and a solid sheet of water washing off the bridge, making me feel like I was walled in by water. A loud crack of thunder made me jump, the wind kicked up causing the water to spray mist on my face. I huddle tighter into a ball, trying to hide my face in my jacket. No matter what way I turned the wind and the water found me. This would be a long night.

The storm raged all night long. I had given up trying to weather it shortly after the sun went down. My robotic legs carried me quickly to the nearest hotel. After acquiring a room, it took me some time to find my warmth. Sonja turned from a cat to girl and helped me disconnect my legs and arm so that I could take a bath. My arms and legs could function in water and normally I took showers without taking them off, but the water wasn't good for them. They would require oiling, oil cost money. After drying off, Sonja and I huddled together on the bed.

I broke the silence, "You've been uncharacteristically quiet."

She shrugged, "I've been waiting for your teeth to stop chattering."

"I appreciate that."

Another moment of silence passed between us, Sonja asked, "How might you kill this lady?"

I eyed her, "You heard that." It shouldn't have surprised me. I often didn't see her, but she was always around. "I don't know if I will."

She spoke carefully, "You spent more than half of what you were willing to take from your brother, for *one* night in a hotel. I know how to live on the street, in the alleys. If you need, I will show you how to live that way."

I didn't like what she said, true or not. "Perhaps, I can survive that way if I need to."

Sonja chuckled, "It's not a matter if you can survive, it's a matter of being miserable for the rest of your life. Plus, what about your brother?"

"What about him?"

She explained, "Well, do you think he'll let you live on the street. Your brother should have made you his sister when he took on this new life, but he didn't."

I defended Tom, "He didn't for a good reason. I would have dragged him down. I hypnotized him, he couldn't have accomplished all that he has, by being my nurse. He has always believed once he made the money he would be able to help me out. It's that wife of his that got in the way. She's so, damn, controlling."

Sonja threw her arms up, "So, it's your fault, and now you're on your own. Still, your brother needs your help. If you walk away and lose yourself in the street, he might not be able to find you, and perhaps that would be best, but he is in love with this Green-e. He will get caught. It's not just you that needs this, you must both be free. He used this Vicky to get ahead, but now for both your sakes you must get free of her."

I laid down and pulled the blanket over my head, "I know this… I'm tired."

Sonja gently rubbed my back. In a soothing tone, "Rest, we'll talk later."

As I drifted off I couldn't help but think. Why was this girl trying to talk me into murder? Was it truly my only choice?

Chapter 15 Finding Morgan

Tom Weaver

Why, why did I even say it? How could I've asked my little handicapped sister to murder my wife? That is what preoccupied my thoughts. Green-e's face brought my attention back to the here and now. I was greeted by that smile, not any smile, but the smile of my dreams. I wanted to grab her and pull her to me, feel her body pressed against mine. All I could manage to do was, remove my hat, "Good evening, Lady Green."

She smiled politely, but her eyes screamed for me to kiss her, "Good day Dr. Weaver. Cindy is waiting."

I followed her towards Cindy's room. I was in a hallway inside Castle White, without even looking I knew that it was decorated beyond imagination, but I could not see it. My eyes tuned everything out, until the only thing in focus was Green-e walking in front of me. She opened the doors to Cindy's room, she closed them behind me. I caught her hand, almost out of reflex. Realizing what I had done I gave it a slight squeeze and released it.

Cindy had a large room, with many different levels. The many different times I've been here, it normally took us some time to locate the girl. She could be sitting in her doll room, or her library, so many rooms, but not today. Today she stood just ten feet away, with a funny look. She had seen me take Green-e's hand. I hid my emotions away, and stepped toward the girl. As if nothing happened, "How is my girl today? It is good to see you up and about."

She smiled, "Thanks to you, that's every day. Come inside, I've made tea."

She turned to lead the way, I turned to spy Green-e, she gave me a tight face. I knew she was unhappy with me, letting the girl see my affections, I tried to give her a reassuring smile. We arrived in Cindy's great room. It was large, great windows lined the wall. It was one of the highest rooms in the tower, right below the great garden above. The view was breath taking, you look over the walls of the Enchanted Garden, and all of Eden lay below. The outer walls of the great city looked tiny in the distance. You could not see the outer Territory walls, they were too far away. The world seemed endless up here.

Cindy sat down, then motioned for me to join her. There were only place settings for two. Tea and cakes were laid out upon a small table with a white frilly table cloth. Cindy looked up at Green-e, Cindy never used her nickname, "Lily dear."

"Yes," Green-e answered anxiously.

"I will require some private time, with my doctor."

Green-e was nervous because of what Cindy saw, or perhaps there was something more to it. Being only two place servings laid out, told me that she wished to speak to me privately before witnessing me taking Green-e's hand. Green-e started to disagree, "My lady, I cannot leave you alone with a man."

Before she could state any other reasons Cindy raised a hand. "I wasn't asking." Cindy turned to me. "I have selected several different kinds of tea. You must pick carefully, each is rare."

Green-e was stiff, the emotion of anger and fear washed across her face, but she had been dismissed. Realizing that Cindy was treating her as if she was on the way out, she turned and left. It took all my will power not to get up and go to her. I replied to Cindy, "Thank you for your hospitality." I picked up a tea bag marked, *Marvelous Green*. "This looks good."

Cindy approved, "Good choice, one of my favorite." I was about to say something when the door shut, and we were all alone. Cindy reached over and added the hot water to my cup, saying, "And here I thought you were saving yourself for me."

I tried to remain calm and play it off, "Whatever do you mean?"

She laughed, "Come on, I didn't need to see you take her hand to know the truth about you two. Before you bother to deny it, let me tell you, I don't care. I think it's cute."

"You must understand," I tried to explain.

Cindy hushed me, "None of that. I told you, I don't care. This is not what I want to talk to you about. I would gladly take a secret to the grave, I owe you my life. Believe me when I say, I'm not the only one thankful."

I nodded in understating, "Thank you. So, what is bothering you, have you been in pain?"

She smiled, "Always the doctor. No, ever since you, I have felt better every day. I do think you are close to healing me. Am I wrong in that?"

"No my dear, I'm afraid soon enough I'll have worked myself out of a job."

She laughed, "Oh, I doubt that. As long as the sickness is in the world, there will be work for Dr. Weaver. We digress, what I really need to talk to you about is your part in the revival."

"The what?"

Her face was very serious, "Revival. Let's not get caught up in the details. I have chosen you to turn me into a vampire on my sixteenth birthday. You and you alone."

My mind spun, I had no idea what she was really asking. "I've healed you. Why turn so young? I thought your kind had children first?"

A shadow of regret crossed her face, "Details, don't worry about the details. If not for you, I would have never been healthy enough to survive the turn, let alone live long enough to have children. You have made me whole, but not to live the life of my ancestors, or family. Do not worry about the details, except for one."

My heart pounded, I didn't like this. I was being involved in something, something I didn't understand. "I don't know, look, this is a great honor, but I'm a doctor, not a vampire... Maker."

She gave me a small smile, "Sorry. This is my will."

I looked at her, she stared at me. Finally, I broke the deadlock, "Ok, what detail must I worry about?"

Her eyes filled with intensity, "Find a place to put my body. A place only you know of, and prepare it for me."

I stared at her, why would I have to hide her body as she went through the change. It could take years for her to become a vampire. Why would they want me to be responsible for her well being? Whatever the reasons, they were not good, and she would not tell me. I responded the only way I could, "Perhaps another cup a tea before your treatment."

Her smile was genuine, "Good idea." She giggled, and before I could ask what was so funny, she told me. "I was just thinking. I have some tickets to a show, at the college. You and Green-e might have a good time. It's tonight, it's Alan and DJ Walker, in concert."

I smiled, "I truly am thankful, but I am a married man."

She laughed, "I'm going, so Green-e must be there, I have guards… and a private booth. Lots of opportunities for clients. Come on, Doctor; I'm sure you can come up with a few lies." She winked as she said the word lie.

I chuckled darkly. This girl has my number, "What time does the concert start?"

Chapter 16 The Concert

Alan Walker

I watched the young girl walk out on stage from behind the curtain. DJ and I have never put on a show like this, with a crowd like this. Hundreds of heads laid out before me, fanning away from the stage climbing upwards in shadow and darkness. No faces could be made out, if I had a heart it would be skipping beats. An audience this large was one thing, but this was the upper class of Eden. We were invited to the, Caster school of magic, the largest and only magic school in all of Eden. This could make or break our music career.

I heard that royalty was here tonight. I have never been this nervous. I was about to use my magic in front of some of the greatest wizards. I had always wanted to go to a school like this, but I had been born in the outer territories. My father never had money, but I do. Between my factory and my music career, I would never be like my father. I snuck another look at the crowd… this was so off the gear.

The young girl stood at the mike and began the introductions. "Welcome to Caster Theater," the crowd cheered, "We are proud to have some talent from the outer rings come and play some music for us. These talented brothers come from Carpenterville. Not only are they talented musicians, but they bring forth the art with steam, gears and magic. I have to say, we couldn't imagine a better show to have here at our school. So let's give a big round of applause, and welcome, Alan and DJ Walker."

The crowd went wild as the lights on the stage went dark. The curtains pulled away and I flashed to the center of the stage, the crowd went silent. I was an elementary wizard, controlling Fire, Wind, Water and Earth. This on its own would not be exciting, but thanks to my children, we would blow their mind.

The curtains opened. They stared up at my image, I was a black outline and a light cast directly behind me. I raised my hands up, the stage shifted, boxes with the pipes came down, landing right and left of me. A large tower structure arose from behind me, standing upon the top was my son, DJ. Long flowing robes came off of him, steam rose up from around the tower. The steam made his robes move around him like a tornado. I used my magic to bring forth great flames that heated the giant tanks of water.

DJ was surrounded by levers of his own design. His genius was second to none, but I was the musician. What I lacked in technical knowhow, I made up with pure musical talent. Flames burst free in all directions, the stage lit up and the crowd came to their feet screaming. Specially designed glass boxes captured the light of the fires, turning making beams of light. A spectacle of color bringing the stage to life. At the same time DJ pulled levers, the boxes moved, the lights danced everywhere. Pulling more levers DJ sent steam through different pipes and boxes. The pipes blew and the bass shook the stage. The large steam engine burned behind the stage, the pressure was released into the tower, and DJ mastered the controls, releasing pressure, controlling the hundred of pipes and boxes.

Using my power over the air I controlled the sounds coming from the machine into a rhythm. My earth power I used to enhance my movement as I danced. Long waves of silk came down from the ceiling. Moving in time with the song, I spun up through the air using the material to hold me. Wrapping my body up in the silk I could spin around in almost any direction. Steam was air, but it was also water, thanks to this mechanical creation of DJ, I was in control of all four elements in a way that any wizard would be proud of.

From the ceiling more machines lowered down. They were strange, filled with hundreds of tracks and large tubs of water at their base. Dancing over to them, I pushed levers, timing them to the beat. Steam forced its way up small pipes that moved gears. Hundreds of wheels turned, lifting metal balls up the tracks. The balls rolled down to the blocks that DJ could control. Each time he opened a block, the balls would fall. The metal balls would land upon strings, some landing upon small drums, and others hit bells of different sizes. The music came to life.

I walked forward, my long robes flapping from all the wind and heat being generated upon the stage. I concentrated on my energy, DJ's machine would continue to play my music. Fire burst forth and light engulfing me in flames. Growing ever taller, a woman of flames and multi colored light rose above me. She was in the likeness of my daughter, Evie with her big curls and doll face. Her mouth open, and she begins to sing. Evie back stage, singing into a tube and playing through the giant music machine. With hundreds of hours of practice, DJ and I weaved our dancing, sound and magic. Creating a picture of a thirty foot women singing, now that's always got the crowd's attention. The crowd responded and moved by music, totally in awe. I stepped forward in front of the giant girl of flame and began to dance, commanding the music changes with a twitch of my hand. The audience bounced in time with the song.

My nervousness gone, I was lost in the music. My hands moved as I pushed the beat through me and around me. That's it, now I feel it, the rush of living. DJ's head just bobbed while he stood upon the tower, keeping the music in time. The crowd swayed, this is what I lived for.

By the time the curtains fell, I was beyond jubilant. Moving back stage I joined my son and daughter. The stage hands clapped and congratulated us for a great show. We moved through the crowd of people and to our dressing rooms.

Evie shut the door and squealed, "What a show. That was your best by far, out of this world." She hugged DJ, "Wow, that song was off the gear. Can you believe how they cheered us?"

I teased her, "You're part of the band?"

She stuck her tongue out at me, her doll face animated. She said, "I wasn't asking *you*. I'm sure they were wondering where we attached the strings that held you up."

"I hope you know that my dancing is captivating." I stuck my tongue out..

She sneered, "The talent is DJ, everyone can see that."

Before DJ could respond, "We need to shower and clean up... That means you need to go."

She shrugged, then pointed her thumb at me, "What's the big deal. I won't look, at *him*." She said this as she stared at DJ.

DJ very plainly pointed out, "I'm your brother."

Her curls bounced as she laughed, "No your not."

I put my arm around her and started to push her towards the door. "I adopted both of you, so he is your brother, and you're my daughter, and that makes us family. You can't date, family, it's gross. Then again, you're gross, so that may not be a good reason for you."

She scratched at my arm as I pushed her out the door, "He is not my brother… And adoption does not make him my blood brother. Only a Mom and a Dad can do that. So stop…" Before she could say another word I shut the door and locked it.

I shook my head, "Whew, she's never going to stop."

DJ shrugged, "She is correct, I am not her brother."

I narrowed my eyes, "Do you want to date her?" He shook his head, "Then son, you need to stop pointing out she's right. I am going to shower first. Let's hurry up, I bet there is going to be all kinds of pretty ladies at the meet and greet."

DJ was not into dating, and he hated crowds. Looking distressed, "Must we go?"

I grabbed him by his shirt and pulled him towards me. I growled, "College girls… What's wrong with you man? Hurry up and get ready."

I looked myself over in the mirror. I was short, only five three, a narrow face and dark brown hair that would not be tamed. DJ on the other hand was six feet one and built like a dreamboat. His black hair looked good as soon as he got out of bed. He kept it just long enough to hide his face from time to time. DJ has no personality, not like me, I was nothing but personality. It didn't matter, all he had to do was stand there and say nothing and the ladies swarmed all over him. It took all my charm and considerable talents, just to get a date. Even my pretty daughter wanted to date him.

The party was off the gear. I mean everyone was there. The teachers were so impressed that the Dean offered us a place at the school. In many ways being from the outer rings meant that I might never make it this deep into the city. With my children's help, and my music, I was finally being noticed.

The party went on into the early hours, everyone was taken back by our music. A lot of people wished to know if we had any wax cylinders for sale. We hadn't got around to recording any of our music yet, but I let them know it was high on our priority. Four pretty girls, all dressed to the hilt approached us. I grabbed DJ over the shoulder and turned him towards the approaching ladies. They giggled, and I announced, "Why hello there pretty ladies. I'm Alan, this is DJ. We are the Walker brothers." I didn't like to seem that much older when the ladies were in sight. In fact, I was only ten years older than my children anyhow.

One of the prettiest girls spoke, "I'm Victoria, and this is Elizabeth, Elizabeth and Dote."

One of the Elizabeth gushed, "You two were amazing, truly, I've never heard music like that. I swear you've changed my life. Truly talented… And, do you, never mind."

The other Elizabeth finished her question, "Do you have girlfriends?"

With that all the girls burst into giggles. I smiled, "No, not at this moment."

Dote grabbed my arm, "Come on then, hang out with us."

I smiled, "You don't have to ask me twice."

DJ was unsure, "We do have an early morning appointment."

Just like him to ruin a moment, "Ignore him ladies. The sleep can wait."

"Can it?" A voice boomed from behind me. It was full of good humor and without looking I knew who it was, Ezra. He went on, "Come on boys, don't keep me waiting."

Ezra was tall, really tall, with a thin frame. He stood a head taller than anyone I have ever met. That made the fact I was short all the more apparent. His long brown hair hung loose around his white face, his brown eyes too big to be human, but still, few recognized him for what he was. Little to do with his tall, handsome features, but more to with the fact he messed with others minds. I looked over at the ladies, "I'm afraid we will need to get together at a later time."

They laughed, then gave me their numbers and names. Ezra waited, once out of earshot, he added, "You know I would have let you go…"

I finished his sentence, "I know, Ruby would be disappointed."

Ezra added, "Plus my young one, this upper class society. You could get in trouble being with the wrong daughter, if you know what I mean. I hate for you to be accused of being with the wrong girl. Here I am lecturing, and it is the first time you've been in the inner circle to visit me."

I eyed him, "Not by choice. Not exactly easy to get in, unless invited by the great Ezra."

He shrugged his shoulders, "Let's not keep Ruby waiting."

Ezra being a vampire had turned Ruby recently. She could not stand crowds, she was too new of a vampire. Unlike other young vampires, she married Ezra, and found herself a spot in the inner circle.

We loaded up into a large steam coach. The whistle blew and we were off. Ezra and DJ started talking numbers and facts about the city, these things bored me. Between the rocking of the coach, the show, and those two droning on, I was having trouble keeping my eyes open. Looking out the window I watch the city go by, it would be my new home, perhaps. Here in Eden there was more than a few vampires, Wizards, and Enchanters. What adventure awaited me here?

Ezra, how old is he? He had known my great, great, great grandfather over two hundred and thirty eight years ago, he would never give me a straight answer. He had turned many young women and men throughout the years. Many died without changing, even more were killed on the outer wall protecting the city. His wife, Ruby was twenty-five when Ezra turned her, and she has been a vampire for ten years. She didn't have enough control, not to go to a concert full of food. I got to know Ruby pretty good, Ezra would come several times a year to check on the cotton mill. Had to make sure I wasn't running it into the ground.

He also had many other duties at different cities on the outer wall. He would not bring Ruby to the other cities, he felt they were too dangerous for his love. Plus there was a lot of interaction with humans and Ruby had control issues. So it was often that Ruby would stay with me for months at a time. I enjoyed it, even if the workers did not. This fact, along with the my ability to create music is why Ezra has helped me move up. Dealing with Ruby had been a chore, and a dangerous one. The payoff was worth it.

Of course, this reminds me of the biggest problem of staying in Eden, the mill. Would Ezra allow Charley to run the factory without my oversight? Ezra owned a large Mill in Carpenterville, it made most of the fabric in Eden. Boats came up the river full of cotton and left full of clothes.. Charley was the man I left in charge of the factory. He was a good man and the best choice to replace me, but still he wasn't me. Ezra knew my heart, he knew why I bought such talented kids to move up in the world. I guess the word adopted sounds better.

I watched DJ talk with Ezra, and realized another thing to worry about. Could I trust the people of Eden with the well being of my children? They were truly gifted, and some might try to take advantage. Evie was talented, she was a great conjurer. Often you would see her with a fairy. How she summoned the magical creature, was beyond me, but what the fairy could do was frightening. The little bug could make you see things that weren't there. Evie had brought the fairy over from some dimension when she was a child. They became fast friends, living out her childhood fantasies with help from the fairy. How her parents died, I didn't know, but I always wondered if she hadn't accidentally brought something into their home. She never told me. Of course her crush on DJ made it hard to hang out with her. She hadn't even bothered to join us, she opted to stay at the party. I don't blame her, I'd rather she was there, plus she and Ruby did not get along.

The hotel we were staying in was the best in all of Eden. Only inside the Garden could you find a better place to stay. Too many secrets, too many agendas, too many strangers. Walking into what felt like a rather large home, we found Ruby pacing the floors. She hurried over to us, hugging me, "Tell me everything, leave nothing out."

I did as she asked. By the time I finished, I about fell asleep, I was dead on my feet. Ruby hurried DJ and I off to bed. My eyes closed as soon as my head hit the pillow.

Chapter 17 Plans in motion

Morgan Jones

It was late April, spring was in the air. The market place was busy, carts filled the street while stands lined every square inch of the walls. The open market was loud with the sounds of animals and people going about their business. Men would yell, *Come and get your fresh Grapes*, or *The best fruit in town*, each trying to attract you to their wares. My stomach growled as I worked my way through the crowd. I had a few pieces of silver and a few pennies left. I was unable to meet up with Tom, partly due to the fact there was little chance of him finding me. It had been over a month since he suggested I kill his wife. I hadn't had the time to work out a plan, it has been a full time job just living on the street. I was putting it off.

At first I scratched all the time, from the fleas that infested the lower alleyways. I was used to the bugs constant biting. My skin was so dirty, it appeared that water had never touched it. I couldn't tell how bad I stank, but others gladly pointed that out to me. When I passed too close to the market stand, the owner would stare at me, watching to make sure I didn't steal. Most weren't even that kind, they would yell out, "No begging, either buy something, or go away." I guess I couldn't blame them, they didn't have time to watch me, they had a stand to run. This life was not for me.

I hadn't even showed up for my delivery job, there was no way I could. Everyone on the street was looking for the boy, Sung, the cops were after me big time. The only thing I had on my side was they were looking for a boy, and for now I would stay as a girl. I let my hair down and wore a dress, it now matched the mud of the streets. I quickly snagged some cooked meat and an apple off two different stands. I was moving quickly and no one witness me do it. I cut down an alleyway and away from the hustle and bustle.

Who would have thought an apple would be a treat, but it was. My mouth watered just thinking about it. Rounding a corner, I came face to face with four young men. Dressed in old suits, that obviously did not fit. They had a swagger about them, and a dangerous look in their eyes. I had seen these kind of gang members around here before. I moved quickly around them, not giving them any eye contact. One of the boys yelled out, "What's the hurry girl. How about a bite of that apple?"

Most young girls ended up in the brothels, the streets were too dangerous, and the gangs would sell a young girl if they caught her. I kept walking, trying not to look as if I were running away. I could hear them, as their old dress shoes clattered down the stone road behind me. They wanted whatever I had, and if they could drag me off unnoticed, they would rape me and sell me. I quickened my step.

The men sped up too, they would overtake me if I didn't run. I wanted to run, I really did, but I didn't. I spun around without a word and ran straight at the group. Surprising the men, I leaped at the first two. Throwing my apple at one of the boys, he caught it square in the face and let out a yelp. They all stepped back, I landed right in the middle of them. "Power up," I said, not very loud, but loud enough that my arms and legs went into overdrive.

The men were quick to recover, one of the boys who stood behind me attacked. My hat, had been enchanted, it would buzz if something was heading toward the back of my head. Spinning to my left, my arm blocked a punch, just in the nick of time. My right arm drove into his chest, I could hear the ribs crack as the air rushed out of his lungs. He couldn't even cry as he fell to the ground.

The next two men fell in similar ways, I moved fast, sure footed and hit like a freight train. I turned to face the last of the men. He was the oldest, and looked to be the strongest of the group, but he wasn't about to fight me fairly. He pulled out a gun, a revolver with a large gas tub attached under the barrel. The steam gun looked old, but I was sure it worked. The man yelled, "That will be enough of that."

He had moved away, as I beat up his friends, it gave him the time to pull his gun. He stood about eight feet away, a long distance when staring down a gun. I kept my hands up, body turned as if I were about to box, "What do you want?"

"How about everything you own? You've hurt my friends, you'll be needing to pay for that." He grinned, showing his rotting teeth. He raised the gun up, then cocked it, "Strip."

I unclench my fist, and raised them palms forward in sign of surrender. Then I started to bend my knees falling towards the ground, and at the same time I cried. I cried like a girl, "Don't kill me, please, I didn't mean to hurt your friends."

He paused, looking at me, "Well, this is my lucky day." He was now grinning, looking down upon me with evil in his eyes. I only cried so that he would relax his gun hand, and so he would not shoot me as I bent my legs. I pushed up with all my strength, my body flew up into the air. He fired the gun in surprise, but I was well above where he was aiming. His bullet flew under me, colliding with the alley wall. I flew towards him, arching through the air. I could have leaped over a six foot man if one were standing between us. He tried to raise his gun, but he was too slow. As my body crashed into him, I swung my arm smashing it into his gun hand. The gun clattered across the ground.

The man was quick to react, his left arm sprung towards my face, but my right arm blocked it. Now both my arms held him back and before he could figure out what to do, I kicked him, a straight kick right into his chest. His body flew back into the alley wall, his head whipped and smacked hard against the bricks. He staggered forward, only to get another punch from my left arm straight to the head. His body fell limp to the ground.

I recovered his gun before any of the men could get up. I looked at the weapon, a five shot, four left. The perfect murder weapon. Two of the men were getting to their feet, while the other two stay on the ground, one knocked out, the man with the gun was most likely dead. I pointed the weapon, "Let's see what you have; strip."

One of the men came to, and under closer examination I found the gunman was still alive. Three men in their underwear did make for a queer sight as they ran down the alley mumbling curses. The fourth man was still out cold. Meanwhile, I quickly headed my own way, half wondering if the man would be ok? I now had a pocket full of silver, three weeks worth of Zen, a gun with four bullets, and a bag of crystal blue. I stopped on top of a bridge, once I was sure no one was looking, I dumped the bag of crystal blue. I had no use for that kind of drug. I would take the drug dealers money and weapons, but not that crap they peddled to the poor.

I walked down the street feeling good about myself. I took my first dose of Zen in a week, which made me feel oh so much better. It also broke my heart that those gang members were selling it for profit. People needed it to live, they shouldn't have to buy it. I slipped down another alley. It was overgrown with vines. Looking back and forth making sure the coast was clear, I slid down onto the ground right under one of the buildings. A missing piece of wall made for a nice door that led under the building, it was impossible to see because of the vines. Behind the crack in the wall the ground went down below the structure. There in between some very old stone pillars that formed part of the foundation, I had made my home.

Sonja was curled up as a cat, she barely blinked at me, then went back to sleep. I slid my body onto the pile of old blankets, then took off my hat and jacket. Pulling the gun and a bag of coins out, I lay them out before me. I tapped into one of the building steam lines, I plugged myself in to charge.

I now had what I needed to kill Vicky, the only question was; could I?

Tom Weaver

The voice broke my chain of thought, "Where are you?"

"What?" I hadn't understood the question.

Green-e smiled, then pulled me to her. "I asked, where, are, you?"

Still confused, "Lying in bed with the love of my life. Where else?" In the last month I was only able to sneak away with Green-e three times. All I could think about when I wasn't with her, and now that I'm with her, all I could think of was Morgan.

"I'm not playing games with you Tom. Tell me what's going on, if you can't tell me the truth... then tell me who you do confide in? Then I'll ask them."

Her tone was lighthearted, Green-e never forced anything from me. And yet, all I wanted to do was share all my darkest secrets with her. I thought that was odd the way she asked, "I don't understand, there is only you and no other."

Her face tightened, "I wonder. I sometimes I think it's your wife." I must of made a face because she laughed. She went on, "I only think that when I hear others talk. They say, that Tom is a wonderful husband, and loves his wife. I guess you play your part well, but when I'm with you and I say her name, I can tell from the look in your eyes that you don't love her. Still, there is someone in your life you care about, and you haven't told me who. Perhaps another woman?"

Odd, I thought, "Why would you think that?"

She shook her head, "It's obvious. You are deeply worried about someone, I can tell by how distracted you've been. I don't know of anyone you care about this much, so who is this person?"

Green-e; little in my life means more. I said it without thinking it through, "My sister, Morgan."

Her eyes narrowed, "You have a sister. Why haven't you mentioned it before? Is she in some kind of trouble?"

I was stressed, unbelievably stressed. I had asked my sister to murder my wife, then lost track of her. I had no idea where she might be, I didn't even know if she had a place to live. My life was a lie, and I had no one to talk to, at that moment my wall cracked. "No one knows of my sister... My life is a lie. I'm not Dr. Weaver, that's not my real name. I lied, I lied so that I might..." I couldn't finish as I burst into tears.

Green-e held me, "There, there now. Calm down, and start from the beginning. You can trust me, my love, I don't care what your name is, or where you came from. I love you, tell me why you're in so much pain. Let me help you."

It all poured out. Everything, my parents' death, my younger brother Darrell, my sister Morgan, and so much more. Green-e listened, sometime wide eyes and amazed, but never in anger. I finally ended my story, explaining that I could not find Morgan and worried about her well being. I did leave out the small detail of asking her to kill my wife, I wasn't ready for that kind of honesty. She was silent for a while. I was nervous of her reaction, fearing the worse, "Should I leave?"

She chuckled, "Don't be daft. You've given me a lot to take in, yet it explains so much. Too many things I could never understand, like why on earth did you marry that woman? I suppose it looks obvious for your career, but that reason didn't seem to be enough to put up with Vicky.

"I have always loved you, from the moment we first spoke. At first, because you came from such an upper class background, I thought we might not get along." She pulled my face to hers, looking deep in my eyes, "Understand this, no matter what you have done, I love you. Sometimes I wonder why. I can't help how I feel. I know better, but I don't care."

I cried, I could not remember crying, not since the death of my parents. "I love you so much. I was sure you would turn me in, or worse, leave me."

"Never," She was now crying. She embraced me, "You can count on me, I'm a fool, your' fool."

"I only hope that you can count on me." I felt better, better for telling the truth. At the same time worried that she knew my secrets.

She slapped me playfully, "Stop that. If you could figure out how to get free from your wife" She paused, "I can help you with your sister more freely, let me help. I have free time coming up, and no one will question me if I say I'm going into the city for some shopping and entertainment. I could help look for her."

I didn't want to get Green-e involved, but it was impossible to get away from prying eyes. Worst of all, I had used my few free moments to sneak away to see Green-e. I relented, "Ok, but I don't want you going anywhere dangerous in Eden. Eden is not the Gardens, and I will lose my mind if you go missing." I pulled out my pocket watch and flipped it open, inside there was a picture of my wife.

Green-e's face wrinkled up, "Ew, gross."

I laughed, then said, "Morgan." The picture swirled around in the watch and Vicky's face became Morgan's. "This is my sister, take my watch so you know what she looks like. She will know you by my watch."

Green-e took the watch from me, "What a cool watch. Where did you get it?"

I hadn't told her about Morgan ability to enchant. That was not so much a lie, as an omission. It was dangerous to know about Morgan. I simply answered, "A gift." She didn't question it anymore.

We hadn't much time after that, we both were expected elsewhere and like always, our time together was too short. I couldn't help but worry after I left Green-e. Should I have involved her? And what might she think of me asking Morgan to assassinate my wife? I had this strange feeling she would only partly hate it, she would hate the part where I ask my little sister to murder Vicky for me.

Morgan Jones

I watched her from a park bench. I knew her at once, Green-e. I have made more than one magic picture of her for my brother. Pictures hidden in items that only he could see. Plus, I had never seen anyone with green eyes like her. It made me wonder. He was so in love with this beautiful creature. Not that I could blame him, I was jealous. Her body moved like she was floating, and I noticed many of the men sneaking a look at the girl when they thought their lover's eyes were elsewhere. Single men stared, and a few even approached and tried their luck. She was quick enough to dismiss them. She approached me, I wore no disguise and I knew she was looking for me. She was holding my brothers watch, and glanced down at it often. It worried me. Was there something wrong with my brother? At the same time I've never met the women and did not trust her.

She was closer now, she wouldn't recognize me, I was too dirty. My hair was a beehive and it had been some time since I last bathed. I went to say something to Sonja, but the cat disappeared again. I really wish she would quit doing that. I was sick of living under a house, in the mud and cold. I was half hoping that perhaps my brother had just sent her out with more money. Still, better not chance it. I need information if I was going to go through with the murder... What should I do?

I continued my internal debate about talking with Green-e. As if a cosmic force heard me, Green-e all but passed me by, then she came to a stopped, turned her head around and eyed me. Turning her whole body towards me. She walked over slowly, without a word. She stopped just a few steps before me, in a soft voice, "I was worried I might not find you." I didn't reply, she then went on, "You look like you could use a meal, and perhaps a bath." She held out her hand, "Come on sister, don't keep me waiting."

It was the word sister, and the look in her eyes, the look of true concern. I took her hand and she helped me to my feet. Without a word I went with her, and my heart leaped at the hope of a meal and a bath. She led me to a local restaurant without a word. We were quickly seated. I hadn't realized how hungry I was. Even though I had some coins, most places won't let me eat because of my physical appearance. They didn't want me to come in now, but when Green-e said, "She's here with me." The head waiter turned white, then apologized many times as he found our seats. Good seats. Tom had told me who she was, but I now realized how powerful the Dare's must be if their nanny gets treated like royalty.

Green-e ordered, she didn't even ask me what I wanted. I shoveled the food in my mouth as soon as it was put before me. She took small careful bites, staying quiet, which I appreciated. I was too busy to talk. At one point she called the waiter over, she let him know that she would require a room with a hot bath, also a tailor who could fit me with a dress. The waiter hurried off, happy to fill her request. I had cleared my plate when Green-e asked, "Desert?" I shook my head, I noticed her eyes fall to my right arm. It was covered by my dirty long sleeve and I wore a glove, just on my left hand. "Do you think you might show me?"

I knew she meant my robotics, "Like a freak show?"

She frowned, "You are a beautiful girl, a little dirt can't hide that. I must say, I'm just curious. If it makes you uncomfortable, never mind."

I suddenly felt bad, she had been so nice, "Maybe."

She smiled, "It's truly up to you. We have more important things to do."

That made me wonder, "Like what?"

She narrowed her eyes, like she was trying to read my mind, "We'll talk about it later. Somewhere more private."

The rest of the evening was grand. The dessert was delicious, and I ate like I was a wild beast. Partly because I could tell it was upsetting the other guests, which in turn took it out on the manger. All the times he had kicked me out and not let me eat, this time he could do nothing. It was hours later before my bath was complete and the tailor fitted me in a very nice dress.

While I got measured I did not send Green-e away. Not only did the tailor get an eye full of my mechanical parts, but so did Green-e. For her part she did well, she didn't look disgusted. The tailor on the other hand could not hide his discomfort. It made me smile when Green-e pulled him aside and scolded him for it. Whispering I should have not been able to hear her, but I had enchanted small ear studs to enhance my hearing. She told him, "Sir, if you are to keep tailoring, I would suggest your behavior to improve. My sister in there is a rare beauty, understand? Perhaps the outer wall needs a good tailor?" I did not hear the man respond, but his face was full of false flattery for me when he returned. I could see why Tom loved her, she was amazing.

Green-e told me to make the dress in any fashion I wanted, and not to worry about the cost. It was wonderful, she didn't even bat an eye when I told the tailor to make pants under the dress. Or when I added laces, which held the lower part of the dress on. This way I could take off the bottom and wear pants and tops like a boy. The tailor thought this all to be highly irregular, but he was paid enough not to complain. It was a dark brown dress, highlighted with lighter browns, good colors for being outside. It would not be ready until tomorrow, but I was given a beautiful blue evening gown.

Once the tailor left, Green-e had a table and chairs placed outside the room and onto a very small balcony. It was meant for standing, but if we left the door open, there was enough room for the table and chairs. Once room services brought us tea and left, I thanked her for what was perhaps the hundredth time, "Thank you."

She smiled and politely, "Enough of that. The room is yours until you do not require it. No matter how long. Do you understand?" I nodded my head, she added, "Also, the room is in my name. I have not given your name, nor are they in the need of it. They will remember you." She said the last part with a wink.

"Thank you… again," How much had Tom told her, "So I'm guessing my brother told you a lot about me."

Her eyes narrowed, "Yes, and no. He is leaving a great deal of information out. At first when he was secretive, it hurt my feelings. I thought, why can't the man not trust me? Now I realize… he can't chance it, he was protecting you. I don't know all the trouble you and your brother are in to, but realize, I love Tom. I love him enough to risk my well being."

"I see," understanding that Tom had withheld information. Most likely she did not know I could enchant, and perhaps he withheld the fact I am supposed to kill his wife. I better be careful, she must be after information from me.

She took another sip of tea, "Tom sent me out today to find you, nothing more. I have done much more, why, a gift to the man I love. Still, there is one thing I want from you."

"Ask away."

She looked around, as if to check there was no one listening, she was nervous. "The truth, does he love her?"

At first I didn't understand, then I realized that she was talking about Tom. Did Tom love his wife, I laughed. Shaking my head, "No."

She looked abashed, "Oh, well, sometimes, it's hard... Never mind."

I fixed a second cup of tea for myself, "Tell me, what made you doubt his love for you?"

She shook her head, "You misunderstand me, I know he loves me. I would never doubt that. Still, there is room in most men's hearts to love another. Maybe not in the same manner. He does show his wife... how would you say it, affections. He takes care of her, and she is so happy. How can a women be this happy, and feel that loved; but secretly not be loved at all?"

I didn't know, but she talked as if she knew Vicky. "I hadn't realized you were so close to Vicky."

"Not Vicky, but her father, Marvin. He has been telling me about Tom ever since he started dating his daughter. I'm being silly, by the way, this Saturday, Tom, Vicky and her parents are going out to Palermos to celebrate his partnership. Are you familiar with this place?"

"No, I've never heard of it."

"It's a high end restaurant located close to the entrance of the Gardens." She dropped some coins on the table. "You should go check it out, get a meal. It's right next to Grand Central Station, pretty easy to get in and out. No one would notice you. You could sneak over and say hi to Tom, let him know your ok. I might not get a chance to speak with him for some time." While saying the last part I could see her sadness, and her need for my brother.

I looked at the coins, "Thanks, you've done enough. I mean I get the fact you have heard of the love my brother has shown Vicky. My brother is good at it, but trust me, I know him, he can't stand her."

She gave me a sideways smile, her tone was bitter, "Should I be worried? Such a great actor, perhaps I've fallen for his game as well?"

"Well, if you ask me, he loves you deeply. Then again, would you be sitting here if you believed anything less."

She let out a deep breath, "Unfortunately for me the answer is yes. I'm a fool in love. I don't want to share him. Or why he takes her to dinner…" She paused, she looked like she might cry.

After a moment I wondered, "I don't understand why Tom is going out to dinner with Vicky and her family would make you think he really loves her."

"I'm jealous, I want to celebrate this moment with him. The fact he is with her… Well, it sucks. I know why he married her, and if he hadn't I would have never met him. I think about it all the time. I just don't know how much longer I can share him, or, how much longer I can play this game." A tear betrayed her and she quickly wiped it away, "I'll lose him. He means the world to me.." She shook her head, then looked out over the city no longer able to look at me.

I took her hand and held it while she held back the tears. I knew why I would kill Vicky, another reason, I had another reason. With a reassuring voice, "It will be ok, and sooner than you might think."

She turned her head and looked at me, "Why do you think that? Is there something I don't know?"

I just smiled, and thought, Saturday at Palermos. Sounds like a night to die for. She was giving me a time and location, and had no idea what I was up to. Or did she? Either way, no time would be better.

Chapter 18 A Call to Duty

Tom Weaver

The day was taxing, I had been called to Castle White, but given no reason why. I had half hoped that it was Green-e again, pretending to be a patient in order to see me. There had been no word on my sister, and my worry was ever growing. Arriving at the Castle I was led in by one of the servants, then told that Cindy was awaiting me in her tower. This seemed strange, I was worried. I have never gone to see Cindy without meeting up with Green-e. Also, I have never been asked to come at night.

A few things came to mind, I couldn't help but think that Cindy was having a medical emergency. I realized that would be the best thing. What a life, when my hope was a young girl was suffering, for I was consumed that one of my lies would come back to haunt me. I was shown to one of the doors to Cindy's quarters, the servant opened the door, "Cindy awaits your arrival."

"Thanks," I stepped inside as he shut the door behind me. Hanging my hat and coat, I was surprised at how dark it was. The rest of the castle was so well lit, it was always bright through the hallways even though few hallways had windows. I had been in this part of Cindy's room before, it was like a living room, only larger. The door I came in was attached to a long hallway, that was normally bright, but not now. I almost had to feel the wall to find the hooks for my hat and coat.

I started down the hall, it led to the large living area, full of couches and seats. Two large fireplaces sat at either end of the great room, and the ceiling stood at least twenty feet high. The ceiling was one large arch, starting from where the hallway spilled out into the room. The wall was nothing but glass over a hundred feet long and twenty feet tall. It curved along the tower wall and looked over the city below. On this side of the tower you couldn't see the enchanted garden, but instead looked over the city of Eden. It's truly a breathtaking sight, especially at night.

The large room was dark when I entered it. My hair stood up on end, I tried to stay calm. I walked across the room to the large window, that looked over the city. Their lights flickered away with large black clouds of hundreds of chimneys burning throughout the city.

I jumped, "Doctor," it was Cindy. I turned to see her sitting in a chair. "Pardon, I didn't mean to startle you."

"It's no problem, I just didn't see you there."

She grinned, "It's a little dark. I like it dark, but that's not what you want to know. You would like to know why I've called you here, so late."

I took a few steps closer so that I could see her. I wanted to know why she brought me here, but I was afraid to find out. All I could say was, "I am concerned, are you ok? What ails you, that you would have me come in this late?"

"I'm fine," Cindy gestured to the seat next to her. "Sit; we have important business, and it cannot wait."

"Of course," I sat, and tried my best to remain calm. If she wanted to arrest me, or call me out for a crime, this would be a strange way of doing it. No, this all had to do with me keeping her body as she went through the change.

She asked, "Tell me, have you found a place to hide my body?"

"I have, I figured the best…" But before I could finish a man cleared his throat, it startled me. The man was standing right where I had just come from, practically in front of me.

He said in a deep voice, "I apologize, I did not mean to startle you, but you must never speak of where you plan on hiding her body. Especially here, only you are to know."

The man was of average height and build, thin with a smooth face. I took him for a middle aged man, perhaps in his forties, but after closer inspection, I could not be sure how old he was. He had long blonde hair that hung freely. He looked young, except he was too pale, the lighting was bad, but even in the dimly lit room, I could tell he was white as a stone. His face looked like he might be twenty, yet, his skin looked aged somehow. Not wrinkled, but like chalk full of hairline fractures. I stood up, "Sorry how rude of me, I am Dr. Weaver."

The man took my hand into his hand, it was cold, and felt like dried leather. "I am Jeffrey Dare, Cindy's Uncle."

I almost fell over, "Jeffery, you're the leader of the house of White." I was talking to the most powerful man in the world, and if the legend was right, the oldest. Jeffrey was the vampire who started Eden, over six hundred years ago. "It is truly an honor."

He smiled, "I thank you, but unfortunately we do not have time for pleasantries. Please sit down." After taking my seat, Jeffrey sat next to Cindy and continued. "What we're about to ask you, will be hard for you to understand. Perhaps even harder for you to do, but there are rewards. When Cindy and I first came up with this plan we were under the impression we had more time, then she got sick and the plan was forgotten."

Cindy chimed in, "Now that I'm better, we can make our dream come true. Sadly, things have gone… Well, sideways."

Jeffery squeezed her shoulder, "We would love to explain everything to you, but we don't have time, and we are afraid that if you knew too much, it might do more harm than good. I hate to do this to you, but tonight you must kill and bury Cindy, furthermore, no one can know about this. You will have help sneaking her out of the Enchanted Garden, but after that you must do the rest. No one must know where you hide the body, not even me."

Cindy pulled out a parchment and handed it to me. I pulled it open and looked at it, but my eyes couldn't concentrate, I could barely believe what they were asking me to do. Cindy spoke, "It's a list, how often to feed my body, blood, and what you should do if I awaken… I know this is a lot to take in, but we have run out of time and we don't know anyone else we could trust."

I shook my head in disbelief, "What about Green-e?"

Jeffrey answered, "We don't have time for this. All you need to understand is there's about to be a civil war. Most people in this city won't even know it happened, but I will no longer be in power. I've lived long, and unlike most people believe, I am not immortal. I'm dying. Protect the last living heir of the Dare line. It's not just for me, but for humanity. Trust me, she can save the world. People that are coming after us might suspect Green-e, that is why you must leave with Cindy now. They will never suspect that we have started the process so early… and used you to do it."

I didn't know what to say, but it still seemed wrong and I didn't want to get involved. "Won't they come after me? I mean, they know about me."

Cindy chuckled, "They do know, and that's why it will work. You have only known me for mouths, not even one year. They would never expect that we would use someone we barely knew. Also, I have a feeling your hiding place is better than anything Green-e could find, seeing as she lives in the castle, and rarely leaves the Garden."

I tried to gather myself, my head was spinning. I had my sister to worry about, and what happens if Vicky finds out about Green-e… Or better yet, what if she doesn't? How do I get free of her and still help my sister? "Look, I don't mean to be rude, but my plate is kind of full. When do you expect me to do this thing? What exactly do you expect from me?"

Jeffrey answered me, "All fair questions. The thing in question will happen tonight. Do not worry about your family, I will talk to Marvin myself. I plan on staging Cindy's death, you were called in tonight to try to save her from a suicide attempt, but unfortunately you failed. We have a body that we will burn, as it is our custom when we cannot be revived.

"The burning of the body will happen quickly. They will expect foul play, but they will never guess your part in it. They'll expect that you witnessed her dead body, but not that you are hiding her, so that she might rise again. You will take her to the place you have prepared, then you will strangle her. You will leave here, being nothing but a witness to a suicide that never happened."

"You expect me to kill her!" My voice broke as if I was thirteen.

Cindy's voice was small, but sweet, "I would be honored if it were you."

I shook my head, "Well, thanks, but, I can't kill you. I mean I could... I just don't know about all this."

Jeffrey stood up and walked over to me, my heart skipped a beat. He moved unlike a man, but more like leaves in the wind. He came before me and bent down until he was eye level, putting one hand on my shoulder. I was stunned into silence. In a quiet voice, "This is why we have picked you. You have a good heart, you may not show it to the world and hide behind lies, but we see it." I was stunned, his eyes were glowing, actually glowing. He went on, "We don't ask you because of our need, we ask you for the need of all men. There is no time to explain, but once this deed is done, look out for the church of seven. You will be not only the keeper of my family legacy, but the hope of men.

"One last thing. I would owe you, you never know when you might need the help of the most powerful man in Eden. Even after my fall, my allies will live on, and they will remember your name. We know about your sister, we can help you."

Cindy was standing next to me now, laying her hand on my other shoulder. "We ask you to believe in us. Can you do this?"

I sat there confused, but something became clear. They knew I wasn't who I said, they understood that and yet they still thought me worthy. I nodded, "I'll do this, but not for men or the world. I'll do it for Cindy, and my sister."

They both smiled, Jeffrey stood up, "That is a good enough reason for me."

Chapter 19 Trust

Morgan Jones

Saturday morning, I had only one day to plan my attack, Tom's dinner was tonight. Walking across town in my beautiful new dress, I couldn't help but feel thankful for Green-e's help. The day was gloomy and I brought along my umbrella it certainly looked as if it might rain. Passing by a store window, I caught my reflection. I was pretty again, between my spells and this dress my spirits have been lifted. I walked away from the image, the image of a girl who was planning a murder.

I still was so uncertain of my course of action. Yet, I headed towards Palermos, so that I might scope out the area. It hadn't been easy to figure out the best method of escape. In fact, I planned several just in case. The restaurant emptied out into Grand Central station, depending on which direction I chose there would be countless avenues of escape. It seemed that my course was set.

I had lots of work to do, magical disguises that I could employ at a moment's notice. Clean the gun and make sure that I wore gloves when handling the murder weapon. I would drop it after shooting her. Needing to head back to my hotel room so that I might finish the many tasks at hand. I started going over the possibility of getting caught. I suddenly realized my biggest mistake, Green-e. I don't think anyone at the restaurant or hotel realized I was a cyborg, but the tailor knew. If I were caught, he could put me with Green-e, this could lead to problems for her and my brother. I needed to deal with the tailor, I needed to deal with him tonight.

It didn't take me long to get the tailor's name from the front desk of the hotel. I flagged down a rickshaw and told the driver, "Please take me to Sunrise Tailor shop."

"Right away," the man touched a stone located on his cart, then repeated my location. A little arrow attached to one of the pulling arms of the cart, spun around then stopped pointing the way. We hadn't traveled far when a large cat jumped in the passenger side window. After turning into Sonja, she closed the blinds. This was an enclosed cart and apparently she didn't want to be seen. I ignored this by leaving my blinds open, I wanted to see the outside world and smell the city. Well, maybe not smell all of it.

Sonja spoke, "Hello... What are you up to?"

I eyed her, "You pop up whenever you want, then expect me to pay you attention. Not today. I have a problem to solve. I have to hypnotize the tailor, or perhaps figure out how to erase his mind."

"Oh," she said with a very strange look.

"What do you mean by that?"

She gave me her best innocent face, "By what... Oh." I gave her a look. "Ok, ok, I hadn't thought you would realize that problem."

I was surprised, "You realized it, when? I swear you must be snorting cat nip all day long."

She grinned, "Well, right after he finished measuring you. I thought to myself, this man knows too much, if you get caught, he'll be a problem. So, who would have guessed after oiling yourself up you could have put that together."

I barked, "And you plan on sharing this with me, when?"

"Well, honestly... never. Perhaps it's all the cat nip." I was about to yell at her when she tossed her hands out, palms up. "Wait, before you break a gear, let me explain."

I hissed like a cat, "Explain."

She put on her best innocent face, "Well, realizing how full your plate is, I figured I could help you out. So, I handled it. No reason to get all your gears out of wack my little machine."

I took a breath, and for the first time I realized how little I trusted this magical creature. "Took care of it how?"

She gave me a sly look, "You need not worry about it. Go back to the hotel. No need to waste time on the tailor."

"That's not an answer," I growled.

Her look was unconcerned, "It's up to you if you waste your time. Trust me, you have nothing to worry about. I'm on your side, I'm here to help. Try not to get your springs to wound, you have some serious business tonight."

I looked out the window, "We're almost there. I think I'll check out your handy work. Let me add, I don't trust you."

Her voice was low and dangerous, "Don't you trust me? Why do you insist on wasting your time?"

The cart stopped and the driver yelled out, "Miss, we have arrived."

I turned back to Sonja, "Time is irrelevant, this is about trust."

Without another word I stepped out of the rickshaw. The driver came around to meet me and collected payment. I handed him the required amount of coins, when I turned my head Sonja was no where to be seen. I figured that, she disappeared whenever someone else was around. They never would see her in cat form or otherwise. I wonder why that is? That was a mystery for another day.

I turned to the storefront and was confronted by a small crowd of people standing out front. I wondered what this was about and how it might delay me. I walked up to the crowd and stood next to a woman who was craning her head around trying to get a better look. I asked, "What is going on here?"

The women turned to me and gave me a big smile. Eager to share her gossip, "Oh, you haven't heard. Billy Maker, the owner of Sunrise Tailor took his life last night. They said he hung himself right in the middle of the shop."

Without thinking, "That can't be right, I received this dress from him this morning."

They lady took a longer look at me, or perhaps my dress. "Perhaps the carrier got it earlier. They found his body last night. They say the family is inside his shop now… There talking about a big sale. The daughter wants nothing to do with the shop. Some savvy shoppers are hanging around… Just in case."

I turned and walked away, she was too busy paying attention to the shop to see me leave. I was angry, who was this cat? She killed a man. Why was she so eager to help me? It made me wonder if I should go on with the plan of killing Vicky. I felt like a snowball falling down a hill, the whole thing seemed hard to stop, and kept on getting bigger. This much was for sure, I could not trust Sonja.

I hurried, I had lots of things to do. Trust her or not, I have no choice.

Tom Weaver

It was a surreal feeling to walk next to Cindy, knowing full well I was taking her to a place to kill her. It was Friday night, tomorrow I had a big dinner with my family. How could I endure acting normal with all this going on? Cindy picked up on my nervousness, "Relax, this isn't a bad thing. I look forward to this change."

I shook my head, "Easier said than done. I'm afraid I've been in the business of healing people, not killing people. Before you say it, I know, this is like a change and not a death. Still, it could be your death."

She added with a smile, "Like a butterfly. Have you ever heard of a butterfly?"

I smiled back, "I've seen them before. Green-e showed them to me. They live in one of your gardens, she explained how they started from a caterpillar, cocoon, then turned into a beautiful butterfly. I wonder if any survive outside the walls?"

Cindy shrugged her elbows, "Who knows? It's a large world and we are blind inside our bubble. If God is good, perhaps one day man will reclaim the earth."

"Perhaps," I agreed.

She suddenly sounded older, "It's a lot of responsibility, but I must try. The power that runs through my family's blood can save the world." I couldn't help but wonder, how much responsibility could they lay on this girl's shoulders?

We traveled together in silence. Stopping before a large painting of a beautiful woman, with angles flying up behind her, Cindy reached to one side of the painting and pulled on the frame. With a creak the large painting swung open, revealing a dark corridor. Cindy grabbed a torch from the wall, and I followed. Upon entering I found that it was not a corridor, rather a circular staircase. Shutting the painting, I followed Cindy down. I thought we were heading toward the center of the earth, my toes hurt from going down. Cindy announced, "Almost there."

When we reached the bottom I found myself in what appeared to be a cave. We must be far below the castle I thought. This is where humans found refuge at the beginning, deep in the earth. The tunnel we enter snaked back and forth, sometimes moving upwards, sometimes down. At first I noticed many passages breaking off, but the more we delved, the less adjoining tunnels. The passage straightened, and felt as if it might be going up. No more adjoining passages and the air smelled old and stale. The tunnel now narrowed and I removed my hat, the ceiling was too low. Eventually, I was forced to duck, or hit my head upon the rocky ceiling. I was thinking we might never find our way when Cindy called out from ahead of me, "We're here, hurry up."

I grumbled, "Some of us are taller than others." She didn't need to duck and had moved some ways ahead. I popped out of the tunnel to find her there waiting. I asked, "Where are we?"

"Under an old manor, that sits right outside the wall of the Garden." She walked into a wall, pressing on a brick which slid away to expose a lever. Pulling open the door, she said, "Lizzy is waiting for us, she will help us navigate to the place you have chosen." After she said that I realized that we were standing in what appeared to be an old cellar, minus the wine. Spider webs filled all the empty wine racks the whole place was forgotten and unkempt. Spying a staircase across the cellar I headed towards it with Cindy in tow.

Realizing what Cindy just said, I stopped suddenly. Cindy banged into me and whispered, "Ow, what's wrong?"

"No one told me of another person. I was told that I would be the only one involved, and no one but me will know your place of rest." Cindy chuckled, I held back a wave of fury, "This is not funny. I risked everything for you."

She stopped laughing, "Sorry, you're right. We haven't had time to explain everything. Lizzy is not a person, but a doll. She is a magical thing, made back when modern man still ruled the world. She is the last one, the last one we know of. She is just an old body, sewn together and animated by magic. She will rest in the grave with me, to protect me, like she has done for hundreds of my kin. In preparation, we had her moved here, to guard the house and be in place for us to take her with us."

I shook my head, "More surprises. A doll, well it shouldn't surprise me. Let's get going."

She grabbed my hand, "Tom, don't be grumpy. I know I ask a lot."

The look on her face and her kind touch made my anger turn to shame. I nodded my head, "I'm just stressed, I am proud to be the one you have chosen."

She smiled, "Then let us hurry."

Without another word we headed up the stairs. When we entered into the home what I found surprised me, it probably shouldn't have, but it did. The home itself was empty and the windows were boarded up. Anyone who could afford a house this large would have to be extremely wealthy. Of course the fact there was a secret entrance into the Garden told me that anyone that stayed here would be well connected as well.

In the living room, standing in the center of the room, was a girl. Average height and build, she stood in a black dress, motionless, in the dark, she made no move as we entered the room. My torch cast a weak light and shadows danced against the empty walls. Yet she did not move and my heart filled with dread the closer we came to her. The light finally illuminated the girl, she was pretty, pale as a stone. I came to realize her face and hands were covered in scars held together with stitching. Her dress had full sleeves, so I could not make out any other part of her, but I knew she had been sewn together by some terrible magic.

Her head jerked towards us, lifeless eyes stared at us with daggers, Cindy held one hand up saying, "I Cindy Dare, princess of the Castle White, command you to obey."

Lizzy's eyes twitched, then she spoke with a strange accent that I had never heard before. "Cindy, I have waited for your command. Should I kill the man?"

Cindy stuck her finger to her chin, "Hmmm, let me think."

I was truly scared of this thing, "Not funny... Cindy."

She giggled, "No, do not kill him Lizzy. This is Tom Weaver, and he will be your master. Do you understand."

The girl simply said, "Yes," but I swear I could see the defiance in those eyes.

Cindy clapped her hands together, "With that settled, let's get a move on."

Alan Walker

"Wake up," I heard. I realized someone was shaking me. Looking up I stared into Evie's Doll eyes and her large curls hanging in my face. "Wake up," she demanded.

"What... What time is it," I asked in confusion.

She growled, "Three o clock," she then added, "Saturday."

I had been up all night. After the concert we had spent the rest of the night animatedly explaining how the concert went to Ruby. I complained, "I sleep during the day."

I must of dozed off, because she was shaking me again, saying, "Come on, wake up. You have some explaining to do. You can't sleep the whole day away."

I sat up, and she handed me a hot cup of coffee. I looked at her funny, "Why thank you." I was suspicious, she was being nice. I eyed her, "So, what do you want?"

"Want? Can't a daughter get her father a cup of coffee? The only reason I'm waking you is because of your appointment."

Yep, she was up to something, "What appointment?"

She eyed me, deciding whether or not I was lying or not. She finally said, "Well, there was a message at the desk this morning. You and DJ, are supposed to go to the college at four to talk to the Dean. Something about getting enrolled. Enrolled into Caster College."

I sipped my coffee, "Unless I've slept for a day, that's not until tomorrow."

She blew up, "When were you going to tell me?"

I was defensive, "Never… I mean, I haven't had a chance."

Before I could explain further she interrupted me with, "What about me? You can't expect me to go back to that backward town and work at the mill, while DJ goes to a college. A college with people who have all their teeth no less… And live in the city!"

I sipped my coffee. Not able to hide the smirk, "I'll miss you." She punched me, "Ow, ok, ok, no need to get violent. I'll ask the Dean, with your abilities, I'm sure you could go to school also. You are a part of the band." She was smirking, "It was always my intention to get my children enrolled."

She jumped up with a yelp, throwing her arms around me. Fortunately I had finished the coffee, or I would be wearing it. DJ came in my room, apparently already awake. He looked at us and in his dry manner, "Good, she has woken you up. Get ready so we're not late to meet the Dean."

Evie asked, "What about me?"

DJ answered, "You will need to attend as well, that is if you wish to go?"

She narrowed her eyes, "For someone so cute, you're really daft sometimes."

I was about to correct him, and tell him it was tomorrow, but then I remembered who I was talking to. If anyone knew when and what time I needed to be somewhere, it was my son. Without him I would be late to my own funeral. "Ok, I'll be ready shortly."

Dean Alexander Shipwrights, was the standing Dean of Caster School of Magic. I waited nervously in the waiting room, DJ, was calm, like always. How he did it was beyond me. Evie paced the floor.

Our meeting, if you could call it that, was nothing more than a welcome to the school. It appeared that all the details had been worked out by Ezra. In fact, he rented us a small flat right off the school grounds, so that we might stay together. DJ was less than happy to hear about this, Evie would be around every corner. Still, a place in the city with my children, this was my chance to move up in Eden. Things were looking good.

Friday night concert, then a meeting with the Dean, what a way to start my stay in Eden. It looked to be a busy week. Evie was overjoyed with her acceptance into the school. She announced that Ruby and she would be off to find some suitable clothing for the new school year. DJ and Ezra had left, often DJ accompanied Ezra on a late night walk.

Finally alone, I fell back on the hotel bed, when a head appeared above me, "What, are you doing?"

"The day was going so good," I moaned. "Go away."

"Wow, that wasn't nice. I should claw you in the face." She scratched me, but not hard enough to hurt.

"Sonja, what are you doing? I haven't seen you in days. Starting to think you abandoned me, or perhaps went off to have a litter."

She hissed, "Funny, you're *real* funny. I've been busy, and I think I might need your help."

I narrowed my eyes, "You need my help? Or does she need my help?"

She flipped around, landing with a thud so now she lay next to me on the bed. "There is no difference. Everything I do is for her… and you must help me."

I grumbled, "What do you need?"

"I'll let you know the details later. For now, go down to the Grand Central Station. There is a restaurant named Palermos, wait out front for me."

"I have plans, really need to catch up on sleep," but I realized I was talking to a cat. She jumped off the bed and onto the window sill. Leaping out the window, even though we were seven stories up. The cat vanished into thin air.

I wondered, would I ever be free of the debt I owed that angel? Or whatever she was. I thought of the power I had, it had been a gift for serving her. No, I would never be free.

Chapter 20 Dinner Time

Morgan Jones

I walked around Grand Central Station, my mind a flutter. My stomach hurt, twisted in knots. I kept whispering to myself, "You can do this," over and over again. I was going mad, or perhaps I was already mad. Furthermore, I hadn't seen that cat. I didn't trust that damn cat, but, who else do I have? I was walking through the mall, where hundreds of shops lined against each wall and carts filled the isle. They sold everything you could imagine, and the stream of people made it hard to move.

I was forced to a halt by some window shoppers, the crowd kept me from moving. Frustrated, I turned to the window display, only to see myself looking back at me. I was dressed like a fine young gentleman, yet, I still appeared to be female. My long hair and woman figure was plain for all to see. Many people had said, "Excuse me, ma'am." No one had mistaken me for a boy.

My long jacket hung loosely to my side, ash gray and matching my pants. White shirt and a a dark brown vest I looked smart indeed. I was also armed to the teeth, including the stolen gun with five remaining shots in it. It hung on the inside of my jacket. It felt like it was getting heavier by the minute, pulling down upon my soul.

It wouldn't be long now. I finally was free and moved quickly away, to a less crowded area of the station. I found a quiet park bench and took a break, only to find Sonja. The cat came from thin air, as she often did, then turned into a girl and sat next to me. "Aren't you afraid someone will see you?"

She shrugged, "No one seems to be paying us any attention." We were quiet for a moment, "I realize you don't trust me. Perhaps there is more to my tale than just being a standard cat tail, if you know what I mean?"

"Ha, ha," I responded dryly. "Why are you here? Or better yet, why are you helping me?"

She smiled slyly, "I've been waiting for the right time to tell you this." She paused.

"And," I demanded.

"This is not the right time." She laughed.

I shook my head and growled, "Go away. I don't need the likes of you right now."

She argued, "But you do. In case you screw this up I brought help, hopefully you will never need him. His name is Alan, and he's resourceful." Before I could respond, she blurted out, "The best of luck to you."

She turned into a cat and jumped into the air. I reached out to grab her yelling, "Hold on…" But before I could finish she disappeared into thin air.

I shook my head. How? I look around and noticed a few people giving me strange looks. I lowered my gaze and they hurried along. I don't know why, but I knew they could not see that cat, or Sonja. I must of startled them jumping up and grabbing at thin air. I don't know why it took me this long to realize that I was the only one who ever saw her.

I cleared my mind. I couldn't think about all this, I had to concentrate on the mission ahead. Instead, I found myself thinking about Sonja and all the times I have seen her. I could not remember seeing the big cat before I died, but afterwards I saw her everywhere. It did put my mind at ease, at least I knew she wasn't out to get me. It's what she wanted from me that scared me. This was my price to pay, for my sin. I owed Tom.

I sat there in self debate, when my stop watch alarm chirped. It was time.

Dr. Weaver

I stared into the mirror, waiting for my image to scream back at me. I took a deep breath, then another one. Last night was a horror story. After I snuck through town with Cindy and that abomination, we finally made it to my father-in-law's estate unseen. In the garden there was a large steel door that leads underground to the crypts. We made it down to the lower chambers without a hitch.

Once inside we headed down, and traveling further away to the old chambers of long ago. To the ancestors that no one even recalled. Here she would be safe. From the layers of dust and cobwebs, no one has been down there for a long time, perhaps generations. I had cleared out an old stone coffin, only bones and tattered old clothes remained. The coffin itself was carved right into the wall. I lined the inside with pillows and a clean sheet. Cindy seemed pleased by the attention to her resting area, even if it was unnecessary.

We talked for an hour. Personally I was trying to put the whole affair off for another day, or never. In the end, I did it. I had never killed a person, except for my uncle. That seemed so much different, he was attacking us and I hated him. He was a mean old dying man, in fact, you could say I only took a few years off his life. Cindy was none of these things, I loved her, and even though I knew she would rise again... I was still killing her. What if she didn't rise? Does that make me a murderer?

I woke up to many times, tossing and turning. I watched her eyes go blank... choking the life out of her. The way her body went limp... I shook my head, and took another deep breath. I remembered laying her dead body carefully into her resting place, only to turn around to find myself staring at Lizzy. That thing was hard to look at outside in the open air, but in a crypt, dealing with a corpse. My whole body shook with the memories. I jumped as my wife's voice screeched from the other room, "You almost ready pumpkin. We don't want to be late? My father might be here any minute. Are you ready?"

I spat back, "I'll be ready in a minute."

Her voice sounded timid as if she had been scolded. "Are you ok?" Her head came into view as she looked around the corner.

I smiled, "Of course, sweetheart... I didn't mean to startle you. I just thought you were farther away."

The worry melted away from her face, "Ok, sweetie, I almost thought you were mad at me." She chuckled as if the idea was impossible, then added, "I'll be ready shortly."

I nodded, "Ok," but I wanted to scream. *You've been rushing me, but you're not even ready?* I turned back to the mirror, there my image screamed in silence.

It was all I could do to act normal. To play the part of the happy husband, and shake hands and smile. It felt like a long dark tunnel until I finally set down at the dinner table. All I wanted was a drink by this point. I realized Marvin was speaking to me, "Sorry dad, what were you saying?"

He laughed, "My boy, are you feeling ok?"

I smiled, "Nothing a good drink can't fix."

"Now that my boy, I can fix." Marvin yelled a drink order at the waitress. His wife hushed him as if he were being rude, but the waitress didn't seem to mind. Marvin added, "That's how you have to order here. A man might never get a drink. What was I saying, oh yeah, did you see the governor is here tonight?"

I looked around, "The governor of?"

Marvin laughed, "The governor of Eden my boy. Look right over there, Governor Cooper, sitting right over there."

"Well, sure enough, but I didn't vote for him." Marvin and I both laughed as the waitress dropped off our drinks. Well, perhaps tonight was going to work out. I really did need to get my mind off it. I had enough problems with helping Morgan out, and finding time to be with Green-e.

Another thought crossed my mind. Any time tonight I could be called by the local authority. I was supposed to stand before the local sheriff and give testimony to Cindy's suicide. Green-e was sure to be there, remembering this, I decided not to drink too much. This was going to be a long night.

Alan Walker

I could see the girl sitting on the park bench. Sonja was talking to her before she did her disappearing act. So it seems this angel might have other poor saps doing her dirty work. I wonder what her price was? She was a pretty thing. Dressed in what appeared to be a suit, but somehow very feminine. The cat had been clear, only get involved if she needed help. Other than that, she didn't need to see me. I preferred that.

I watched her, she looked upset. No doubt the cat had upset her, I know how she feels. A boy yelled at me, "Get your news, attacks increase at the Southern Gates. Will they hold?" I flipped the boy a coin, he tossed me a paper, "Thanks…" He wheeled off yelling his headlines to the crowd of passersby.

I flipped open the paper and pretended to read. My eyes followed her as she got up and begun to walk. I fell in step behind her. She walked into the restaurant, I found a wall across from the establishment's entrance. Leaning back, pretending to read. I watched her give her name to the hostess. Apparently her name was on the list. She was out of my sight as she followed the hostess. What did that dumb cat want me to do next? I guess I should try to get a seat.

Folding my paper I headed over to the hostess. The lady greeted me with a large smile, "How can I help you?"

"I was hoping to get a seat," I tried to sound charming.

"Do you have an appointment?"

"No," I slipped out a gold coin. "I was hoping you could sneak me in."

She smiled, but did not take the coin. "I'm sorry. Any other night, but tonight the Governor of Eden is eating and were filled up. Truly sorry…"

Looking for a name that I hadn't given her, "Alan, Alan Walker."

Her attitude changed, "Alan and DJ Walker?" Her eyes narrowed as she checked me out.

Seductively I asked, "You've heard of us?"

"You bet, I was at your concert. It was out of this world, such talent." She looked around, "Maybe we could sneak you in." She added with a wink.

I gave her my best smile, "That's truly appreciated, my love." She gently touched my arm as she led me to a table. I might get a date out of this, maybe this night wouldn't turn out so bad after all.

Chapter 21 The Hit

Morgan Jones

I looked over the edge of the menu. I could see my brother and his family. Sitting at a U-shaped booth, Tom sat on the inside edge between his father-in-law Marvin, and his wife. Next to Marvin must be his wife, I had never seen her before, she was gorgeous. Vicky had missed all the gifts of her parents, Tom had said this many times. I understood that she was an idiot, and Marvin was ugly, but somewhat of a genius. Until now, I hadn't understood what gifts; she had missed from her mother.

The restaurant was crowded, I ordered a glass of wine and an appetizer. My stomach twisted, the food and wine hadn't helped. I watched him laugh from an unheard joke, he looked happy, but I knew better. I knew that he was putting on a show, a show for all his fake friends and family. Only I knew, and perhaps Green-e, on just how truly unhappy he was.

I swallowed, I had a plan, it would soon be time. I made up my mind. I would not be stopped. I killed my mother and ruined my brother's life. I was a burden, I would be free of these debts. She was starting to explain why, when it happened. Vicky stood up and along with her mother. They were excusing themselves to go to the ladies room. The time was now, I stood up, prepared to go through with my plan.

I put my goggles on, then pulled out my enchanted marble. I walked forward, matching my steps with Vicky's. If I had a clear line of site for a clear shot I would act.

Dr. Weaver

I watched as my wife and stepmother left for the restroom. I couldn't wait for the guards to come and get me. I need to see Green-e, I need to talk with someone who would understand. How can I live in this life of lies? Marvin broke my chain of thought, "What's bothering you my boy? You seem to be somewhere else tonight. Don't forget, this celebration is for you… Partner."

I gave him my best smile, and started to say, "Well…" But then the world went black.

Alan Walker

The whole restaurant was crawling with vampires and security. The governor of Eden was eating here tonight, out of all the places to be. Stupid cat hadn't even noticed, not until it was too late. I never even understood what the girl was trying to do in the first place. I was only a few feet from her, I walked quickly, trying not to bring any unneeded attention to myself. She was intent on a target, there was no way she would kill anyone here? I had to stop her, she would get caught. Only feet from grabbing her, I watched something drop from her hand, the world went dark as I reached for her.

Morgan Jones

I had my shot, dropping the marble, the world went black for everyone around me. With my enchanted goggles, I could see just fine. I pulled my gun up to eye level, then cocked the hammer. Seeing Vicky just a few feet in front of me, groping though the air, lost in darkness. She couldn't see me aiming the gun right at her head, all I had to do was pull the trigger.

At this moment my heart sank when I realized I couldn't do it. All the reasons in the world, were not enough for me to kill her in cold blood. She was smiling, she thought it kind of funny that the lights went out. She giggled when she banged into an unseen chair. She was a child, in so many ways. And what had she done? Other then love my brother… who had done nothing but lie to her.

Someone slammed into me, grabbing at me. I turned my head to see a man I have never met before. I pushed him… he grabbed at me, pulling my robotic arm. I twisted my arm around breaking free from his grip which jarred me. I realized that the sudden freedom was accompanied by a loud bang. It took me a half of a second to realize that I had accidentally pulled the trigger.

The horror went through me, when I looked at where Vicky had been. She was no longer searching in the dark, instead she lay in a pile on the floor. Everyone around was still lost in the dark, some were now screaming, I froze.

What have I done?

My mind went into autopilot. The boy was coming to his feet, reaching as if looking to grab me again. I elbowed the boy with my robotic arm, clocking him upside his head. I had no more time to deal with him. He fell to the ground with a moan. I took off towards the door, all I need now was not to forget my escape plan.

I hadn't made a dozen more steps before something else smashed into me. I lost balance, crashing into a table. Dishes and food went flying as confused people just screamed and struggled through the darkness. I pushed off the table, spinning around, only to find myself face to face with what hit me. My stomach dropped as I realized I was staring at the vampire. The same one that tried to grab me in the alley. He might not be able to see me, but he knew where I was, I barely lifted my arm in time to block a blow.

I blocked with my left arm, and even though my robotic arm was strong enough to take the impact, the vibration traveled through my whole body. Before I could recover, he struck again, hitting me square in the chest. The blow knocked all the air out of me. The vampire grabbed my left arm and twisted it, putting me in an arm lock. Unable to twist my robotic arm with one hand, he grabbed on with both. With great effort I could hear the metal in my arm tearing in defeat. My arm came off with a horrible ripping sound. I screamed in pain.

I fell to the ground. In pain, I tried to rise to my feet. The blow came from behind me, hitting me in the head. The world spun and now my world was lost in darkness.

Dr. Weaver

The darkness that enveloped the room was strange. At first I thought that perhaps the gas that feeds the lamps had gone out, but as we sat in the darkness, listening to the sound of panic, I realized something was off. It was too dark, under darkness, I pulled out my lighter flipping the top sparking it to life. Only it didn't light, it didn't even spark. I yelped in pain, "Ow."

Marvin asked in concern, "You ok my boy?"

"Yes, just burned my finger on my lighter." Yet I could not see the flame. "What kind of magic is this?"

Marvin yelled back, "I could not tell you. I wonder what's going on?"

Before I could reply a loud gunshot filled the air, followed by screaming. I yelled out, "Vicky... Marvin, you ok?"

I could barely make out Marvin's voice as the restaurant filled with screams, "Yes, yes I am."

It felt like an eternity, but the darkness went away, as quickly as it came. The light was blinding at first. Across the room there were soldiers dragging someone off. I heard a man yell, "Is there a doctor?"

"Yes," I replied. Standing to my feet a waiter hurried me over to the patient. There on the ground was Vicky, a puddle of blood forming under her. I heard Marvin's scream from behind me, "Vicky, what happened? Vicky," we both went to her.

I could see that she was shot in the chest, close to the heart. I reached down for that magic, holding my hands over the wound, I began to save her. Marvin eyes were full of tears and fear, "Please save her Tom, please save her."

I looked at Marvin and promised him, "She'll make it... I won't let her die."

Chapter 22 The Beginning of the End

Alan Walker

I had gotten to my feet, in the darkness, no one witnessed my struggle with the girl. Wow, she was strong, I couldn't believe she had gotten the best of me. I came to realize that a doctor was trying to save the woman that had just been shot. Poor girl, she walked out in front of the would be assassin. Obviously, she was targeting the governor. If that girl hadn't taken the bullet, the girl might have killed him. Which made me wonder, why did the cat want the Governor dead?

I snuck out of the crowd, then out of the restaurant. I could move quickly. The other vampires in this room were busy capturing the shooter, or securing the governor. There was nothing left for me to do, security had her. Still, I followed, watching them drag her limp body, they surrounded her as they quickly moved her through the station. I saw the cat, moving in and out of people. I couldn't help but wonder, what she would want of me now?

A door opened into a secured area, the men rushed her in. Two men stood guard as the door slammed shut. There was no way I could follow. I moved out of sight and found Sonja in her human form and looking quite irritated, "It's all gone sideways. How will we get her back?"

I chuckled darkly, "You're asking *me*? I don't even know who she is, or why *we*, need her back?"

She narrowed her eyes, "Go back to your life of music and games. Without her it will all be over before you know it."

I barked, "And what's that supposed to mean? What do you think I could, or should do? It's not my fault you can't even plan a murder. Perhaps a smaller target to start off with."

She shook her head, "I don't have time to fight with you, but your right, there's nothing you can do. For now, follow the doctor. When you get a chance, tell him that Morgan was the one who shot his wife. This is the important part, he is to do nothing, but ask for help from the Dare's. He'll understand. Also, don't let anyone see you or hear you."

Full of contempt, "Not a problem. What else can I do for you? Perhaps clean your litter box?"

She turned into a cat and quickly bounced away, then faded into nothing. I'm not sure what happened tonight, except, that it was about to directly affect my life, and I had no idea why. I rubbed my temples, this was going to be a long night.

Did she say the Dare's. Maybe, just maybe this could be a good thing? Only one gate away, from a life in the Enchanted Gardens.

Morgan Jones

I could hear men speaking, my eyes felt like weights were upon them. My head pounded, the more my world came into focus the harder my head pounded. It sounded like the men were in another room. Somehow I knew they were not, my eyes opened only to see blurry figures standing over me. I could feel my right arm tied down along with my legs. It was strange, my left robotic arm being torn off reminded me of losing my real arm. I missed both and had neither.

As my head cleared along with my vision, I could now make out the men. One was that vampire, the one in the alley. He was leaning against the wall with his arms crossed over his chest. He looked handsome and young, but his beauty was marred by the fact I knew he was a monster. The other two men stood above me talking back and forth. One was porky and bald, his skin was pink, he looked as if he had never been outside a day in his life. He wore what appeared to be a fancy robe. He made my skin crawl. The other man was nothing like him. He wore a fine suit with a frock jacket. His gold chain ran across his chest. His suit was black, white undershirt with a red tie and matching handkerchief that hung from one pocket. He was thin, his face was pointy and his skin darkened from the sun. He was obviously rich and his eyes had no compassion in them.

As they spoke back and forth, their words became clear in my mind. The rich man was saying, "She tried to kill the governor, and yes she is obviously a pawn. That is not what worries me, what worries me is; Who is this unknown enchanter? He must be our top concern. I see no reason to keep, her… We should just kill it. Most of this poor girl is a machine and dangerous to keep around."

The bald man spoke carefully, "Yes, Lord Abbett, you are very wise. As you said earlier, there is no chance this poor creature would remember her creator. Still, this was a very public attack. Would it not be better to try this girl? A show, perhaps, otherwise panic may set in. If it takes us time to catch the true attacker, this could buy us time with the public."

Lord Abbett was not happy with this, "How much time should it take for us to bring this man to justice?" The bald man shrugged and gave him a very apologetic look. Lord Abbett's face went tight, "Very well, I see your point. Take her to the court of Dolls, try her fast, we must make it look like justice was served. We must not seem weak, not now. You understand Theo. It cannot seem like someone in our city that can enchant is outside of our control."

"Of course," Theo replied with a slight bow.

"I swear, if it wasn't for Peter, nothing would get done around here." Lord Abbett's eyes had shifted over at the vampire when he said Peter. I now know the monster's name, something I never cared to know in the first place. He moved to leave, "I will leave you to this… mess." Peter followed Lord Abbett and left me with Theo.

Theo looked down, then smiled, "I see you have finally decided to join us."

I felt a chill run through my body.

Tom Weaver

I had to use my magic to stabilize Vicky. How could I not? We rushed her to the hospital, the fact that I saved her life… Ironic. I came up with excuses on why. Marvin was there, and he knew about my magic. How could I explain a reason for not using it? Of course the answer was easy, all I had to say was, it was beyond my power. How would he know? I sat in the hospital, this time in the waiting room, instead of a doctor saving lives. Both Marvin and I were refused entry on the grounds that we were emotionally compromised. Who could argue?

This internal argument changed nothing. I had used my magic to save her. I had stopped the internal bleeding. All they needed to do now, clean her wounds and hook her up to fluids. Perhaps some blood. Marvin was still freaking out, I was too, but not because I was worried she wouldn't make it. I couldn't understand why I saved her. I missed my chance, a random attack on the governor, no one would have looked my way.

Laying my head in my hands, I came to a conclusion. I saved her, because I was not a murderer. I have lied about everything, but I have never truly murdered anyone before. I thought I had, because of my uncle, but until this day I hadn't realized how different that truly was. Vicky was innocent, killing her was only for my personal gain. To think, I asked Morgan to do this horrible thing. I must communicate with her soon, she must not try such a horrible atrocity.

Marvin was speaking with one of the local officials and the doctor who was overseeing Vicky. I could tell it made Marvin extremely happy. He looked over at me, I was already heading over. "What's the news?"

Marvin beamed, "She'll be fine, resting. All thanks to you my boy." He pulled me over in an awkward hug.

I chuckled, "As if I would let some crazy man kill my wife."

The official corrected me, "It wasn't a man." He then looked over at Marvin, "I'll let you fill him in, I need to get back."

Marvin shook his hand, "Of course, and thank you. You'll keep me updated?"

The official tipped his hat, "Will do doc."

The doctor excused himself and left Marvin and I to talk. It wasn't a man? That's what he said. A slow panic was starting to set in. I asked Marvin, afraid of what he might say, "What do we know about the attack?"

Marvin explained, "Not much. It was a young woman, would you believe that? I guess that's not too surprising, a woman can pull a trigger as well as a man. It's just odd, not only because it is a woman, but because she has no legs and only one real arm. The best part is, her legs and one of her arms, are robotic. A cyborg, my boy, I never thought I would live to see a cyborg, let alone one trying to kill the governor.

"She used magic to create that blackness in the restaurant. It must have been some powerful wizard to put that girl together. Of course, I think they're trying to frame this on a lone killer. That my boy is hard to swallow. All I know is that I hope they find everyone involved…. They almost killed my girl."

I put my hand on his shoulder, "I'm sure they'll round them up."

He nodded, "You're right, not for us to worry about."

My mind was spinning, they had Morgan. I have never felt so helpless, not only could I not save her, but I was sure to be next. How long before she tells them everything? What about Green-e, how would I keep her safe? Then it hit me, at any minute the city guards would be looking for me, but not to arrest me. I was to be called to confirm Cindy's suicide. Cindy, I was the only person who knew where her body was.. The Dare's had much to lose with my arrest.

They couldn't let me be arrested, I knew too much. They were my last and only hope in saving my sister. Cold sweat ran down my face, how long would I have to wait for them to fetch me.

Alan Walker

I went to the hospital to find this doctor. I couldn't lay my finger on why, or how this man could help that poor girl. Furthermore, why would he help? I meant the girl just shot his wife. I guess that doesn't matter, I'll just deliver the message as the cat instructed. All he needed to know was that Morgan was the one who tried to kill his wife and she had been arrested. I felt like I had came in a motion picture halfway through. I was a pawn, in a cats game. Soldiers riding a steam tank pulled up in front of the hospital. What now?

I have never seen this type of steam tank. There were hundreds of different models. The large tanks were used on the outside of the wall for taking more territory. I remember the kids playing on an old tank that sat half buried and rusting, near the mill. It was from hundreds of years ago, when men broke free from the inner circle to create the massive outer circle. It was rusted and the earth had reclaimed most of it. It was hard to imagine what it looked like when they used it. This machine tonight was much different in design. Square except for the front where it swooped down into a large scoop, that way it could push its way through large crowds. It was an unfinished looking machine, the rivets were mismatched and roughly done. The back door dropped down and soldiers rushed into the hospital, led by a well dressed officer. I just knew they were here for the doctor. How could I follow him? Or get him a message?

To top everything off, the night was more than halfway over. Looking at my watch, it was three in the morning. I had little time to wait, the soldiers came out with the doctor in tow. He didn't look under arrest, but none the less they loaded him into the back of the steam tank. The smoke billowed from the top as the machine lurched forward. The wheels were made of steel, and made a horrible sound as it banged down the road.

Following him would be impossible. That machine was heading towards the Enchanted Garden, and there was no way I could sneak in. I decide the best course of action was to head back to the hotel room.

Chapter 23 The court of Dolls

Morgan Jones

Theo looked down upon me like I was a starving dog. Two guards came into the room, they untied me then pulled me to my feet roughly. One of them threatened, "Just try something, I dare you." The other guard's eyes felt sorry for me, but not enough to do anything about it.

Theo reassured the guards, "Come now, she's a smart girl." He came face to face with me. I could smell the perfumes that tried to mask his body odor. He tried to sound like my friend, "Now my sweet girl, this is what's going to happen. We're going to take you downstairs to the court. There you will be tried by the court of dolls. I'm sure they will find you guilty, then sentence you to death. By morning you'll be beheaded." He waited for me to speak, but I just blankly stared at him. I was too scared to move, let alone speak. He spoke again in the same even tone, "I don't want to see a beautiful young girl such as yourself, put to death. If there is anything you could tell me, anything, it might help. Do you know the name of the man who did this to you?"

Funny, they were sure it was a man who did this to me. I had read the names of many enchanters who worked in the Enchanted Gardens, and most of them were men. Yet, the person who started the Enchanted Garden was a great female enchanter, Summer White.

What could I say, without getting my brother killed. I would die for him, I hope he knew that I didn't mind. He had always taken care of me and in the end, I had failed him. Tears ran down my cheek, my voice cracked as I tried to speak. I tried again, "No, I remember nothing."

He shook his head, "That's a shame. Take her away."

The guards dragged me none too nicely, I tried my best to think of a way to escape. The further we traveled, the more hopeless, I became. There were guards posted every twenty feet, one, on each side of the windowless hallway. I couldn't be sure where we were, I sensed it to be underground. They had stripped me of all my clothes, and dressed me in a plain brown dress with long sleeves. The dress was fine, but with my clothes went my weapons. My robotic arm had a lot of tricks, but the vampire had ripped it off. All I had was two strong legs that didn't have a place for me to run to. I thought of my enchanted wand, hidden in my right arm. What good would that do? I wouldn't have time to enchant anything before they beheaded me.

I was transferred to a large white room. We came from a side door into the great hall. Long rows of seats, rising high above, filled with onlookers. Large white columns lined the wall holding up balconies. My eyes filled with tears and my heart beat so hard it felt like it was going to pop out of my chest. Then I realized, everyone was wearing masks, creepy masks. They were doll faces, of all shapes and colors. Hundred of dolls stared at me, unblinking, unmoving. If I thought I was afraid before, I was now struck with terror.

The two guards brought me before a large tower, and sitting above it was a doll. This was no person wearing a mask, but an enchant doll. It was the most elegant doll I have ever seen, its dress was white, with so much decorative embroidery, it was hard to describe. The doll had been placed in a large white chair overlooking the room. The doll spoke in a young girl's voice, no lips moved, just sound. "Who is this, and what has she done?"

Theo, who had been walking behind us, stepped forward. "She is unnamed your honor. She made attempts on the Governor of Eden's life. She did not succeed, but managed to hurt a young bystander in the process. She has given no defense for her action, and there were many witnesses to her act. Let there be no doubt, she did commit these crimes with intent to kill."

The doll spoke, "Unnamed girl, what name do you give? What defense do you give?"

There was dark magic in this room. No lie would work here, how I knew, I couldn't say. I looked at the doll, "I am no one. I am innocent…" I almost said of the crime of the attempt on the Governor's life, but it hit me. I need them to believe that was my target, they could not know about Tom.

The doll replied, "Everyone has a name, not to give it means you have much to hide. Did you mean to kill tonight, yes, or no?"

"Yes," it was the truth. A gasp echoed in the room.

The doll asked the crowd of people wearing doll masks, "How do we find her?"

A voice, yelled out, "Guilty." He was followed by a chorus of, "Guilty."

When the noise died down the white doll spoke again, "You are found to be guilty. For you crime, you will be sentenced to a life of imprisonment in Nemos. With no chance of parole."

Theo spoke up, his voice was different, concerned. "Your honor, is this not a death sentence? Her crime was to kill one of our leaders. The crime has only one punishment."

Just earlier, he was asking for information to help me, what a louse. The doll went silent, and the guards grabbed me. The entire time they pulled me along Theo complained, "There's some kind of mistake. Give me time to sort this out... let me get a hold of Lord Abbett, so that he might clear this up. She must die for her crime."

The guards took no heed of Theo and pushed me into a square room. A steel gate slid closed between us and Theo left in a huff. The box lurched, then quickly moved upwards. Fear had my teeth shattering, never had I thought an elevator to be a scary place. Moving up into the darkness, knowing something horrible awaits me. Somehow I knew that Theo would catch back up, and whisk me off to the death chamber.

The elevator shook as it stopped, the gate clattered open. As soon as I stepped out I saw her, dressed in a beautiful green dress. I could hardly believe my eyes, my voice trembled, "Green-e."

She smiled, then nodded at the guards which stepped back, giving us some space. She smiled, "We haven't time. Things being what they are... A week ago I could have set you free." She shook her head, "Time is short. The Dare's family six hundred year reign of power is coming to an end, but, we still have friends." She turned and began to walk, she beckoned me to follow her. She spoke quickly and I listened closely knowing that my life depended upon it. "One of those friends happens to be the warden of Nemos. Her name is Rose, most know her as Thorn. Understand that as a favor to us you will be treated better than most, still, you will be in prison. Hopefully not forever. One more thing, your brother, he knows your plight. He went to Jeffery Dare for help. Luckily, I had already dealt with it, but I thought you should know."

We came out a door, heading onto a large balcony. I could barely believe my eyes. This whole time I had been in the enchanted Garden, not just the Garden, but Castle White. We were standing on the side of one the large towers. A bridge hung out from the balcony, leading to a small airship. I didn't need to ask, I knew where it was heading. Knowing I had no time, "Green-e, thanks, you have no idea. Tell my brother, I love him. Watch out for him, please."

She took me by the shoulders, "Don't, don't you worry about him. He's better off than he deserves. I love your brother and I will watch over him…. And you, my sister… take care."

Tears streamed down my face, "Thank you. You have no idea…"

She cut me off, "We're out of time. You must leave before that clown Theo has you executed. Be safe."

No more was said as a man came from the ship to escort me back. I watched the tower in all its beauty as the airship climbed into the sky. I would have continued to watch, but a bad tempered man announced to me,"Prisoners go below deck, off with you."

I scurried below, a crew member followed me, locking me into a cabin. Inside there was nothing but a small bed, jug of water, with an empty glass next to it. I sat on the bed, wiping the tears away. A smile crossed my lips, I still had my wand and my legs… Most importantly, time.

Chapter 24 What Next?

Alan Walker

I only made it halfway through my story about the cyborg assignment when DJ freaked out. I have known the boy for years and not once seen an emotion. He was nothing but a computer, all about the numbers. He asked none too kindly, "What was this cyborg's name?"

I was flustered by his tone and action, "I'm… not sure. I forgot. What's going on with you? I've never seen you act in such a manner."

Evie, wide eyed in wonder added, "Someone has oiled his gears. I can't even get that kind of reaction out of him, and the seven Gods know I've tried."

Ignoring her Darrell unleashed his fury at me, "Was her name, Morgan?"

"Yes, I think," He was about to yell at me again. "Wait, hold on here. You stop it, right this minute. I don't know what has your gears all out of alignment, but remember who you're talking to."

I watched him taking calming breaths, then he growled, "Sorry."

"Ok then," wasn't much of an apology, but the boy was very upset. I needed to understand what would cause my boy such pain. "Yes, her name was Morgan. I can't say that she gave me her last name."

"I know her last name," DJ said. "Her name is Morgan Jones."

When I meet my boy, his name was not DJ, it was Darrell Jones. With his abilities, I had purchased him off some pig farmers. I detested slavery, but with the boy's talents it was the easiest way to acquire him. I had heard of his hardships with brother and sister, but with lack of emotions I was never really sure if he cared. It all added up, I put my hand on his shoulder. "She's not dead." His eyes lit up and I added, "They've taken her to Nemos."

"What?" He gasped.

Before he could get upset I quickly added, "She is safe there. Stay calm my boy, listen to me." He shook his head, "It's ok, we will get her out."

He quickly asked, "How?"

"I don't know, " I answered honestly. "I don't know, but damn it, we'll figure it out."

Evie added, "Hell yeah. Just remember, they design prisons so you can't get out. So getting in will be easy."

Darrell looked confused, then realized what she was saying. "You want to commit a crime?"

She laughed, "That's one way in."

I smiled seeing that Darrell had relaxed a little. "Before you two rob a bank, let's come up with a plan. You know, the part about getting out. We need to figure that out before we get in."

My head was spinning, this would not be easy. I reached to take another drink, but my glass was empty. How would breaking someone out of Nemos help me move in society?

Dr. Weaver

Finally the dust had settled. I was in a room in Castle White, with Green-e. I yawned, I was so tired, bad dreams kept me from my sleep. I had told Green-e of the constant nightmares of my sister; naked, cold and laying behind bars. No matter how much I pulled and screamed, I couldn't get her out. Green-e smiled, "She's ok, you can trust me."

"I know that," I paused. If I knew that, why the nightmares? I shook my head, "Last night was the worst. I dreamed of that creepy doll that guards Cindy's body. I woke up, she was standing over my bed, with this look on her face. It was almost human, I went to say something when it smiled. It covered its mouth... like she was a school girl. I jumped up, but it was gone like a wraith in the night. That's when I realized I must have been dreaming."

Green-e shook her head, "We must not talk about such things. It didn't happen, you know that. Dolls have no personality, your mind is playing tricks on you. Now remember we must never be overheard talking about that."

She was curt; something was off about her behavior. Ever since I got here, I could feel, but in a way I didn't want to deal with one more problem. There was no way around it, "Are you ok?"

She answered quickly, almost defensively, "Yes, why?"

"Just worried, that's all," I was unsure of what to say.

A moment of quiet passed between us. I got up and poured her a drink of wine. Handing her the glass she looked up at me with pain in her eyes. "Thanks... By the way, how's your wife's recovery?"

There it was, "What did you expect me to do? Let her die?" I was tired and I hadn't meant to be so blunt.

She didn't yell, but she couldn't hide her anger, "Of course not. You wouldn't want anything to happen to her?" Her face went tight, "Sorry, I didn't mean like that."

I sat next to her, on the verge of tears, "I love you, and you alone."

She was crying now, "Is there not room in your heart, to love another?"

"Not Vicky," I defended adamantly.

"Why not let her die? Not kill her, just... Why save her?" I was quiet, she continued, "I know what I'm saying is wrong. By not doing what you did, well, I guess it would be like killing her. I feel such guilt, not only for feeling the way I do, but because of what I said to your sister. Or rather, thought she might be up to and hoped she would succeed. It's my fault she tried to kill Vicky!"

I was stunned, "What did you say to Morgan?"

Head hung low she answered, "It's not so much what I said... more like what I felt. I knew what she might do, but didn't do anything to stop her."

I felt the anger in me, she could see it. I said, "I asked her to kill my wife first? Never could I have imagined I would have plotted to kill anyone, for any reason… I try to kill Vicky. What does that say about me? I plotted, stood aside, and for what? Just to save her and watch my baby sister go to prison." She got up, I begged, "Don't leave." Standing I took her in my arms. "I love you. You are right, I should have let her die. I will make this up to you."

She smiled, but there was worry and sadness in her eyes, "I know. I love you more than anything in this world. You should not have to murder for love. I shouldn't have to be angry because you saved a life."

I knew our time was up. We had to leave, she kissed me passionately. We planned our next rendezvous for Saturday. She handed me her empty glass, then left. Standing with the empty glass in my hand, I needed to tell my wife why I would be out next Saturday. No worries, I would come up with the perfect lie.

Epilogue

Big John

    It was an easy job. That's what I was told. A poor caretaker named Lily Green. Luke asked me for the fifth time, "So all we have to do is kill one girl? That seems kind of overkill to me. Why send Big John and three guys for one woman?"

    Everyone called me Big John, what can I say, I'm big. Still the way Luke said it was as if I could take on the world by myself. In truth, I always felt better when Luke was with me. The man could out shoot me with his eyes closed and I knew my size didn't protect me from bullets. In fact, you might say it made me a bigger target. I told Luke, "Settle down. It's not every day the world has a new leader. Lord Abbett will soon be over Eden. It's past time, the Dare's have been in control too long. This kill might just get us a promotion. Kind of sick playing second fiddle to the vampires."

    Luke added, "Not like the blood suckers can work during the day. If it weren't for guys like us; the secret police would only operate during the night." We laughed. "Perhaps we'll be allowed into the inner chamber?"

    I smiled at the thought, "You never know." Looking at my watch, "It's time, let's do this. Go get Nick and Beck. Tell them to make sure they clear the passenger car before any harm comes to this woman. No witness, and no fooling around. We kill and dispose of the body, nothing else. Make sure they understand."

    Luke nodded, "No problem boss."

    The plan had been easy, two on both sides of the car. We ushered all the passengers out. At first I thought this would be the hard part. Telling the lady to stay as we ushered everyone out. What if she made a scene before we could empty the car? First the car had a few passengers, second the lady set quietly staring out the window. Off to a good start. She took no notice as we empty the car. Once it was done, Nick and Beck blocked one door while Luke and I had the other.

I pulled my dagger and said to Luke, "I have this."

He chuckled, "Go get her John."

I moved down the aisle way toward the lady. What a shame, so beautiful. I truly didn't want to do this, but what choice did I truly have? The woman looked up at me, her dark green eyes... never had I seen eyes like that. It made me pause. She stood, moved from between the seats and into the isle. She was stern, "Don't do this. Please."

Even though she said please, she had no fear in her eyes. Instead, she seemed to pity me, that anger me, which was good. I moved forward, brandishing my blade. "Sorry, it's just business."

No reason to prolong this, I moved forward and struck out my knife hand. My blade strike was true, my blade sunk into her chest. I was a strong man, her body flew back. I had expected her to fall to the ground, but instead she caught her balance and remained standing. The tip of my blade bent, hmm, perhaps she wore armor under her corset. No matter, I will slice her throat.

She was angered now, "You really don't want to do this."

I moved forward and grabbed her. I should have been able to overpower such a little woman with no effort. I found myself wrestling with her, unable to bring my knife arm to slice her throat. I heard Luke tease, "Big John, need some help with the lady?"

The woman threw me back, I had to grab a chair to keep from falling on my butt. She stood before me, she was enraged. Smoke, smoke was coming out of her nose and mouth. What the hell? I was told this was an easy job. The boys had figured out this was not a joking matter and pulled out their guns. I yelled out loud, "Shoot her."

The car was filled with gunfire, followed by flames and a mighty roar of an unknown beast. As the hot fire wrapped around me, I screamed in pain... my final thought, what just happened?